FILTHY

Rich

Dawn Ryder

sourcebooks
casablanca

Published by Sourcebooks Casablanca, an imprint of Sourcebooks, Inc.
P.O. Box 4410, Naperville, Illinois 60567-4410
(630) 961-3900
Fax: (630) 961-2168
www.sourcebooks.com

Library of Congress Cataloging-in-Publication Data
Ryder, Dawn.
  Filthy rich / Dawn Ryder.
    pages ; cm
  (trade paper : alk. paper)
  I. Title.
PS3623.I6255F55 2015
813'.6–dc23

                    2014036339

Printed and bound in the United States of America.
VP 10 9 8 7 6 5 4 3 2 1

Chapter 1

"ADMIT IT," SABRA DONOVAN, very soon to become Sabra Nektosha, coaxed her companion. "It's perfect up here."

Celeste toyed with the stem of her wineglass and looked over its rim at the expanse of Alaskan perfection that surrounded them. "Point taken. It's breathtaking."

The testing and development cradle of Tarak Nektosha's all-terrain business was in a pristine setting. So was the house he'd built overlooking his entire operation. Huge floor-to-ceiling double-paned windows gave Celeste a bird's-eye view of the dozen huge warehouses where Tarak's line of monster vehicles was produced. The warehouses were surrounded by a test track, complete with viewing platform.

But what claimed Celeste's attention was the granite bowl surrounding everything. Sometime in the distant past, it had been carved out by a glacier. Now it was green with new grass and tall timber. Overhead, the sky was a majestic deep blue, looking close enough to reach up and touch. In the distance were glistening white glaciers.

"Pure paradise," she added, to her friend's delight.

Sabra beamed. Celeste offered her a toast. "And you look happy."

"Told you. There is nothing here not to love."

"You did promise me that." Celeste took another sip of her wine. "I'm planning on testing you, though. It's been ages since I took a vacation."

She seemed to have picked the right spot to remedy that.

The main house was a mansion constructed of large timbers and offering even more floor-to-ceiling windows to let viewers take in the surrounding scenery. The air smelled clean and fresh, even if it had a bit of a chill, but that was also a slice of perfection for Celeste, since she'd just left the heat of the Southern California summer.

This was all good, given that a portion of her motivation for making the trip was to check up on Sabra.

Sabra was her best friend, so Celeste didn't plan to apologize for showing up to scope out the situation. Or for tucking an extra credit card into her purse in case they needed a couple of emergency plane tickets. That was the maid of honor's duty too—driver of the getaway van in the event of a change of heart. In the remote Alaskan wilderness, Celeste had recognized the need for a getaway plane.

But one look at Sabra, and Celeste knew that wasn't going to happen. Sabra was glowing, and not just about the amazing house her soon-to-be husband had built in the middle of the wilds of Alaska. No, Sabra's eyes sparkled with joy—true joy. The sight made Celeste realize how long it had been since she'd felt anything close to that sort of elation.

This vacation was definitely overdue.

Even if it was immeasurably sad to be so jaded. Celeste could only believe in love as something that blinded you to men's flaws while you were busy feeling deliriously happy.

"Jaded" was the word, alright. She took another sip from her wineglass and tried to let the flavor fill her senses and restore her faith in life. But the hard facts of her past remained unchanged.

Love had been nothing but a toxin for her, and that just seemed to be her piss-poor luck. So she smiled brighter to avoid being a killjoy while her best friend was in love. She was the maid of honor, after all.

Tarak Nektosha, the object of her friend's affection, was

leaning against the kitchen counter on the other side of the room with his best friend, Nartan Lupan. Turning her attention back to the scenic view took more effort than it should have, but there was no way she was going to admit that she couldn't look away from Nartan.

She so wasn't going there.

Their first and only meeting was branded into her memory, which pissed her off. Nartan Lupan was everything she needed to stay away from. Tall, dark, and handsome, with the kind of money a gold digger would be willing to undergo plastic surgery to get her hands on. His kind understood their power too. They wielded it like a whip, expecting women to be their pets. They only wanted control in a relationship, not equality or partnership. No, Celeste would never again submit to that kind of subjugation.

You're accusing him without evidence…

Her inner voice had a point, one a lawyer would agree with.

She'd already admitted to herself that she was jaded. It was on her to-be-dealt-with list, emotional baggage she knew she needed to let go of if she was ever going to be truly happy. Even though she knew she would end up independent and taking care of herself, Celeste didn't ever want to turn bitter.

Things were going well, though. She was on her first real vacation since her divorce. Her boss was likely still in shock. Maybe it was time to really cut loose. She looked over at Nartan again but lost her nerve and looked back at the scenery.

One step at a time, she decided.

Chicken…

Yeah, but better safe than stuck in a relationship with a psycho.

Men with too much money tended to slip into that category all too often. Celeste looked back at Sabra, giving her friend another quick once-over just to make sure everything was good. Tarak Nektosha was loaded and a noted recluse.

But Sabra was swirling her wine around the inside of the glass, a perfect look of relaxation on her face.

"Told you the trip up here would be worth it," Sabra crowed, glowing with her victory. "I find it so peaceful."

"It's that."

"But you're still worried about me," Sabra said. "Don't be. I'm happy. You'll see. Tarak isn't like your ex-husband."

A huge diamond flashed as Sabra moved her hand. She extended it so that Celeste got the full view of the three-plus-carat center stone.

"I thought it was too big at first, but it's growing on me."

Celeste took a long sip of her wine to ease the knot that had formed in her belly. Sabra knew her too well and raised an eyebrow.

"Don't hate the diamond just because Caspian was a total prick about making you wear yours like an owner's label." Sabra suddenly grinned in a very menacing way. "When is he due out of prison? I think I know just the right girl for him…"

Celeste gave a husky chuckle. "Thinking of setting up Anastasia?" She offered the name of Tarak's last girlfriend, who had done her best to scare Sabra off. "They might just deserve each other, but trust me, Caspian wouldn't go for someone who just took his shit."

No, her ex-husband liked to break down his pets, crushing their spirit a little at a time to make the experience last longer. The harder the chase, the more he was interested.

Oh yes, she'd been a prized possession.

One of his favorite toys.

He'd courted her for two years, and she'd been stupid enough to think that meant he loved her. No, he was a collector and she had merely been a challenge.

Her insides chilled for a moment. She hated these echoes of being traumatized. She didn't want to live the rest of her life bitter, angry, and afraid. She knew how to defend herself now, and she was never going back. She had a bright future ahead of her. She told herself that again and again, but the wound was still healing. The moments when it reared its ugly head were less frequent now, but no less dismaying.

Yeah, the to-be-dealt-with list.

It was like a flashing sign that wasn't going away until she faced it. Master Lee often reminded her that martial arts training needed to be total and complete and more than just the physical body. True peace came from within.

But Sabra was looking at her suspiciously.

Celeste fluttered her eyelashes and wrinkled her nose, the way they'd both done when they were eight, and that was the perfect moment to change the subject. "It took all day to fly up here. My backside is numb."

Celeste offered Sabra a grin to let her knew she was teasing, then forgot what she was thinking as someone cupped the right side of her bottom. She nearly jumped out of her skin, whirling around instantly to come face-to-face with the person she'd been spending a lot of time trying to avoid thinking about.

"Definitely not numb now," Nartan Lupan observed as he reached out to take the wineglass away from her before she spilled the dark contents all over herself—or him.

Celeste automatically raised her opposite arm and adjusted her stance to keep him from claiming his prize. She was pleased with how her martial arts training had become almost instinctual, and she allowed herself a gloating smile.

But she was less than pleased to notice that his cobalt-blue eyes and coal-black hair were a stunning combination, with an added hint of boyish mischief that was almost endearing. Her eyes narrowed. That observation wasn't going to keep her from killing him. Sabra slid between them while her groom-to-be choked back something that sounded suspiciously like a chuckle.

"Okay…" Sabra hooked Celeste's arm and tugged her away. "I think it's girl time."

"More like pest-control time," Celeste grumbled loudly enough for Nartan to hear as she fell into step with Sabra. He offered her a smug smirk that said he'd welcome any attempt on her part to bring him to heel. The hint of boyish playfulness melted and forged into something harder, something far more mature.

"Bring it," he challenged her softly.

Sensation slithered through her belly, one she pointedly refused to name because she wasn't answering any challenge that concerned him.

"Don't get your hopes up."

Because she wasn't going there. But a gleam entered his eyes that caught her attention. Sabra tugged on her wrist again.

Shit.

She turned around to follow her friend. Had she really just let the guy mesmerize her?

That was off-the-scale stupid.

She wouldn't be answering a challenge that rose up from inside herself. That was just nature's way of leading her into trouble, and she had no intention of being controlled by her hormones' reaction to a gorgeous hunk of ultra-alpha male—even if he was one of the most striking men she'd ever seen.

Even if he made her shiver for the first time in far too long.

There was something about the way he moved that made her think of an animal on the prowl. He kept his hair long enough to brush his collar, but it didn't strike her as messy like a teenager's, or overly styled like a metrosexual trying too hard to be something beyond a boardroom jockey. Instead, she discovered herself recognizing that he wasn't quite tame. He'd conquered the business world, but he was still Apache and proud of it.

The distrust that had sent her flying up to check on Sabra returned, only now it settled on a much more personal target. Money often translated into power for a man. A normal man wouldn't have reached out and touched her. Nartan was arrogant enough to think himself entitled to that kind of uninvited intimacy because he was master of his world.

Awareness rippled through her again, awakening urges she'd thought long dead. It was sort of a relief to discover herself emerging from the coma her failed marriage had left her in. But with another look at Nartan, she dismissed the idea of having anything further to do with him.

Really, it was a no-brainer.

Pure and simple, she outright rejected the notion. He was dominant and just waiting for her to show him she noticed, daring her really. It was there in the way he watched her. His focus was unnerving, which alone was a good reason not to have anything to do with him. Some women were foolish enough to think a man could change, that he'd settle down once he connected with the right girl. Stop playing games, become docile. She was no longer that naive.

Nartan's boldness hinted at what could be an impressive experience. But knowing she needed to let go of her reservations about men didn't mean she was getting anywhere near someone like him. There wasn't any inner peace connected with that blue-eyed Apache. He was a bundle of fire and ambition, and proud of it. For just a moment, she considered making an attempt to shove her fears aside. It wouldn't kill her to flirt with him. It might even be fun.

It would be a kick-ass ride and you know it…

Temptation was like rich food. It might taste divine, but you'd pay for it the next day when you looked in the mirror.

Still, she lost the battle to ignore him and sneaked another glance. For a moment their gazes fused, and she felt the connection like it was physical. Sensation rippled across her skin, awaking a thousand little nerve endings while her heart accelerated. His lips thinned, hunger darkening his eyes as the unmistakable glint of demand entered them.

He'd heat her to the melting point and mold her to suit his whims if she let him get too close. It was his nature.

So she wouldn't engage him. No, she'd had a taste of his elite world and didn't want another sample. Getting on with her life would require someone a little more run-of-the-mill. That might translate into boring, but it also could be defined as steady and reliable. Two things she was positive she needed for inner peace.

Still, she couldn't deny that the current between them left her breasts feeling heavy and her clit sensitive. Honestly, she didn't want to deny it. It was selfish of her, but she clutched the knowledge to her heart and enjoyed the evidence that she wasn't so scared. She pressed her tingling lips together and reached deep within for her self-discipline. She was going to condemn herself to disappointment. The reason was simple. If the man could affect her so strongly from just being near, she'd be helpless against her own desires once she was in his bed.

She wasn't going there. She didn't trust herself to make a wise judgment call.

And that was sad because it was going to cut her off from something that might have been mind-blowingly intense.

Completely pathetic.

"That was a little bold," Tarak observed as his bride took Celeste off to explore the house.

"Couldn't resist." Nartan slid onto a barstool in front of the marble-topped breakfast bar while Tarak tended a pan on the range top. "She's such a tempting little bundle. You can hardly blame me."

"Work a little harder on that self-discipline, would you?" Tarak slid a salmon steak onto a plate and sent it across the counter to Nartan. "Holidays could get tense if you piss off my soon-to-be wife's best girlfriend, and I don't need my wedding ruined by a death in my family. Namely yours. I understand Celeste is a black belt."

Nartan made a little sound of appreciation, earning him a warning look from Tarak.

"She needs to grow a sense of humor, but I'm open to the idea of her trying her luck at taking me down. Might even lie down for her."

"That will be the day," Tarak countered. "You never could lose with any amount of grace."

"Guess that's why I'm the one who stuck it out with you when the rest of the tribe told us we were never going to strike gold up here."

"Maybe," Tarak agreed with a satisfied curl to his lips.

Nartan lifted a bite of the salmon to his mouth. He chewed slowly before nodding. "I might have a job for you at Angelino's if you fuck up your own business."

"Very funny." Tarak took a clean pan from the rack and set it on the range. He tossed butter and olive oil into it and swirled them around with a practiced motion of his wrist before adding another piece of freshly caught salmon. "I'll have you know that my profit is four percent above what I predicted for this quarter. We're completely in the black. Solid. So don't look for me to be joining you at your cliffside restaurant."

"Not too bad," Nartan remarked as he polished off his meal. "Nice to know we're not heading back to that shack on the claim and to winters of blackened mountain goat."

Tarak ate his meal leaning against the kitchen counter. He surveyed the house, and satisfaction covered his face. They were both a long way from the reservation they'd grown up on.

"Nice to see you've made peace with the past at last," Nartan remarked before standing up and taking his plate to the sink. He washed and rinsed it before depositing it in a drying rack.

"Yes," Tarak agreed, his eyes on the back patio where Sabra and Celeste were settling into two of the lounge chairs. "Feels good."

Nartan only glanced momentarily at Sabra. She was her friend's opposite, with dark hair and full curves. Celeste had blond hair and a trim figure. He would have questioned if blond was her natural color, but she had a pair of light green eyes to go with it.

But there was more to her that he found worthy of a second glance. She was fit and toned, like an elfin princess. But one of the warrior class. It wasn't the sort of tone a woman got from marking time on the local gym's exercise machines to burn calories. She trained her entire body, and the stance she'd taken when she turned on him told him exactly how she got the body she had. Martial arts training made sense to him, while at the same time she didn't look like the sort of woman who would mix well with an all-male crowd at a dojo. That only made her more intriguing.

"Here." Tarak tossed something at him.

Nartan caught it, scowling when he realized it was a dish towel.

"You look like you're about to start drooling," Tarak informed him.

Nartan thought about flipping him off but settled for a shrug instead. "Can't tell me she's not worthy of it. I know quality when I see it."

Celeste suddenly turned her head and caught him watching her. Nartan held her gaze, curious to see what she'd make of his interest. He wanted her to see it, wanted to watch her reaction to him. Her entire body tightened, the tension clear and almost palpable. She turned her back on him, but not before he caught the hint of awareness in her eyes. An unmistakable flare of interest that she shoved aside, denying it, denying him.

Staying in the kitchen took a little more effort than he was comfortable with.

"What's the deal with her?" Nartan turned back to Tarak. "First time I met her, she burned my business card like it carried a contagion. Lesbian? That would be such a waste. Maybe I can talk her into giving men another try. Go for bi. I could share her with a girlfriend. In fact, I know a few girls who would love to double-date with us."

The words rolled off his tongue but left a sour taste in his mouth for some reason. The idea of sharing was suddenly unappealing. He was used to possessiveness in business, but he avoided it like the plague with women. Getting caught up in anything more than sexual interest with a woman would be nothing but a time-sucking nuisance.

"Something about her ex-husband. Sabra didn't go into details," Tarak answered. "I understand the prick is in prison for assault. On her."

Nartan felt the muscles in his neck tighten. Rage flashed through him a second before a detail about Celeste surfaced from his memory.

"That explains the black belt."

And the reservation flickering in her eyes.

Nartan felt something new filter through his brain. Lust he was used to. His upscale restaurant and spa attracted gold diggers and trophy wives who spent a lot of time and money making sure their assets were in prime condition, so he wasn't really surprised to feel his cock twitching over someone as delectable as Celeste.

But there was something else now. A feeling that he'd almost forgotten he was capable of. It was the distinct sensation of protectiveness, one that had nothing to do with being a decent human being whose hackles rose in the face of injustice. This was deeper. Far closer to the part of him reserved for family. It was striking dangerously close to what he'd call personal.

It wasn't welcome at all.

In that respect, he and Celeste had something else in common besides attraction. Now that was twisted humor from fate.

"I haven't seen that look on your face in a long time, Nartan."

Nartan turned and gave Tarak a blank look.

Tarak shook his head. "We've played too many hands of poker. I know you, Nartan."

"I don't do relationships," Nartan cut back. "She's put together nicely. I'd have to be blind not to enjoy the view, but that's all I'm interested in."

Tarak folded his arms across his chest and pegged his friend with a dark gaze. "Bullshit."

Nartan felt heat gathering on the nape of his neck. "You want to get married, fine, but I'm not following you this time. Hope you have a prenup because a divorce at your financial level would be hell on your bottom line. I've worked too long for what I have to see a failed relationship take it away after I let down my defenses enough to share my personal life with someone. Like I said, I don't do relationships, just hookups. Celeste looks like fun. That's all I'm interested in."

Tarak shrugged. "Keep telling yourself that." He looked out at his soon-to-be wife. "I used to think the same way." Tarak turned his attention back to Nartan. "I don't regret changing my tune."

"I didn't come up here for a matchmaking session. Leave that to my grandmother," Nartan warned. "She's got the guilt tone down perfectly."

Tarak snorted. "Agreed. Nothing like tribal guilt. Your grandmother has already called me to ask if we're going to start a family, since I don't have a grandmother and you and I are as close as brothers. To her way of thinking, I'm her son now so I need to think about putting family first. Seems I'm not getting any younger."

Nartan held up his hands in mock surrender. "Like I said, she's the master."

"She'll be here in another day." Tarak's eyes narrowed. "She won't miss the charge in the air between you and Celeste."

"She will if I avoid Celeste."

Which didn't give him any satisfaction. In fact, it was irritating the hell out of him. Tarak was watching him, his lips slowly rising into a knowing grin.

"You know, a true friend would have eloped."

Tarak shook his head. "Having the ceremony up here in Alaska got me a long enough lecture."

"I bet."

Nartan took one last look at Celeste before turning his back on her. Once the wedding was over, he'd be on his way back to Southern California and the plentiful contact list he had stored in his phone for times when he wanted female companionship. The last thing he needed was the complication of a relationship. Or the risk of letting someone close enough to his heart to sink a knife into it. Women like Celeste were dangerous because they were quality, and dismissing her wouldn't be possible.

His damned fascination with her would die. He was sure of it.

———

Celeste skipped down the stairs the next morning, eager to enjoy her time in Alaska. Seeing the last frontier was on her bucket list. So now that she didn't need to implement the escape plan, there was nothing to do but enjoy her trip.

Let the fun begin.

She'd dressed in sweatpants, layered a sweatshirt over a T-shirt and a long-sleeved shirt, and tied on some good hiking boots. She tucked her cell phone into her pocket and made a stop in the kitchen to fill up a water bottle. Snapping the lid shut with a satisfied smile, she was ready to begin her adventure.

"Wait."

She thought she might have imagined the curt word, but when she turned around, she discovered Nartan Lupan in the oversized living room of the house. He'd transformed a corner of it into an office and stood typing on the keyboard of a laptop placed on a raised desk.

That suited him. He didn't strike her as the type to drive a desk. No, he was the one in the position of control, no mistake about it.

But he had his back to her and had still noticed her. That sent a little chill down her nape. No matter what she'd decided about ignoring him, men who had sharp senses were just damned sexy in her book. That sense of awareness was building inside her again.

The sound of him tapping the keyboard filled the room. He continued, his attention on the screen in front of him. Celeste turned toward the door, taking her chance to escape from the sizzling aura he radiated.

It was practically tangible. Her awareness increased with every second she shared air with him. Her heart was accelerating as Nartan pressed against her comfort zone. She was responding to him, feeling like she was being drawn to him. And the longer she stood there, the more aware she became of details about him. Tiny things that shouldn't have drawn her attention, like the way he used his fingers on that keyboard so precisely, so expertly. With just a hint of excessive strength that sent a curl of heat across her clit. She turned and headed toward the door before her self-control crumbled any further. Either he had some imbalance in his pheromone levels or she was more desperate than she'd realized.

She needed to upgrade his priority on her to-be-dealt-with list.

"I told you to wait, Celeste."

She stiffened and fought the urge to snap at him. He was being arrogant, and she was ultrasensitive about being ordered around by men. Especially when she wanted to leave the house. A dark memory stirred, and she pushed through the entryway door before her past got its claws into her.

She was going to enjoy her Alaskan vacation, and she was going to let go of her emotional baggage. A hike into the pristine wilderness would be perfect. Maybe she'd find some of that inner peace

Master Lee was so often telling her about. As much as she loved her martial arts training, she had to confess that meditating to calm her inner spirit was something she still struggled with.

The air was crisp when she exited the house—a sharp contrast that helped snap her out of the trance Nartan's presence had sucked her into. She drew in a deep breath, closed her eyes for a moment, and did her best to hear Master Lee's voice instructing her.

The beauty of the forest and the granite outcroppings was a welcome distraction. The freshness in the air smelled fantastic, and she felt her troubles dwindle in the face of the timelessness of her surroundings. There really was more to life than a bad choice in her past. She set off, smiling as the gravel crunched beneath her boots.

Nartan snapped his head around as Celeste disappeared into the entry room. Arousal surged through him, taking him by surprise. It was intense and sharp and shouldn't have been so acute, considering he'd tried to take the edge off his appetite in the shower.

That had pissed him off.

He'd worked his ass off for years in the Alaskan wilderness so he'd never have to jerk off again. He liked success and women and all the comforts that went with making sure the gold he and Tarak had unearthed was invested in businesses that would continue to increase his fortune. Women were plentiful in his world, and he gave them only as much as they gave him. A balanced, fair exchange.

He walked over to the entryway doors and pushed them open. Celeste was already gone. He stopped in front of the outer doors, looking at the Nektosha test track, but she was nowhere in sight. She'd gone around the side of the house and out into the forest to avoid him.

Alright, he was being a little dramatic to take it personally.

But that didn't stop a second wave of heat from rising along his cock. It thickened behind his fly, beginning to ache. He should forget her. Women who wanted to be with him were a lot easier to deal with.

That thought didn't stick because the intensity of their connection lingered, with a sting that wasn't fading.

He debated for a moment. His childhood was full of stories about listening to his instincts. Those memories conflicted with the logical side of his brain that knew without a doubt how much trouble following Celeste promised.

It promised something else though, something that made his blood heat with anticipation.

He should walk away. Sex shouldn't be controlling, only enjoyed.

His lips curved into a very confident grin. He'd enjoy the hell out of Celeste's delectable body, that was for damned sure.

He reached for a rifle sitting in a gun rack by the door and checked it before slinging it over his shoulder. Celeste was inexperienced at hiking through the Alaskan wilderness. A gun was as essential as a solid pair of boots. Nartan opened the front door and went down the steps to the edge of the driveway. He crouched down, studying the dirt until he found a set of fresh tracks. Satisfaction moved through him, surprising him because he hadn't expected any sort of challenge in tracking her. But it was there, warming its way through his blood, a level of enjoyment he hadn't felt in a long time.

Just maybe, his buddy's wedding would have some fun attached to it after all.

Celeste smiled.

Once she'd hiked up to the ridge above Tarak's massive house, she could see the ocean on her right and glaciers to her left. The forest was thick, rising high above her head. Birds were calling to one another as a breeze moved the branches to produce a rustling sound. For a moment, she closed her eyes and let the sounds fill her senses. She drew in a deep breath and smiled at the earthy scent of the air.

Now this was vacation. No sounds of cars, no smell of exhaust fumes, and she didn't need to check her inbox every half hour. Her clothing was designed for practicality instead of the ability to impress her next client. It was the whole "escape from reality" package.

Nartan Lupan could put the cherry on top of it all…

She laughed at her own thoughts but realized she was avoiding admitting just how much the guy buzzed her system.

There was nothing tiny about the disruption he was sending through her. In fact, it was really starting to snare her curiosity because it was such a change for her. It wasn't as if she hadn't had opportunities to date in the last month. But having her sexual appetite turn back on so suddenly was actually sort of a triumph, proving that Caspian was losing his grip on her more and more. It was a moment to be celebrated, but all she ended up doing was shivering as the memory of Nartan's hands on that keyboard surfaced.

She noticed details about him. Too many of them. It had to be an unhealthy level of attraction.

Like an addiction.

She went down the other side of the ridge, leaving the house behind.

Okay, the house and Nartan Lupan. Fine, she was a chicken, but the guy oozed sex appeal, as well as arrogance. There was no way she was going to do anything about what she felt for him. The bottom line was that she wasn't going to play with fire.

Chicken.

Guilty as charged.

But better safe than sorry.

Sabra and Tarak had left early that morning to run errands for the wedding, including fittings on Sabra's bridal gown and Tarak's tuxedo. Celeste was just happy to have some free time. She had no problem being alone, and she loved to move her body and feel her own strength and limberness. Her childhood had been a series of foster homes, which had taught her to enjoy her own company. So had her marriage to Caspian. Today, she aimed her attention at the wonder surrounding her, snapping a couple of pictures with her phone before setting off again.

She walked further along and heard water rushing in the distance. As she got closer, it turned into a roar. Just over another ridge, a massive, bubbling river was being fed by the glaciers high above them. The water was moving at an incredible speed, tumbling huge boulders that clunked together every now and then as she watched. The energy was raw and hypnotizing, drawing her closer to the display of nature's power.

"Be careful, Celeste."

She jumped, stumbling as she landed on the uneven bank.

"Even shallow rapids can sweep a full-grown man off his feet."

Nartan was poised halfway down the ridge in a low crouch. She blinked, doing a double take.

"How did you find me?" she blurted out, betraying just how startled she was.

He slowly grinned, the curving of his lips arrogant and full of pride. He pointed at the dirt he was crouched over. "If you want to give me the slip, better learn to cover your tracks, Celeste."

Something slithered through her gut again, just a little stronger than the first time. This time, there was no way to avoid facing what it was. Sexual hunger gnawed at her insides, refusing to be ignored. She didn't need it complicating her life, but it rose from some dark corner where instinct refused to be ruled by logic, leaving her with one irrefutable fact.

Cravings didn't have rules or respect for her desire to play it safe.

The guy was so damned sexy, drawing her attention to every detail of his person. Logically, he was everything she didn't want anything to do with, but that had no effect on the excitement the sight of him set off inside her.

Every detail about him was mesmerizing. She knew he was full-blooded Apache, but somehow seeing him so confident outdoors drove that home. It struck her deeply. His high cheekbones and sharp features made him more attractive than any man she'd ever seen. He was dredging up an approval rating from some deep, dark part of her mind. It was pure reaction, and it shocked her into stunned silence. He held himself in that half crouch without any effort, proving he had serious strength, and no one got that strong without training.

The clothes had to be throwing her off balance. The first time she'd met him, he'd been in an Armani suit. It was a far cry from the jeans and cotton button-down shirt he had on today.

But that wasn't the reason she was having trouble dismissing him. Even in the suit he'd looked primal. She'd sensed something about him that made her stomach flutter.

Her gaze traced the expanse of his forearms where he had the shirtsleeves rolled up to his elbows. Sharply defined muscles were on display, covered in cinnamon skin. Nartan let his hair grow until it was brushing his collar. It was almost as if he was making sure everyone knew he wasn't tame and had no desire to be.

"I told you to wait."

She jerked her attention to his face but found his expression unreadable. She expected her temper to flare, but instead she had to fight the urge to prop her hand on her hip. The desire to flirt rose up, recklessly tempting her to engage him. The problem was that she had no doubt he'd rise to the challenge.

"Tarak didn't need to set you to minding me. I'm just fine on my own." Celeste turned and began hiking along the edge of the river, breathing in the beauty of the scenery, the rushing water, the brisk air. Okay, and doing her best to clear Nartan out of her senses.

But she only felt the charge that came with knowing his gaze was on her.

It was like an advanced game of chicken. The urge to turn her head was driving her insane. She was stubbornly determined to prove that she could and would ignore the riot he was causing inside her.

Which unveiled another problem: she was enjoying the challenge of pitting her will against his.

Celeste headed back toward the top of the ridge. She could feel her heart working harder to fuel her body as she pushed herself. Heat moved through her legs and sweat coated her forehead, but the effort was worth it. The hours confined in an airline seat melted away.

Her sense of triumph was short-lived. Just before she made it to the crest, Nartan came into her peripheral view, his longer legs allowing him to overtake her and reach the ridgeline first. He scanned the area on the other side before nodding and looking back at her. She felt the connection between their gazes, his cobalt-blue eyes stunning her with their brilliance and the unmistakable energy burning there—burning for her, she realized with a sense of shock and even, if she were honest, satisfaction.

Playing with fire…

"You can't be full-blooded with those eyes." She bit her lower lip, trying to get a grip before exposing herself any further. Any curiosity about him was bound to land her in a situation she'd already decided she wouldn't be stepping into. But logical choices weren't sticking. They were just slipping aside as her hormones raged and need tried to rule her.

"According to the books, I am." He offered her a hand and she hesitated for a second before stepping to her left to avoid joining him.

Avoid touching him, you mean…

Guilty as charged.

"Blue eyes are recessive," she said, but found herself wondering why that mattered so much if she wanted nothing to do with him.

Actions spoke louder than words, and her curiosity was proving her interest. His lips twitched up, proving he'd noticed her lapse.

"Apaches used to like to take captives," he countered. "My ancestors enjoyed a challenge and had a taste for the unique."

A ripple of anticipation moved across her skin. There was a hint of promise in his tone, along with something else that stroked the heat flickering inside her belly.

"You do too," she remarked, pointing toward the mountains above the test and development center. "Sabra told me you and Tarak stuck it out on a claim up there." Changing the subject was pathetically chicken of her but no doubt a wise course of action.

"Three long years." He looked toward the spot Sabra had pointed out to her. "They seemed longer when I was living them."

"There are times like that." For a moment, it felt like they had something in common. Conversation felt so natural with him, so very comfortable. "Time has a way of dulling the blunt edges of reality."

"I'm not sure about that," he offered with a flash of a smile that gave her a peek at the boy he must have been. "I think...I'm close enough to smell blackened squirrel." He sniffed the air and shuddered, shaking his body like a large dog after a bath.

She laughed at him. "I hope it isn't on the menu tonight. Dining-out options look limited."

"I'll give you the un-blackened portion of my squirrel."

She propped her hands on her hips and planted her feet wide. "I came to the last frontier. I expect my share of hardships."

He took a moment to sweep the area before returning his attention to her. His smile was gone, a pensive look in his eyes.

"You burned my card the night we met. Care to tell me why?"

"It wasn't personal." She replied as if her boundaries were being pressed. "Everyone has one or two skeletons. The important part is that the skeleton is dead."

"But the ghost haunts you," he stated firmly, with a little too much truth to suit her. "I see it in your eyes."

Celeste shrugged and didn't care for how forced the action felt. Her confidence was trying to desert her, leaving her feeling exposed. "It's on my to-be-dealt-with list."

Nartan's eyes narrowed and his lips thinned. She could see the truth of his nature in his eyes. He was used to being in control and getting whatever he wanted. At the moment, that was to unmask her, something she wasn't going to let him do. The truth was, she didn't think she could bear being stripped down to such an unguarded position again.

But that was her failing, not his, and it didn't give her the right to be bitchy.

"It's nothing." Her tone was even and devoid of emotion, which was a major accomplishment. She felt like she was boiling, the heat twisting through her, increasing with every second he watched her. Peeling away her facade with nothing more than the force of his nature.

"I'm sure you don't need any female issues to deal with."

The ghost of a smile touched his lips. They were full, sensual lips that looked like they tasted fantastic. There was a restless energy pulsing around her insides that she recognized from a time when she hadn't forbidden herself impulses or playing with fire.

"You think I'm like most men?" he questioned smoothly.

Definitely not…

Not that she was going to admit it to him.

He moved closer, the gun making a soft sound as he gripped it. It was a metal-on-metal sound that made her flinch because it fit the hard nature of the man holding it and the uncivilized location. Everything was different here—basic, blunt…savage. And that suited him perfectly.

He stopped next to her and she fought the urge to step back.

"I'm not like any man you've ever known."

Her mouth went dry.

But her temper came to her rescue at last, flickering to life and burning through the haze of attraction dulling her wits. "I think you're used to being the boss. Understandable. Angelino's is impressive, but I like to keep my private affairs—private. Along with my vacations."

So maybe it wasn't the flare of temper that was sizzling inside her. Maybe it was pure panic, but she wasn't in a position to quibble over details. She needed her head cleared before she did something…impulsive.

She started down the incline, intent on discovering where the river was flowing from. Intent on anything that wasn't Nartan and her reaction to him. She dug deep, trying to gather enough focus to control herself. The sound of the rushing water filled her ears as she dug her feet into the steep incline and concentrated on her footing.

She felt Nartan behind her, shadowing her…stalking her. He made sure she caught sight of him from time to time. It was an exquisite sort of torment, that moment of having him in sight before he'd fall back and leave her with the knowledge that he was watching her with those intense, cobalt eyes.

Well, she wouldn't be turning around to engage him. She kept moving until she made it to the next high point and paused on the crest to savor the view. The wind blew into her face, chilling the sweat that had formed in her hairline. She smiled, enjoying the proof that she'd pushed her body.

"You enjoy a challenge too." He inserted himself back into her world. Okay, so she hadn't really been successful in ignoring him but she wasn't ready to admit it.

Nartan stepped up beside her, standing only a pace from her. Sensation rippled across her skin and down her body. She'd never been so aware of a man before. She wanted to be irritated, but all she could do was feel the way he was pressing against her comfort zone. Like some ultra-high-stakes game of chess.

She moved aside, but had her attention on Nartan rather than on her footing. The rough wilderness was unforgiving. The eroding granite shifted beneath her boot, ready to take her down the slope with gravity's help. A startled cry escaped her lips as she felt her body weight dropping, but it turned into a muffled word of profanity when Nartan curled his fingers around her bicep and yanked her back up.

Breathless and panting, he held her tight for a moment, seeming to allow his own surge of adrenaline to subside. She knew he'd seen her almost plunge into danger, and if he hadn't been right there, she could have been seriously injured, maybe killed. Nartan seemed to know only too well that this beautiful wilderness could turn deadly in a moment.

She lifted her elbow and dropped it on the other side of his hand. Honestly, she wasn't sure if she was breaking his hold or just responding to the panic rushing through her.

"You're welcome," he mocked.

"Thanks." Her tone was less than gracious.

He studied her for a moment, his eyebrows lowering in contemplation. "You need to deal with that ghost."

"Actually, that's sort of the idea behind being here." She opened her hands wide. "A soul-seeking sort of adventure." She straightened her stance and faced off with him. "I believe the custom is to undertake such journeys alone."

He shrugged, unrepentant. "This is Alaska, not Southern California. Your martial arts skills aren't going to be much use against a bear. Even if you know how to use a gun, you didn't take one with you. I told you to wait because you're green."

It was a blunt fact that made a lot of sense, but she didn't care for the direct blow to her pride.

"An explanation would have cleared that up," she said and rolled in her lower lip because she was itching to bicker with him. The urge was almost impossible to ignore, even though she knew it wasn't rational. She wasn't going there, to that place where she lost control of herself and started going after him because she just couldn't quell the urge.

"I enjoyed hiking with you more." He was testing her. Tossing down a gauntlet to see if she'd reply. "The journey you need to take is one that leads you back to the thing that left a scar on you."

"You're getting a little too personal." The words slipped past her lips. The moment she heard them, she shook her head, but he reached across the distance and caught her chin.

She shivered, the contact as jarring as she'd suspected it would be. His skin was warm and smelled enticingly male.

He turned his hand over and stroked the back of his fingers along her jawline. She felt like she was on the edge of bursting into flames, at the point when all the heat was trapped inside her, ready to flare up.

"Really…" She struggled to find the argument she needed to make but got lost in the intensity of his cobalt stare. It was stripping her bare.

She dragged her gaze away and turned back toward the house.

"You really need to stop running."

She wanted to. The desire was welling up inside her, flooding her.

Terrifying her with just how close she was to letting go of her control.

She couldn't.

Wouldn't, actually.

She just couldn't risk trusting again.

She headed back toward the house instead. For a moment, she thought she heard a soft, male chuckle. She ended up tightening her hands into fists and increasing her pace.

The man had just sent her into a full retreat.

———

Nartan fell into step behind her. He wanted to reach out and drag her to a halt.

He found himself battling the urge as she took to the uneven ground with a strength that turned him on even more. His cock thickened, hardening as he watched the way she moved. He was no stranger to admiring the backside of a woman, but here was something completely different from what he'd been enjoying in feminine companionship. No sleek dress fell over her curves; no delicate ankles were set off by fuck-me stilettos.

There were only slightly baggy warm-up pants, just big enough to need a drawstring to keep them around her trim waist. He caught a glimpse of her firm bottom as she moved, but what triggered another wave of lust in him was the realization that she had selected those pants with function in mind. He didn't doubt for a second that she could get her leg up into a deadly kick. His cock hardened to marble. He lost the battle to let her make her getaway cleanly.

"The ghost wins when you let it control you so well," he said.

The house was in view, along with the huge all-terrain tank that Tarak drove. Celeste hesitated, flashing him a quick look. She was shaking her head, but he reached out and hooked her elbow. "I bet the prick would love to know that you're running away from what I make you feel."

She smacked his hand so quickly that she surprised even herself, the sound loud now that the river was not close enough to drown it out. But her lips parted in shock as she stared at the spot she'd struck on his forearm.

"Shit." She was out of control, exactly the way she'd feared. She turned away from him, the need to escape driving her. "Look…I'm not ready for this. Sorry. It's nothing personal."

It was a nice, polite way of chickening out.

"You're having the same effect on me." He spoke clearly from behind her. A jolt of excitement shook her, freezing her in place. Her knees went weak and her nipples drew into hard points as excitement swirled through her thoughts, clouding every rational thing she'd been thinking. "And I find it very personal."

She whirled around and almost crashed into him. He was right behind her now. Far too close for her unsteady emotions. But losing control wasn't going to be the answer—it never was, never had been.

"I'm not interested in a fling." She made sure her words were clear and precise and delivered in a smooth tone. "Not with my best friend's husband's best friend. That could get messy."

Her statement was a perfect execution of what she'd decided she wanted, but looking at him undermined her determination. He was just so damn attractive with his inky black hair and the way he exuded power. Two midnight-black brows lowered as her statement sunk in. Something about his physique, his energy, his whole demeanor was pulling her toward him.

"Liar," he accused her, with something between a smirk and a determined grin. That glitter of mischief was back in his eyes, making her nipples tighten even more.

She wanted to label him arrogant, but the truth was the truth. He turned her on more than she had ever been before. And he knew it, which only made her hotter because she wanted to know just how sharp his powers of perception were when he was making love.

"I thought you said it was on the to-be-dealt-with list…" His tone was smooth and silky soft.

Suspicion prickled down her spine. She lifted one finger. "Don't."

He cocked his head to the side. "Don't remind you that you're running, or don't notice how charged the air is between us?"

He surprised her by chuckling. With amusement sparkling in

his eyes, he was even more attractive. "Or don't notice how good it felt to touch you?"

Shit.

"I'm really more trouble than you need, Nartan." It was an admission, one she felt was ripped from that spot inside her soul where she had shoved every last bit of emotional turmoil still clinging to her. "Or deserve," she interrupted him when he opened his mouth to argue. "You're right. I need to deal with things, and you rescuing me isn't going to accomplish that. I have to take the journey myself."

Disappointment was raking its claws across her insides, but she dug her feet in and pushed off with every step to widen the space between them. She made her way back into the house and up to the guest room Sabra had given her. Celeste flopped back on the bed, staring up at the ceiling as heat teased her clit and need gnawed at her. It had been a long time since she'd actually desired any man in particular. Sexual tension was something she normally satisfied with her vibrator, but she knew today she'd end up nursing an appetite long after climaxing. The need was deeper. More intense. Just like the man who had unleashed it.

It intrigued her beyond anything she could remember, and at the same time, it scared the hell out of her. But what stuck in her throat the most was the way that it challenged her. A challenge was something she just couldn't ignore.

What made her worry her lower lip was the fact that she was practically certain Nartan knew her weakness.

Tarak raised an eyebrow when Nartan pushed through the mud-room doors into the house.

"By the look on her face, I think you made a good call in taking the gun."

Nartan put the gun in the rack by the door and shrugged. "I'd rather use my bare hands on her."

"Any chance you could wait until after my wedding to get your arm broken?" Sabra asked from across the room.

"She took off without a gun," Nartan defended himself. "I did her a favor by following."

Just because he'd enjoyed it, that didn't change the facts.

And he had enjoyed it.

Nartan took a walk out onto the back deck in the cooling evening air to help ease the heat coiled in his gut. He and Celeste had more in common than she realized. He was just as uncomfortable with the level of attraction between them as she was. But he grinned as he contemplated telling her that. He just might do it for the pleasure of seeing her spit at him.

Spitfire.

Maybe it was an outdated word, but somehow it suited Celeste. In fact, he liked the ring of it.

Too much. He didn't need the complication of being involved with a woman beyond casual sex. Really, he didn't. But the look in her eyes haunted him, pulling on his resolve even as he tried to reason out why he needed to remain steadfast in his choices.

Weddings were a bloody pain in the ass, he decided.

Chapter 2

THE HOUSE TARAK NEKTOSHA had built was massive, but Celeste found it crowded. The knowledge that Nartan was there was the same as knowing there was a bear loose in the hallways. Dinner conversation flowed, but she was on edge, fighting to keep her gaze from drifting to Nartan's. It was a draining effort, and she felt wrung out by the time the meal was finished.

And that was a shame. She enjoyed the occasional fine meal because keeping fit required strict dedication to calorie counting. But dinner passed in a haze of tension as she battled her rioting hormones. When the opportunity to escape came, she took it. Sabra was leaning against the kitchen island, her groom-to-be next to her. Celeste selected a bottle of wine from the wine fridge and picked up two glasses.

"If you gentlemen will excuse us."

Tarak frowned at her. At least her poise didn't desert her in the face of his displeasure. She moved closer and reached out to pull Sabra away from the island.

"Girls' night," Celeste announced softly.

Sabra laughed and turned to blow her husband-to-be a kiss. "It's a sacred pact. Girls' night."

His features softened, and he relaxed back against the edge of the island. Celeste moved on, but the look was branded into her mind.

That was love.

Not that she had any personal experience with it, at least not on the receiving end. For a moment she was bitter, feeling the bite of loneliness more keenly than she normally did.

But Sabra's presence helped drive Celeste's memories back into the shadows, and she followed her friend down the long hallway. Just because she didn't have a man in her life didn't mean she didn't have fun.

———

"Don't think I didn't notice."

Celeste looked up from where she was painting Sabra's toenails. Her lifelong friend had an empty wineglass in her hand and a knowing look on her face. "Nartan is"—Sabra made a small circle with her index finger—"getting to you."

Celeste finished and sat up. She took a moment to screw the top back onto the nail polish bottle. "Since he has less than twenty-four more hours in my company, it's going to be a moot point very soon."

Sabra finished off her wine. "He owns Angelino's."

"I know." Celeste reached for the wine bottle and poured some into Sabra's glass. "I'm going to have to go into mourning. That was one of my favorite restaurants."

"Don't be such a chicken." Sabra picked up her glass. "It's been a long time since—"

"Not long enough," Celeste fired back quickly. Too quickly. She groaned with defeat. "Point taken."

Sabra toasted Celeste with her wineglass. "You can bet your ass Caspian isn't moping around. Or at least, he won't be once he gets out of prison."

Celeste drew in a deep breath and let it out. "He was never faithful anyway." She took a drink from her own glass but smiled. "I'm over it."

"Not that over it if you're letting Nartan slip through your fingers," Sabra persisted.

"I can be over my marriage and not be interested in Nartan."

"Except for the fact that I saw your face the first time you two met." Sabra refused to drop the subject. "He rocked your world. Admit it."

"Not denying it, just making the choice to say no," Celeste answered smugly. "I have every intention of leaving romance with billionaire playboys all to you. I tried it once, and that was enough for me."

"Tarak and Nartan weren't born rich."

Celeste set her wineglass down and opened the nail polish again for a second coat. She was ignoring the topic, and Sabra wasn't playing along.

"You shouldn't give up. Caspian came from a long line of assholes who thought their shit didn't stink. The look on his face when the judge sentenced him was priceless."

Celeste smiled. "It was. He'd never encountered a situation where his money and connections couldn't buy him out of a mess. Part of it was my fault. By taking his shit, I helped him think every other girl would too."

"You shouldn't have," Sabra replied, her tone hardening. "I can't believe you hid it from me."

Celeste only offered her friend a delicate shrug. "It starts out as pride and only toughens. I didn't want to admit to myself that I'd made such a colossal mistake in marrying Caspian, much less to you or the police."

"The biggest problem is that since you didn't testify against him, no one will notify you when he gets out of prison. But I guess it's good he's got a target for his anger, even if he was cheating on you."

Nothing had ever stopped her ex-husband from doing exactly what he wanted. Certainly not the bonds of holy matrimony. Celeste thought for a moment about the stripper who had testified against Caspian. The rest of the world might think that her ex would go after the girl, but Celeste wasn't so confident. Caspian separated people into groups, and most of them fell into the "disposable" one. He never spared them any more of his time beyond what would benefit him.

"Any friend of Tarak is someone you can trust."

Celeste focused on the purple nail polish she was dabbing onto Sabra's toenails. The scent rose up to tickle her nose as the light glistened on the wet surface. "I'm not ready for any sort of a relationship, and since he's your husband's best friend, it would be a lot wiser for me to steer clear of any entanglements that might make for awkward moments in the future."

Neat, logical, and complete bullshit.

"A good argument, counselor, but as your best friend"—Sabra shook her finger at Celeste—"I have to deliver a firm kick to your ass on the general topic of getting back into the dating world."

You have a ghost in your eyes…

Nartan's words rose from her memory, sending a shiver down her spine.

Celeste screwed the cap on for a final time and found Sabra eyeing her with suspicion.

Sabra nodded. "Sacred friend duty. You'd do the same for me."

Celeste laughed. "I've done the same." She lifted her wineglass and leaned back in her chair. "I'll take it under advisement."

And reject the idea for all the right reasons, no matter how frustrating it felt.

"You do that."

Long after Sabra had wandered down the hall toward the master bedroom, Celeste was still having trouble dismissing Nartan Lupan from her thoughts. It was like an annoying itch in the middle of her shoulder blades that she just couldn't reach. Even the relaxation techniques Master Lee had taught her didn't help. So it remained to bug her.

At least she would leave Nartan behind in another day.

But somehow, she wasn't entirely convinced that distance would solve the problem. The reason was simple: he was correct. She had noticed the pulse between them. It was unruly and intense. Sinking into her in a way she'd never encountered. Utterly and completely uncontrollable.

But she was never going to admit it to him.

—ᴡᴡ—

A howl woke her.

Celeste sat up and looked around the room.

The sun had finally gone down sometime after ten. Now the stars were brilliant, and a yellow moon was casting an amazing level of light in the nighttime hours.

There was a whimper and then another long howl.

Alaskan wolves.

She could sleep when she got back to Southern California.

She got up and hurried into her jeans. Only the range light was on in the kitchen, but with so much moonlight coming through the windows, it was easy to get to the mudroom and lace up her boots.

She opened the outer door slowly, sliding through to keep from moving it too much. A howl sounded, so much louder now that she was outside. She pressed the door shut and knelt down.

The starlight illuminated the wolves. At least six of them were pawing the ground as they moved along the road that connected the house with the test facility offices. Those offices weren't even in sight.

But the wolves were.

And so was Nartan.

He was crouched down twenty feet away. Her breath caught as she took in the way he blended with the moment. The wolves made yipping sounds as they came closer, smelling the road and the air as they went.

Nartan lifted his hand and beckoned her toward him. Her steps seemed too noisy, the crunching sounds grating on her ears. A wolf looked toward her and she froze.

Nartan beckoned again, turning to look at her.

The animal was still fifty feet away, but it was looking toward her. She bit her lower lip, afraid of spooking the animal.

Nartan closed in on her, moving right up next to her.

"He can smell you. You're upwind. Come down here with me. He won't worry about you then."

"Oh…"

Nartan clasped her hand and pulled her down to where he'd been. He lifted his head, judging the wind. The wolf let out a yip and joined the rest as they scratched at the dirt and one another. Two of them would circle another, lowering their heads and yipping. The wolf in the center was the one who lifted its head and let out a long howl.

"The alpha…" Nartan whispered.

He had his arm draped around her, his scent filling her senses. Why did he smell so good?

Not that it really mattered. He was still as pond water but his skin was warm. His attention was on the wolves, but she felt like it was on her as well. He shifted just a bit, and inhaled next to her hair.

Fresh from bed, it was a soft cloud. She reached up, self-conscious about how messy it was. He caught her hand and stopped her as the alpha looked at them. The animal's eyes were pools of moonlight. Its mouth was open, giving her a glimpse of its long canine teeth. It made a low sound before pushing its front paws out and stretching its neck up and tilting its head until its nose pointed at the moon. A long, mournful cry filled the night.

It felt like she was suspended in time. They might have been anywhere, in any year.

"Lower your head."

He tucked his chin and cupped her nape.

"To show submission…"

Celeste stiffened. Nartan chuckled in a bare whisper next to her ear. "To the alpha."

She bent, the wolf watching her before losing interest and moving along with the pack.

Nartan massaged her neck, his fingers working the stiffness from the muscles as she straightened. "Well done."

It felt like there was innuendo in his comment. But maybe she was just being too sensitive.

To-be-dealt-with list.

She drew in a deep breath and forced herself to relax. The wolves were moving away now, heading toward a forested area. The alpha looked back at them before it disappeared into the timber.

"That was amazing," she whispered.

Nartan's hand was under her hair, the touch so intimate that she was loath to pull away. He threaded his fingers through her hair, pulling his hand free as he finger-combed the strands. He watched her as he did it, his eyes reflecting the moonlight just as the alpha's had.

He was in his element.

Call it cheesy or lame but she couldn't shake it.

So she rose, backing away from him as he stood. His shirt was open all the way down his front, his jeans sagging low on his waist because he didn't have a belt on. And his feet were bare.

"Aren't you cold?"

He slowly smiled and extended his hand. "Judge for yourself."

She started to reach for him and froze. Indecision held her in its grip as the wind blew her hair around. One of his dark eyebrows rose as she hesitated.

Chicken…

She reached out and touched him. Allowed her fingertips to rest on his forearm for a moment that felt like a mini eternity. It ended when he twisted his arm around and captured her wrist. He stepped

up to her, pulling her toward him. She could have broken the hold,
if she was able to think.

Which she wasn't.

Her brain seemed to have shut down. Somehow, she was caught
in a storm of sensations, completely unwilling to think about anything. She simply wanted to experience the moment.

Well, it was quite a moment.

Rich with scents and sensations that were intoxicating. His
breath teased her ear and then her cheek. A shudder shook her, sending a tiny gasp through her lips. Nartan took advantage of her parted
lips, pressing his down on top of them and tasting them slowly.

God, how long had it been since she'd been kissed?

Pleasure flowed through her, gaining strength like a flame catching a wick. Sure, she knew that a candle was for lighting, but until it
was lit, the memory of how bright it could shine was dim.

She stepped back. Startled by how much she liked his kiss.

She wanted more.

A hell of a lot more.

But she turned and headed back into the house before she could
do anything impulsive.

Moon madness. That was all.

Only she wasn't really sure if she would ever be sane again.

She really hated weddings.

Celeste plastered a smile on her face and ordered herself to let
the past go. She wasn't the only one in the world who'd married the
wrong guy. Weddings as a whole shouldn't be hated, especially when
they were as polished and upscale as the one Tarak Nektosha was
willing to pay for.

A huge warehouse had been transformed into a dream wedding
venue. It came complete with lighting and a sound system hoisted

into the rafters on stage rigging. The normally practical walls were hung with hundreds of yards of satin that reflected the lights perfectly. Candles lent their soft flickering light to the scene as a small army of catering staff made sure the guests all had seats for the ceremony.

The ceremony went off without a hitch, and Celeste had to admit to a moment of softness when Tarak took Sabra's hands in his and spoke his vows. Something in the way he looked at Sabra almost made Celeste believe they might be destined for a true happily-ever-after.

Who knew? Maybe they were. Maybe she was the only one who didn't know how to judge a man's true character before she was in too deep to get out.

But you did get out.

Yeah, she had.

That thought lifted her spirits as the ceremony concluded. The moment Tarak took his bride into his arms and kissed her, the assembled guests broke into a cheer, dominated by the sound of Nartan's voice letting out a deep and savage cry.

Celeste was mesmerized by the sight of him tipping his head back, exposing the deep bronze column of his throat. She found herself wanting to taste it.

She still wanted another taste of his kiss.

Heat rose in her cheeks, and she looked at the ground to conceal her confusion. When she raised her head again, she found herself looking into Nartan's cobalt-blue eyes. The force of the connection traveled through her, making her take an unconscious step back. His lips lifted in response as Tarak turned with his bride and faced his friends and colleagues, leaving Celeste directly facing Nartan.

He was in an Armani suit again, but now he struck her as much more intimidating than the first time she'd met him at Angelino's on the California coast. The polite mask he'd hidden behind while overseeing his multimillion-dollar restaurant was gone, allowing her to see the nature of the man who had faced down the Alaskan winter to achieve his goal.

She felt an unmistakable touch of pride on his behalf. She did love it when someone didn't cry quits even though the odds were against them.

Admired it because she knew firsthand how much strength it took to force yourself to face the harsher edges of reality.

Nartan closed the distance between them, cupping her elbow before she recovered enough to realize his intention. But he didn't stop there. He slid his hand behind her, grazing across her lower back and turning her to face the assembled guests before locking his hand around her hip.

A crazy, intense twist of need went through her pelvis.

"I didn't get much sleep last night," he said as the photographer snapped pictures. Nartan guided her away from the arch under which the ceremony had taken place.

Celeste felt a shiver of triumph at that. The sight of him standing there with his shirt open was branded into her memory. "I think you enjoy messing with the boundaries I try to place between us."

The catering staff pulled aside a curtain wall that exposed the second half of the building, where tables and a dance floor had been set up. The freshly pressed tablecloths and silk floral garlands draping the perimeter of the room were gorgeous, but Celeste was far too conscious of the man next to her to take much notice. She felt a hairsbreadth from a full embrace, the sense of intimacy wrapping around her and tempting her to just lean against him.

"True," he confessed next to her ear. "You're enjoying it too. That's why you reached for me last night."

Nartan's body heat was burning along her left side, and she was far too aware of how hard his body was beneath the fine Italian wool of his suit. His tie matched his eyes perfectly, and a pair of gold cuff links caught the candlelight when he bent his left arm. It was all pretty wrapping that she wanted to tear off him to get to the real present hidden inside.

He raised one dark eyebrow when their gazes met. "No argument?"

She turned to face him to loosen his grip on her hip. It worked, giving her the freedom to step back, but he caught her hand as she moved, his fingers stroking the delicate skin of her inner wrist before he carried her hand to his lips and bestowed a kiss on her fingers.

"No."

A single word had never made her tremble before. For a moment they were locked together in a connection that felt soul deep.

"Let's get out of here." His voice had roughened.

But she pulled away, feeling exposed and vulnerable. "A little moon madness doesn't change anything."

He tightened his grip on her hand, resisting her attempt to pull free for a moment. Taunting her, really, his eyes glittering with a promise that was unmistakable. It was a subtle threat, one that she didn't have to deal with because they were surrounded by people. But she knew what he was doing, and part of her refused to ignore it.

She pushed her hand toward him to break his grip and lifted her arm away. But freedom didn't fill her with satisfaction.

Somewhere deep inside her brain, there was the unmistakable hint of enjoyment that he was stronger than her. Both in will and brawn.

Not that she'd ever admit it to him.

It horrified her because it was a preamble to surrender, one she knew she had no hope of controlling. The sensation was there, crackling like a fire getting its start. Something glittered in his eyes, confirming that he was able to look straight into her soul and see it. Their moonlight kiss was testimony to the fact that she'd lose her grip on reality in his embrace.

Distance was the only hope she had.

The fact that she made it to Sabra's side without turning her ankle was a credit to how many hours she had trained, because she was on autopilot. The reception was in full swing around her, fresh flowers filling the air with their fragrance, but all she noticed was the lingering scent of Nartan's skin and how good his hand felt wrapped around her hip.

She really wanted another taste of him.

—⁓—

Nartan wanted to follow her.

The urge was hard and sharp. He stood for a long moment, feeling it roll through his body. It sharpened his senses, allowing him to pick out the details of the way Celeste lowered her chin to keep her neck from being exposed and the stance she adopted to make certain she had him partially in sight while she fought the urge to look back at him.

He didn't need the distraction but couldn't help but appreciate it. Although "enjoy" was a far better word choice.

Maybe "eating it up" was more fitting altogether.

He wanted to taste her again.

But admitting that brought him face to face with his own boundaries. She wasn't a hookup, which turned out to be something else he found attractive about her.

Shit. He liked his life the way he had it. Affairs were like the city bus. There would be another one along if he missed the first one.

But he didn't want an affair. In fact, the idea left a bitter taste in his mouth.

He needed a drink. Before he went back after her.

Nartan turned and made his way to the lavish bar laid out on the east side of the hangar. No expense had been spared. There was even an ice machine that melted chunks of ice into round balls that rolled around in the martini glasses like huge glass marbles. One of the bartenders slid up in front of him, wearing a black vest and a name tag that bore the company name of a very upscale catering outfit.

Nartan pointed to one of the whiskys, a very limited-production run that retailed for more than eight hundred dollars a bottle.

"Neat," he instructed the bartender. The man shot him a grin as he opened the bottle and poured out a double.

Nartan turned around with the glass in his hand. He lifted it and let the pungent scent fill his senses as he closed his eyes to clear his thoughts. But there was something else too. A hint of Celeste still clinging to his fingers. He opened his eyes, finding her instantly, the delicate column of her neck catching his attention because she'd swept her hair up.

He wanted to pull every last pin out of it and gather it in his hand. Bury his face in it and inhale the scent of her skin.

Like he had last night.

Nartan took a sip of the whisky instead. He nursed the beverage, using it as an anchor to remain at the bar. He confined himself to women who made the first move because it removed the need for him to comfort them when they realized he wasn't there for the long haul. He didn't like to mask who he was during sex. When he took home a woman who had stepped up to him, she didn't have any right to expect seduction.

Celeste needed to be seduced. He felt that truth all the way to his bones.

But all he felt like doing was running her to ground. It was a hard, sharp impulse, just like the bite of the whisky.

The DJ fired up the music. Tarak swept his bride around the large dance floor with a confidence that earned him smoldering looks from the women in the room.

Shamus Donovan, Sabra's father, finally cut in. The white-haired man was still barrel-chested and dressed in a Navy dress uniform. Tarak offered him his hand, but the older man shook his fist at his new son-in-law in a warning that sent a ripple of amusement through the guests.

The father-daughter dance unleashed a soft round of applause as Shamus glowed with pride while guiding his daughter around the floor. The moment the music changed, employees of Nektosha eagerly flooded the floor to join their boss and make sure they were noticed.

Nartan chuckled and drew another sip from his whisky.

Tarak didn't give a damn about who had laid out the money to fly up to his wedding reception. In fact, the reason it was being held in Alaska was because Tarak didn't care for schmoozers. His employees were rated on their performance in the workplace.

Shamus swept Celeste into a dance but abandoned her when the tempo changed. Adele's husky voice sang out "Set Fire to the Rain," sending most of the brownnosing crowd toward their chairs. Tarak held his hands up in surrender when Sabra grabbed the front of her long gown and stepped to the beat. She turned around and Celeste joined her.

Nartan's whisky ended up forgotten in his hand.

He was fixated on Celeste. She moved with a sensuality that struck him like a blow to the solar plexus. Every motion was an expression of hunger.

Sexual hunger.

She dominated the floor, daring any man in the room to try matching her. It was raw and savage. One of Tarak's younger VPs slid up to her, and she tossed her head back. The poor fool didn't know he was already defeated. Celeste's body language was already dismissing him as she slid around him and rejoined the girls' group that had formed around Sabra.

Her ignored dance partner didn't give up. He kept dancing, moving around the group of women until one of them broke off with him.

Celeste didn't give him a second glance.

But she did catch Nartan watching her. She arched and turned, the music still pulsing through her body as her motions changed. It was almost indiscernible, the thrust of her hips and the arch of her back, as she pushed her breasts out.

He noticed.

Would have sworn he felt it yanking him toward her.

Daring him to try his hand at winning her.

Desire surged past the barrier he kept his sexual encounters pinned behind. He set the whisky down, uninterested in dulling his wits.

No, what he wanted was a different sort of mind-numbing experience. He wanted his senses sharp when he connected with her, wanted to notice every last detail of their collision. It went deeper than desire, bordering on craving. That gave him a moment of pause, a red flag going up. He liked having his partners sealed behind a wall of friendly indifference that could be used to shut them out of his thoughts when he wasn't in the mood for them.

But his craving for Celeste was already past that boundary. Far past it.

And he always went after what he wanted.

Sweat was trickling down her back and the sides of her face, but Celeste didn't care. She turned her back on Nartan and focused on the music. The DJ kept the tempo lively for several more songs. She threw herself into dancing, enjoying the high it gave her. Her heart was pounding, her blood rushing in her ears, and it was almost enough to drown out the feeling of Nartan's eyes on her.

Almost…

The lights changed as the DJ slowed the tempo. Sabra abandoned the group, her face bright with perspiration. She rustled off in a flutter of cream silk and lace. Celeste turned and headed toward one of the glasses of ice water set out on the tables.

Nartan intercepted her, turning her neatly into his embrace with a fluid motion that stole her breath. One moment she was confidently striding toward the edge of the floor, and the next his arms were closed around her.

Captured…

"So…" She ended up with her hands flattened on his chest as he turned her a few more times to keep her pinned. It was done so damned smoothly that she found herself as impressed as she was annoyed. "Is this your dance then?" Her tone had turned sultry, almost like a purr.

And he did feel just as delicious as she'd felt the night before.

"Dancing with the maid of honor is one of the best man's duties." He smoothed his hand along her lower back, unleashing a torrent of sensation. "*My* dance."

She twisted away from him, unable to quell the impulse. It was just a dance. She should have been able to maintain her composure, but it crumbled like a sand castle at high tide against the sound of possession in his deep voice. She was trembling, instantly vulnerable and on edge.

Nartan guided her back, sliding his hand along her lower back with a motion that made her suck her breath in. There was far more than arrogance in him; there was a hard presence of dominance. What bothered her most was how it sent anticipation surging through her.

She wanted to bare her teeth at him. She needed to get out of his arms before she did something impulsive…again.

"We've passed the ceremonial dances part of the event." She pressed against his chest, making it clear that she wanted to be released. "So…thanks…"

Nartan's lips twitched, rising into a grin that was far from friendly. "No bother at all. In fact"—his eyes glittered with promise—"I'm enjoying myself immensely. But not as much as last night."

Her mouth went dry.

There was something about him, something that made her feel like she was poised on the edge of a cliff. He was like a live wire, and the need to scoot back was so overwhelming that she shook with it.

He was just so hard. His body was big and immovable, and the way he turned her around the floor was downright intimidating because it curled her toes.

He knew too much about how to use his brawn, too much about how to touch her and send her thoughts scattering.

She trembled again, fighting the urge to draw her fingertips down his chest.

Shit!

Her self-control was dissolving, dropping her on her butt and leaving her at the mercy of her impulses. That idea dragged her down into the failure of her marriage. It was a churning pit of impulses that had cost her dearly when she trusted a man enough to let him into her bed.

She wrenched out of Nartan's arms, feeling the parting too damned much, but she shook her head and left. Two couples looked up as she nearly bolted from the center of the floor where Nartan had taken her. The building was too damned hot, so she made her way out one of the huge doorways that was wide enough for a Hummer to fit through and walked toward the far corner of the building. Only after she turned the corner and left the doorways out of sight did she stop.

She closed her eyes and forced herself to perform a breathing routine she'd learned in marital arts. Her heart slowed, her respiration coming back into a normal rhythm.

When she opened her eyes, the great expanse of natural wonder didn't impress her. She was still fighting for control, fending off the attraction that Nartan unleashed in her. She ordered herself to ignore it, but her body was still trembling from his touch. Her blood was hot, her nipples hard; and every bit of self-discipline she'd learned from Master Lee was nowhere in sight.

"Tarak wasn't pulling my leg when he said your ex was a prick."

Celeste jumped, a startled sound escaping her lips, and whipped around to discover Nartan three feet from her. Her eyes widened, shock filtering through the haze of arousal fogging her brain.

"He had no business telling you anything about me," she said. Her temper was nowhere to be found, leaving her sounding like a lost little girl. Which sure as hell didn't mix well with the way she was fighting the urge to look at his lips.

Nartan raised an eyebrow. "So you'd prefer I just feel like a total dick when you take off in the middle of a dance, insinuating to everyone watching that I can't be a gentleman at my best friend's wedding?"

Shame threatened to choke her as she realized how her exit must have looked. Heat teased her cheeks but she lifted her chin, realizing it was time to face off with him before she lost any more of her wits. "We already agreed—"

"Agreed?" he cut in, stepping toward her. "No, honey, we didn't agree on anything."

He was pressing her. She felt him as much as she heard or saw him. Every muscle she had was taunt or quivering. "I made my feelings clear."

"You made it clear that you're afraid to face that ghost. You were just as interested as I was last night."

Her mouth dropped open. "Are you going to double-dog dare me next?"

His eyes glittered with hard enjoyment. "Maybe."

He closed the gap between them again, but she was too stubborn to heed the warning bell urging her to retreat.

Like hell she'd back away from him. "We're a little too old for schoolyard games."

"Agreed. I'm interested in playing adult games with you." He loomed over her. "You're attracted to me, but it scares you."

"I'm not afraid of you."

"Your actions tell another story," he fired back, relentless.

She drew herself up and planted herself firmly. "Not trusting myself isn't the same as being afraid of—" She snapped her mouth shut when she realized how exposing her words were.

"Trust takes time." Nartan reached out and cupped her elbow. She would have wrenched away from him, but his hold was soft and nonthreatening. Undermining. Like it had been the night before. She had no defense against tenderness. Not even the desire to resist.

And it sent a shiver down her back.

"And courage." His tone was deep and husky.

The ripple of sensation stunned her. Somehow, she hadn't realized how lonely she felt, how much she yearned for human contact. She hesitated, held spellbound for a moment, granting him enough time to smooth his hand around her elbow and along her lower arm before sliding his fingers along hers and releasing her. He tightened his fingers into a fist and forced it into his suit jacket pocket. He concealed his thoughts well, but she still saw the tiny signs of strain at the corners of his eyes.

He wanted to pull her toward him.

But he didn't, and that left her open to a new sensation, one she hadn't felt in a very long time.

Trust.

Just a hint of it really, but she rolled her lower lip and set her teeth into it as she contemplated the restraint he was employing.

"I shouldn't have stomped off the dance floor," she offered softly.

He growled softly. "I didn't follow you out here for an apology."

The sun had set and the wind suddenly gusted, raising goose bumps along her bare arms. "So why did you? It isn't like you'd find it hard to hook up with someone else."

She shouldn't have asked, shouldn't have laid herself open so completely.

"Because I liked having you against me."

She'd known he'd say that.

It was like a secret hope, one that sent a jolt of enjoyment through her, but slammed into the wall her fears had built.

"You liked being against me too."

Hard certainty flickered in his eyes, driving that bolt of enjoyment into the wall a few more inches. She fingered the fabric of her skirt as she fought the urge to reach for him but at the same time, enthralled with the effect he had on her reservations. He was so tempting until she remembered that she wasn't ever doing a long-term relationship again.

"Sabra is my best friend too, so let's leave each other alone before things get tense."

His eyes narrowed. "I don't get tense over relationships."

She found herself recovering her poise. "There's my point. If I'd accused you of being the playboy type a moment ago, you'd just call me judgmental."

He offered her a lazy shrug. "True."

He reached out and captured her wrist. Before she finished deciding if she was going to let him keep hold of her, he'd stroked the delicate skin of her inner wrist with his thumb and sent a ripple of awareness across her skin that made her nipples pucker. "There's a charge between us."

There sure was.

Playing with fire…

But it was intoxicating in a manner she'd never encountered before. She really questioned if she was tossing away a prime opportunity to get it dealt with. No strings attached, and a pistol like Nartan might be the perfect remedy for her trust issues.

"We're not going to connect." She twisted her wrist and dropped it on the other side of his hand to break his grip and held a finger up to keep him back while she finished her thought. "Because I would be using you to cross a line item off my to-be-dealt-with list. I don't use people."

His eyes narrowed as his lips thinned.

"Parts of me would really enjoy being used by you…but your point is valid." He nodded and forced himself to step back a pace. "You should get some…therapy…"

She offered him a dry laugh. "I don't need therapy because I'm not interested in a fling with you. It's called maintaining the integrity of my soul."

"You're interested and that scares you," he countered ruthlessly. "That's why you need therapy. You're being a bitch now because I called it on the money."

He saw too much. And she *was* being a bitch.

"I've had some. Court ordered, no less." She felt like her emotions were draining her. "It was just another way Caspian was able to ensure I did what he wanted. Just another hold stuck in the fine print of our divorce papers. So public, but such a private little stab too. No freedom until I performed one final act of obedience."

"What a prick."

There was venom in his tone. It surprised her and nurtured the little spark of trust taking root inside her. He looked sincere, but she couldn't afford to let her budding feelings grow.

"Yeah, but it's over."

She was shutting him out.

Nartan watched the way Celeste tightened her features and looked away from his face. He really didn't need to get involved. But leaving felt like quitting.

That was something he never did.

"It won't be over until you pull that weed out by the root," he informed her. "That's how that ghost maintains its grip."

She started to shake her head. "This isn't your concern."

He stepped into her path when she tried to make a getaway.

"Or maybe I should have said, it won't be over until you find the courage to face your demons."

Her eyes widened in surprise before her temper flickered in her eyes. "Like I said, neither of us needs the tension hooking up will create."

"The way you blush when you look at me says differently." He shrugged and watched the way her gaze lowered to his shoulders. "Am I the first man who's excited you since you left the prick? Or am I just the first one who's made it past your defense system?"

"You don't—" She bit back the lie, a hint of disgust surfacing in her expression. "My sex drive works just fine."

He offered her a raised eyebrow. "You're good at it, the brush-off."

"How would you know?" she questioned. "You don't look like a man who gets told 'no' very often."

He chuckled. "Thanks for noticing."

"Can you even name the last five partners you had?" she asked.

Nartan locked gazes with her. "Now you're back to being a bitch to get me to shove off."

"Maybe I am a bitch."

He studied her for a long moment. "You aren't. I know my share of them."

She drew in a deep breath. "My point exactly. But just in case you don't get it, I'm not interested in joining your list of friends with benefits. I know what it's like to be used, and I won't do it to someone else. Even if you're willing."

Surprise flashed through him and unleashed a wave of need that shocked him with its intensity.

"Tell me you don't want to touch me and I'll walk away."

She'd crossed her arms over her chest. She gripped her own bicep, her fingertips pressing into the skin. There was a flash of guilt in her eyes, a hint of fear over being unmasked, which sent a jolt of excitement through him.

"I want the same thing."

"Yeah, I got that message when you pinched my butt," she responded in a dry tone.

"I cupped it." He withdrew his hand from his pocket and mimicked a little pat. "Only a boy thinks a girl likes to be pinched. I know how to touch a woman."

Her face turned scarlet.

But the tip of her tongue appeared and swept across her lower lip. He stepped toward her and had to force himself to stop when her expression become guarded.

"Touch me, Celeste."

She blinked. "Excuse me?"

He crooked his finger, beckoning her forward. "Come here and finish what we started last night…" He laid his hands on his chest for a moment. "Do what you felt the impulse to do, and don't let that prick keep you bottled up."

"I told you, I'm not interested in doing anything about what I feel for you." She shook her head. "Why would I? Your ideas are clearly different than mine when it comes to relationships. I'm a complication you don't want any more than I want to be disappointed in myself by how I treat you."

"And still, I followed you out here." Determination edged his words.

"All that proves is that you like getting what you want," Celeste countered, doing her best to recall exactly why using him was something she wanted to avoid.

"You think I have to follow you to get it?" It wasn't really the tone of his voice, just the way his features sharpened with confidence. He knew his effect on women and enjoyed reaping the benefits.

"Thanks for confirming what I thought about you the first time we met."

She went to step past him, but he moved into her path. "And what was that?"

"That you are very successful and accustomed to being in control." She sighed and held up her hand when he started to speak. "It's nothing personal. I just don't go for the controlling type."

His eyes had narrowed, but his lips lifted just a bit at the corners. "The hell you don't. That little puppy dog that tried his hand at impressing you on the dance floor didn't have a prayer, because you need someone who is going to impress you before you yield."

"You sound like a caveman."

He reached out and clasped her nape, curling his hand around the slender column of her neck and pressing with his fingers into those points of tension she seemed to always have. He gave her just a taste of his strength, enough to unleash a flood of heat before he released her.

He chuckled softly when she averted her gaze to keep him from seeing what she felt. "What's wrong? Don't know what to do when there's no way to divert your attention away from how I affect you?"

Exactly.

She was forced to admit there was a lot of truth in what he was saying.

"Nartan, this is just going to get messy."

"You don't trust a confident man, but there is no way you'd surrender to one who wasn't confident." His voice hardened. "Your ex is succeeding in getting you to build your own prison."

Was that true?

She hated the fact that it might be.

He reached out again. Doing it slowly, testing her nerve. She felt the distance between them closing, everything slowing down as she became immersed in the sharp sensation of anticipation.

But she didn't pull back. She locked gazes with him. "You might be right."

"And you don't like that?"

"No." She stepped closer to him. "Let's see if it was moon madness last night."

All of her senses were heightened, her skin ultrasensitive when he brushed the surface of her cheek with his fingertips. She shivered, her eyes slipping closed as she savored the connection between them.

For just a moment, time froze and she allowed herself to enjoy the contact. Oh yes, she had forgotten how good it felt to be touched.

Decadent…

She opened her eyes when she realized she'd never enjoyed a man's touch as much. This was more intense and far more likely to explode.

"You're fire." She shook her head, intending to sever the connection between their gazes, but he slid his hand into her hair, rubbing across her scalp before he closed the distance between them and tightened his fist in her hair.

"I could make the same accusation." His eyes glittered with need. "I haven't stopped thinking about kissing you again."

She gasped, the sight of him on the edge driving her closer to it herself. He leaned down and captured the sound with his lips.

It wasn't a hard kiss.

She could have pulled away from a hard, possessive claiming of her lips.

Nartan started with soft pressure that stole her breath. It might have been slow, but he still pressed his mouth against hers with all the solid confidence she'd accused him of. It was there in the way he slid his lips across hers. Once, twice, and then a third time before he teased her lower lip with a soft lick.

Everything except the connection between them ceased to register. She reached for him, smoothing her hands down the cotton of his shirt. She dipped her fingers beneath the blue tie, determined to get closer to his skin.

She could smell him. That musky scent that turned her on as much as the way he stroked her tongue with his. It was masterful and arrogant, and excitement tore through her like lightning and left a burning trail behind.

She twisted toward him, straining upward so she could kiss him. The hold on her nape changed, tightening as he growled. He curled his other arm around her, binding her against his body as she reached for his hair and pulled his head closer against her own.

The kiss became demanding and hard. He pulled her right off her feet and pressed her up against the wall of the building. He reached down, sliding his hand across the curve of one side of her bottom and further down to her thigh. Heat roared through her, her heart pounding as her clit began to ache. The need to press against him was so intense that she never protested when he pulled her thigh up to allow him to grind against her mound.

He hissed, his fingers slipping beneath the hem of her skirt and discovering that one strap from her garter belt was the only thing to keep his hand off her bare skin. She shivered, his skin connecting with hers like a clap of thunder. She jerked her head back, unbearably conscious of how exposed she was. Only a thin triangle of silk covered her sex, just inches from his fingers. She was on edge, completely exposed. Frantic with the need for more. More of him.

"We need a room…now," he growled next to her ear. She felt the words as much as heard them.

He stepped back, allowing the air to slam into her. It was like a bucket of ice water. She struggled against the horror of what she'd allowed herself to do, blinking as she took in the hunger edging his features and sharpening them. Someone laughed nearby and the click of heels against concrete made it through to her at last. Acute embarrassment mixed with the sexual craving tearing up her insides.

"No…"

He reversed course instantly, turning to face her and flattening his hands on either side of her head. His eyes narrowed to slits as he drew in a deep breath and held it before opening his eyes to display a glitter that made her mouth go dry.

"I can smell your heat, Celeste… I want to taste you…every inch of you…"

His voice was raspy and raw, promising her a hard ride. But it was the possessive gleam in his eyes that made her shake her head. He slipped his hand around the curve of her hip and drew her against him, making sure she felt every hard inch of his erection. Her passage quivered, tightening with need so acute that she groaned.

God, she wanted him…so damned much it hurt.

She ducked under his arm and came up a few paces from him. She really hadn't escaped, and that knowledge, mixed with the raging need inside her, made her wonder if trusting him was such a terrible thing after all.

"Find someone else."

It was the kindest, politest thing she could manage. Brushing him off completely felt overly harsh when she knew damned well she was the one with trust issues.

"Because you're right. I have unresolved issues."

She turned and walked away. Her confession rung in her ears, but a little ripple of relief went through her too. She'd said it. Finally admitted it out loud. Nartan might not be the best choice of confidant, but he'd been the one to insist on pressing against her comfort zone.

Hell, the man pressed better than anyone ever had. It was as irritating as it was impressive. She felt wrung out, her emotions raw.

As she rounded the corner of the building, the music from the reception became louder. A few people stood just outside the doors, enjoying a smoke. They glanced her way and her cheeks reddened as she fought the urge to turn and look behind her.

Yeah, Nartan was good at pressing into comfort zones. She'd bet he was damned good at shattering every last illusion she might have about what great sex was. The way he moved, kissed, and touched screamed out his experience level at bedroom games.

He'd be fire in her hands and she'd be putty in his.

It had to account for the way she reacted. That was also why she needed to put space between them. But at least she wouldn't have any problem doing that. Once the wedding was over, she had a tour of Alaska to enjoy. Nartan Lupan would go back to running his upscale restaurant and no doubt find someone less complicated.

Maybe several someones.

That thought gave her enough poise to restore her composure. Rich men didn't sleep alone unless they wanted to. Even if they didn't come in the mouthwatering type of package Nartan did. She slipped into the building and headed toward the ladies' room to check her lipstick.

That was all. Just a reaction to his skill level.

Rationalizing always broke down extreme feelings. At least for her it did. Taking solace in logic might be cold, but she was far less likely to end up in the sort of disaster her marriage had been.

~~~

The wedding reception was in full swing when Nartan reentered the building. The cake had been cut and was being delivered to the tables. Tarak had retreated to the bar and scowled at Nartan when he joined him there.

"Some wingman you are," Tarak growled. But he frowned and narrowed his eyes as he stared at his friend.

"That's not a good shade of lipstick for you, Nartan."

Nartan reached for a napkin and wiped it away. "Tasted good."

Tarak took a sip of his whisky while brooding. Nartan signaled the bartender and soon found himself nursing his own drink.

It wasn't what he wanted. He wanted the taste of a woman's flesh on his tongue.

Hard, blunt, but honest.

His gaze searched the crowd until he found Celeste. The bridesmaid dress was reserved enough in design, but all he saw was the way it flowed over her curves, fluttering and settling against her body to give him a tantalizing glimpse of what her thighs looked like, then swishing and shimmering and hiding what he craved. He got a glimpse of a trim ankle and a brief side look at one mouthwatering breast before Tarak chuckled and distracted him.

"Don't be so amused," Nartan warned.

Tarak set his drink down. "There is nothing on this planet that could keep me from enjoying the sight of you right now. Payback's hell."

Nartan smiled and let out a word in their native tongue. His grin covered the fact that he was telling Tarak to go fuck himself in the middle of a wedding reception.

"Unlike you, my bed is occupied," Tarak answered. "But I am curious what your next step is going to be. She's not going to make herself available for you."

"Actually…" Nartan's voice trailed off as he contemplated Celeste and the way she'd turned her back on him.

He liked the view.

"I think it's time for me to do a sight check on the lodge." He tossed the last of his whisky back and set the glass down. "I wouldn't want you to think I let your wife's best friend stay in questionable accommodations while she's on her vacation."

"Of course not." Tarak narrowed his eyes. "But if all you're interested in is fun, find another toy. She's family now."

It might not have been the most logical of decisions, especially with Tarak's warning, but Nartan felt a burning in his gut that he knew too well. It was a feeling he trusted, one he'd followed in business, and he'd been rewarded with success for doing so.

He wasn't finished with Celeste Connor. Leaving her behind would be a mistake.

Nartan's grandmother walked right across the crowded dance floor. She was all of five feet tall with long, gray braids. She had plump cheeks and wrinkles around her eyes when she smiled. The guests parted, making way. It might have been because of the way age and wisdom seemed to radiate off her, or it could have been the ceremonial buckskin dress she wore.

Celeste found herself mesmerized by the sight, time suddenly blurring as the old woman took the wedding celebration back to traditions that had stood the test of centuries. She looked frail but latched on to Celeste's hand with a strength that was surprising. She pulled Celeste off the dance floor and right back to Nartan's side. She had to be the only living soul on the planet who could have accomplished it, too. A pleased glimmer appeared in her blue eyes as her lips set into a very satisfied grin.

She started chattering in Apache.

Celeste's eyes narrowed suspiciously. "I seem to recall your grandmother speaking English this morning."

The old woman smiled so widely that her eyes ended up nothing but slits in her face. Celeste got the sneaking suspicion that Nartan had learned a lot from his grandmother.

Nartan lifted his hands in surrender when his grandmother looked back at him. "I'm not arguing with an elder. She wants me to translate."

Celeste couldn't help but smile. Okay, the guy was presumptuous, arrogant, and pushy, but he respected his grandmother.

That made him adorable.

Crap.

"The sun is going down. She wants you to go get Sabra and help her change into the dress."

A younger girl stepped up and offered Celeste a bundle. She laid it in Celeste's arms as carefully as she would have a baby.

"That was her mother's dress," Nartan explained. "Made by *her* mother."

"Wow." Celeste remarked, adjusting her hold to make sure she wasn't crushing the bundle.

His grandmother nodded with approval and chattered some more. Nartan listened before translating.

"She says to tell Sabra that Tarak is her son, no matter how he came to this world, so his bride will wear the dress from her family and that the English portion of the wedding is over, so she will speak Apache now."

A little tingle of suspicion touched her nape as Celeste watched the way the old woman's eyes sparkled. The younger girl was looking back and forth between Nartan and Celeste with a smile that matched her grandmother's.

Celeste nodded before turning and moving off toward Sabra. Nartan fell into step beside her. A quick glance to the side showed her the stiff set of his lips, but she took a second look when she noticed the flush darkening the skin of his neck.

She choked on a laugh.

Nartan reached out and cupped her elbow. "Don't be a bitch," he warned in a low tone.

"What? And notice that your grandmother is a formidable woman? Or that you respect her?" She offered him a genuine smile. "That part won you points in my book."

He made a low sound under his breath. "She's also nosy. I forgot just how little respect she has for my privacy."

Celeste missed a step. "Are you saying…"

"That she followed me outside…yes," he confirmed.

Her mouth went dry. Nartan suddenly laughed. "You blush."

"Well, it beats having no shame," she countered.

"Which is how you see me?"

"You're the one who wants to approach sex like a business merger." Why was the bloody warehouse so large? She picked up her pace. "Can't help it if your grandmother doesn't like your lifestyle choices."

"Fifty percent of marriages end in divorce." His fingers tightened on her elbow. "You're a lawyer. You know that."

They'd almost made it to the head table. Celeste stopped and sent Nartan a hard look. "That's a crappy thing to say at your best friend's wedding. Sounds like you have your own trust issues."

"So stop throwing stones because I live in a glass house?" He made a low sound that resembled a growl.

"We do have some things in common," she replied without thinking. Once again, conversation was flowing between them, feeling so natural that she didn't have the heart to stop. "Someone taught you to distrust relationships too. So you're a playboy and I'm a recluse, but we're both guilty of giving in to our… What did you call them? Ghosts."

There was a flare of surprise in his blue eyes before she turned and moved toward Sabra. Her friend looked up and one of the catering staff moved over to pull her chair back for her. There was a rustle of silk taffeta as she moved, and the candlelight flickered on the surface of the pearl necklace fastened around her throat. Deepsea pearls and all perfectly matched. The single strand was worth a small fortune.

Celeste was caught by the way Tarak turned to look at Sabra. There was an unmistakable flash of heat in his eyes and a softening around his mouth that touched her heart. He was always aware of where Sabra was. Devotion wasn't something that could be faked. It was found in the way a person's gaze returned over and over to the object of their desire. Celeste found herself looking back at Nartan, only to feel herself locking gazes with his cobalt-blue stare.

She felt the connection as much as she saw it. The room seemed to shift, the breath in her lungs freezing as her lips tingled.

With memory? Or maybe with need. She didn't have enough brain power at her command to decide. He moved, reaching out to catch the bundle that was slipping out of her distracted hold.

"One good thing about ghosts…" he whispered softly. "They lose their grip in the light of day."

Her mouth went dry as she shifted closer to him, completely on autopilot. His magnetism was drawing her forward and she was finished questioning why it was a bad idea.

He muttered something in Apache, low and almost savagely.

There was a giggle from his cousin before Celeste felt her face go up in flames. Nartan's complexion darkened as his lips curled back to show her his clenched teeth.

"Timing is everything…" he growled.

"We might both be grateful for it in the morning."

He wanted to argue with her. She saw denial snap in his eyes. A soft bubble of amusement escaped from her lips before she realized it. His eyes narrowed to slits, his features tightening with a promise that sent a ripple of excitement through her.

"Challenge accepted." He turned her loose to offer Sabra his hand. Her friend took his hand, using it to steady herself as she descended the three steps that led to the raised dais the head table had been set on.

She had her fingers in the fire now…

But she wasn't entirely sure if she regretted it or not.

Nartan's cousin stood staring at her with dark eyes full of merriment. She was barely a teenager but just enough past childhood to spot attraction. The girl's lips split into a wide smile before she covered her mouth with her hand and giggled behind her fingers.

Nartan stiffened. He sent a stern look at the young girl, but she was unimpressed and just smiled brightly at him.

Celeste tightened her hold on the dress and hurried after Sabra, the giggle echoing inside her head as she fought the urge to join in.

Leaving the room didn't prove to be the escape she intended it to be, though. Sabra barely waited until they'd made it into the office-turned-dressing-room before pegging Celeste with a question.

"Did you go outside with Nartan?"

Celeste set the bundle down on a desk and sent Sabra a withering look. "I went outside and he followed."

"Did you kiss him?" Sabra pulled her veil off and set it aside.

"Sabra." Celeste tried to sound ominous but ended up merely sounding wiped out.

Her friend offered her no mercy. "You did."

"He started it," she groused and turned to help her friend out of the designer wedding gown.

"Ummmm… He looks like that type. The kind who likes to start things, that is." Sabra hummed before ducking into the bathroom and turning on the shower. "Nartan is just the sort of man you need to send Caspian running for the hills."

"He'd shit a brick, and I don't mean out of fear."

"That's the best part." Sabra's head appeared around the doorway. "I hope the idea of you moving on burns a hole the size of Wyoming in him."

"I don't really need him thinking about me at all. Thanks." That was a can of worms she really didn't want to open.

Sabra shrugged. "True. And not true. He'd want you to remain true to him and he wouldn't care about your reasoning, just that you are still sleeping alone."

She disappeared, leaving Celeste in blissful privacy as she faced the truth of her friend's words.

Caspian would love knowing how empty her bed was and had been since their divorce. But what did it say about her if she had sex for the sake of taking a stab at him? That was worse than treating sex like a business merger. It made her petty.

She sighed, feeling half-alive.

"Be right out, it was hot on that dance floor," Sabra called.

Celeste heard the shower door open and close. The water ran for a couple of minutes, giving her time to unwrap the bundle. Inside was a Native American dress. The scent of leather rose from it as the fabric was unfolded. There were tiny beads sewn in intricate patterns and long pieces of fringe. It was darkened by age but the hide had been a light-colored one. The darkening only enhanced it, giving it a dignity at least equal to the designer wedding dress.

"And another reason—" Sabra reappeared in only her underwear.

Celeste lifted the dress and shot her friend a hard look. "Let's get you married today."

Sabra chuckled. "And miss the chance to prod you over your little encounter with Nartan? Never." Sabra waited until the soft buckskin slid over her head. "Although, by the way you were captivated by him just now…I'd say it was nothing little. In fact, I think he rocked your world with that kiss."

"How much champagne did you have?"

Celeste closed the back of the dress and reached over to where the boots were still resting on the desk. They were newer, because Nartan's grandmother had smaller feet than Sabra.

"Nice try." Sabra wrinkled her nose at her and held up one finger. "I didn't want to risk falling off the horse during my Apache wedding."

Celeste pulled the pins out of her friend's hair and brushed it out so that it fell in soft waves to her shoulders. There was a soft rap on the door before the younger girl who had been following Nartan's grandmother peeked inside. She smiled.

"Grandfather says come soon. The sun is setting."

"Ready?" Celeste asked.

Sabra inspected her reflection before turning toward the door. "The question is, are you ready? Oh friend who is avoiding questions."

Celeste shook her head. "You're beating a dead horse."

"According to my reports, Nartan did a good job of breathing life into you."

Celeste groaned but Sabra reached for the door and pulled it open. Her father was there, waiting in his dress uniform to escort her to the last ceremony of the day. He offered her his arm and proudly strolled back into the warehouse with Sabra.

The music had shifted to a soft flute-and-drum song that was distinctly Native American. Tarak and Nartan's kin sat in a half circle with their instruments. There wasn't any wood polish on the instruments, but feathers dangled from lengths of leather as they played music that seemed ageless.

The guests had lined up at the other end of the warehouse. Tarak stood, holding the bridle of a magnificent horse. His tux was gone, a buckskin shirt and pair of jeans in its place. Nartan had changed as well and Celeste discovered herself struck dumb.

Speechless.

She was suddenly caught in a moment that had no time signature. They might have been standing there two hundred years before or any time in the future. All she knew was that she'd never felt as moved by any wedding before. It was genuine and focused on the couple so completely that her eyes stung with unshed tears.

Tarak led the horse down the center of the room, followed by Nartan leading a gorgeous black stallion. Tarak moved closer and closer, his attention on Sabra while the steady beating of the drum seemed to match the rhythm of Celeste's heart. Strength bled off him, and the animal seemed like some sort of incarnation of that power. He held out the bridle, offering it to Sabra.

"I bring you the finest horse I own. You are worth a hundred more."

The intensity in the way Sabra reached for the bridle held everyone spellbound. Tarak's dark eyes followed her every motion and his lips twitched, betraying his pleasure as she wrapped her hand around the leather. Nartan let out another cry, the rest of his family echoing it. The horse snorted as Tarak offered his hand to Sabra's father.

A moment later, Tarak turned to his bride and lifted her up onto the back of the horse. Nartan held out his horse's reins and Tarak eagerly took them. He mounted and settled on top of the animal with a skill that proved how comfortable he was in the saddle. The guests applauded but the gesture seemed oddly out of place. Ignorant, really. The echo of Nartan's cry suited the moment better.

Nartan reached out and slapped the flank of the horse Sabra sat on. It snorted, tossing its braided mane, and headed for the wide-open doors. Tarak took the lead and Sabra's horse followed. Celeste found herself hurrying to catch a glimpse of them against the pristine beauty of the Alaskan wilderness.

It was breathtaking. The horses climbed the hillside easily, carrying the couple away from man-made structures.

Simply beautiful.

"Don't worry."

Nartan had moved close to her while she was absorbed with watching the bridal couple depart.

Awareness rippled through her. "Worry about what?"

"That your friend is heading for a primitive honeymoon campsite." He pointed up to the ridge. "Tarak had a cabin built up there."

A rich man and his resources.

Nartan reached out and cupped her elbow. "Why does that bother you?"

"I was enjoying the simplicity of the moment," she confessed.

"You can't tell me you don't enjoy all the comforts money can buy."

His tone had hardened. She chewed on her lower lip for a

moment. She was on the verge of labeling him arrogant again, but there was something deeper in his eyes, something he was keeping hidden. His gaze lowered to her lip, settling on where her teeth were pressing into it. Heat licked across her face and flowed down her body.

"I don't care for the sense of entitlement that goes with it." She turned and faced him, indulging herself for just a moment, letting herself soak up the raw power radiating from him. It was hard and distinctly male, touching a part of her she'd thought stone-cold dead.

"You don't either," she decided. "That's why you're unhappy."

He chuckled, the sound a warning. "Nothing could be further from the truth. I love my life."

"No, I'm right, as right as you are about me." She cut him off. "You play the game, but it leaves something in you unsatisfied."

His lips thinned and he reached out to cup her elbow. He stroked it, sending a shiver down her. "There will be nothing…unsatisfied between us, Celeste. I promise you. Nothing."

Now there was a promise…

It was tempting. Really tempting. The raw pulse of need pounding through her was sharp enough to make her hesitate. His blue eyes glistened with determination, making her breathless.

She shook her head and his grip tightened. "I've been a rich man's toy. The trappings lose their shine rather quickly, but as you said, you don't have to go far to find company." She lifted her elbow and stepped back. "So I'm sure you'll never miss me."

For sure, part of her was going to miss the charge he gave her. Withdrawal bit into her as she made her way toward the house and escape from her high heels.

It promised to be the only mercy she was going to find.

Chapter 3

CELESTE GROWLED AT HER alarm clock when it began chirping. But if she were honest, it was a relief to be awakened by something other than thoughts of Nartan. Her mind insisted on playing back every touch, every ripple of sensation, until she was ready to scream. She had even tried practicing her tae kwon do forms in an attempt to clear her head. Nothing worked.

At least she hadn't heard the wolves.

She rolled out of bed and shuffled toward the bathroom. Hot water made a huge difference on her outlook. By the time she'd dressed and applied a light coat of makeup, she was grinning.

Her Alaskan adventure was about to get under way.

She zipped up her toilette bag and stuffed it into her suitcase. The house was quiet, the double doors to the master suite open for once, because Tarak and Sabra had taken off on their honeymoon the night before. A house felt different when it was empty. Like it wasn't really whole.

Within an hour she was aboard one of the private jets Tarak Nektosha owned. The sleek aircraft seated eight and even had a steward who served her breakfast once they took off. She peered out the window, enjoying the view of Alaska. After a while, she dug her travel book out of her bag and studied her itinerary. Mount McKinley, Denali National Park, mushing, and a tour of Glacier Bay National Park. If she was lucky, she'd get to the see the northern lights when she reached the edge of the Arctic Circle.

The small plane circled before coming to a perfect landing near a majestic lodge built facing Mount McKinley. When Celeste disembarked and stepped onto the pavement, she was disappointed to see the entire peak shrouded in clouds.

"Don't worry, Ms. Connor. Denali will come out," an Alaskan woman remarked from where she stood beside a small, off-road type of golf cart. She had on a pressed green shirt with "Glen Stoke Lodge" embroidered on the pocket. "The mountain makes its own weather but it's worth waiting for."

The steward delivered Celeste's bag and offered her a two-finger salute. Climbing into the cart, Celeste enjoyed the sting of the cooler weather against her cheeks. They rounded a bend and she gasped with delight. The Glen Stoke Lodge was even better than the pictures in the brochure.

It was built to look like a cabin, with huge logs forming the front and a roof that rose into a sharp A-frame to accommodate snow. The building also had a foundation of smooth, rounded rocks and large picture windows. Off to the right side was a huge viewing area with padded seating and fire pits.

Wings of rooms stretched out on either side of the main lodge, and wildflowers grew all over the property.

"The penthouse suite has been reserved for you."

The woman drove right up to the front steps before putting the golf cart in park and hopping out. A uniformed doorman was already pulling Celeste's luggage from the cart.

"This way, Ms. Connor…"

The interior was just as grand. There was a huge, glass-enclosed fireplace in the center of the lobby. Off to the right there was a restaurant, the sound of dishes clinking and the scent of food drifting out to tease her nose. The desk manager came striding up to welcome her and show her to her room.

The penthouse suite was everything she'd expected. There was a sitting room, and beyond a doorway were the master bedroom and bath. All the furnishings were just a bit rustic, giving the place a frontier feel. Yet it didn't lack for modern amenities. Every detail had been double-checked, and the small fireplace in the sitting room was on, even with the private patio doors open to let in the fresh Alaskan air.

But she was drawn to the valet stand in the bedroom. A pair of snow pants, boots, and everything else were laid out on it. An envelope was sitting on a polished wood tray in front of it. She broke the seal and pulled the card out of it.

> *Please find everything needed for dog mushing. You*
> *will be airlifted to the camp on the glacier as soon as*
> *you are ready.*

She smiled and even squealed. Tossing the card away, she stripped so she could get into the pants. They rustled as she put them on. There was a short-sleeved top as well, and she quickly discovered that she needed it to keep from overheating before she got to the glacier. The boots were a little clunky but fit perfectly. Ready to leave, she folded the jacket over her arm and headed out of the suite.

The helicopter was a new model, its paint fresh and bright, with the logo of the lodge on it. The pilot came out to shake her hand.

"Any trouble with heights, Ms. Connor?"

"None."

A tiny ripple of relief crossed his face. He opened the passenger-side door and offered her a hand in.

She laughed when they lifted off, the ground disappearing below them. The pilot sent her a few looks until he was sure she wasn't going to have a panic attack or throw up. Once they cleared the landing area, his voice crackled to life through the headphones she wore.

"First time in Alaska?"

"Yes."

He kept his attention on the air in front of them. The helicopter felt like a giant bubble moving through the air. They crossed over forest and granite outcroppings. Water was cutting its way down the mountainsides in white, frothy streams that came from the ice field.

"We're going into a fog bank," the pilot warned just before the pristine view was cut off by clouds. He maneuvered his way through, checking the console as he controlled the aircraft.

"Setting her down."

The surface of the glacier appeared right below them. Her belly gave a little twist as the pilot landed the helicopter. Two men were waiting out of range of the helicopter's blades.

When she opened the door, she was glad for the snow pants. The air was crisp and the clouds hung low over them. She could feel the water in the air.

"You'll want that jacket now."

A ripple of awareness went through her. She turned and stared straight into the cobalt eyes she's spent a lot of time trying to banish from her dreams. Nartan stood there, but what claimed her attention was the way the pilot nodded to him.

"You own the lodge." It was a flat statement.

"Tarak would never book you a room in a questionable resort. Trust me, there are plenty of those up here."

There was a glint in his eyes that made her shiver. She wasn't entirely sure whether it was caused by appreciation or apprehension.

"I'll give you points for your extreme setup. I never saw it coming." But she should have. Rich men stayed rich by knowing one another's weaknesses. That's really all a fascination with a woman was in Nartan's world.

A weakness.

She found herself battling the way he made her question her resolve.

"Praise from the lady at last." He performed a mocking bow before taking her jacket from the pilot and holding it out for her.

She turned around and fit her arms into the sleeves. He pointed up at a red snow vehicle of some sort.

"We have to take the CAT up to the dog camp. The snow here is too soft for the sleds."

Her boots crunched on the ice and Nartan steadied her with a hand on her arm as she got the hang of walking. "Yeah, it's practically summer weather..."

The other man opened the door of the huge snow machine, and Nartan clasped her waist to help her up.

She shivered in spite of the layers of clothing between them. There was just something about the way he touched her.

It felt perfect in a way she hadn't experienced before.

"Coming up..." he warned before he climbed in and sat next to her. The driver turned on the engine, and the CAT started to climb over the ice. Celeste wobbled on the long bench seat. Nartan slid an arm around her as she pushed her feet into the floor to steady herself.

"To be honest, I thought you'd be a tad more prickly about my presence."

"You think I'm a sore loser, huh?"

The machine was noisy, grinding away as it moved over the glacier face on huge treads like a tank.

"Glad to be schooled."

She snorted. "I don't think you get schooled very often."

He flashed her a grin. "You can have special tutoring privileges." His eyes narrowed. "I think I might enjoy seeing you in a prim and proper schoolmarm suit...peering at me over the rim of your glasses... Wooden ruler..."

He tightened his arm around her, and she turned her head away so he wouldn't see her amused smile. For a moment, she just enjoyed the embrace.

Crap. It had been a really long time since anyone had held her.

Okay, since she'd allowed anyone to hold her.

He lifted his right hand and pointed ahead of them. "There's the camp."

Just coming into view was a row of round tents set on platforms that looked a lot like loading pallets. When the CAT stopped and she got out to walk closer, she realized that's exactly what they were.

The dogs were barking, most of them jumping with excitement. Beyond the tents, about forty boxes served as doghouses. They were set right on the snow, but the dogs were resting there as easily as they might on grass.

"This is Candace. She's training her team for the Iditarod. She's going to teach you how to mush."

The girl had ice slush up to her ankles and a messy ponytail, but she grinned and offered her hand.

Celeste started to follow the girl, only to see Nartan heading toward a second team of dogs. He caught her look and grinned. But it wasn't the carefree expression he'd shot her when he'd shown up on the glacier. This one was pure determination.

"We're racing," he declared.

Celeste felt her confidence rising. "You bet your ass we are."

"We're betting for dinner."

He turned and strode over to his sled. Celeste focused on Candace, listening to the commands and stepping up onto the sled. The musher stood on the back runners of the sled, holding the reins. The dogs got up, yipping and barking with excitement.

It was a total blast. The rush of adrenaline, the slap of the frozen air against her cheeks. The dogs took off with a jump, jerking the sled into motion before it started cutting across the surface of the glacier like a hot knife. It was smoother than she'd thought it would be, and faster. She held on, not looking down at the ground because she wanted to win.

Nartan's team came up from behind, pulling alongside her. Candace gave direction from the seat of the sled, while Nartan's sled was empty.

Of course. He wasn't a man who lost.

He smirked at her and she gave in to the urge to stick her tongue out at him.

She instantly regretted that because the frozen air felt like it was freezing her tongue. She dropped one of the reins as she slapped a hand over her mouth. The sled veered to the right, her string of dogs tangling with Nartan's before Candace got control.

Nartan scowled at her. "Sabotage!" he yelled over the barking of the dogs.

"Serves you right."

Candace was trying to separate the dogs, and the moment they were facing forward, the dogs were pulling on their harnesses to start going again. They ran up the glacier until Candace grabbed the reins and pulled them around to face back down the valley. She stopped the team, leaving them looking down the face of the glacier.

Celeste found herself breathless. The expanse of ice had streaks of darker earth and stones flowing through it like ribbons. Below them was the forest and then the ocean. She felt insignificant in such an imposing landscape and, at the same time, more alive than ever.

"Are you warm enough?"

Nartan was behind her, his breath warm against her ear.

"Sure."

He pulled one of his gloves off and stroked her cheeks and nose. "You can get frostbite from the windchill."

He rubbed her nose for a moment, warming it.

"I think this is more than the normal tour."

He shrugged. Her belly tightened with him so close, the reaction instant.

"Thanks. This kicks serious ass."

He winked at her. "Does that mean you'll have dinner with me?"

A warning bell was trying to sound, but it was hard to hear with his body heat surrounding her. "And if I say no?"

His eyes glittered with promise. "Candace will end up getting an eyeful when I kiss you right here."

"Dinner," she answered a little too quickly, "but no promise of a kiss."

"I promise you there will be both," he said, and stepped away.

"You've got a one-track mind," she called after him.

He turned and fixed her with a knowing look. One that warmed her cheeks again and kept them stinging on the ride back down the glacier.

But she didn't really dread the coming evening. The truth was, she was looking forward to it.

Her legs felt like Jell-O when she stepped out of the shower back in her room at the lodge.

Candace gained a huge amount of respect in her book as Celeste rummaged through her travel case looking for some painkillers.

But it had so been worth it! Her Alaskan adventure was a blast, and she had to admit that Nartan was doing his part to make it unforgettable.

Someone knocked on the door, so she made her way across the sitting room.

"Good afternoon, Ms. Connor," a woman in a three-piece hotel uniform greeted her. She pushed a rolling cart into the sitting room and transferred afternoon tea service to the table. "Compliments of your host. You have a confirmed dinner reservation in the Denali room at six."

Celeste dug her wallet out of her purse, but the woman shook her head. "Every detail of your stay has been provided for. Please ring the desk or use the touch pad if you'd like anything."

The woman made for the door and disappeared quietly. Celeste moved closer to the table to inspect what had been delivered. The plate was almost too beautiful to disturb by eating from it. Small slices of cheese and fruits were artfully arranged. There were afternoon tea cakes that smelled divine. They were so delicate that she snapped a picture with her cell phone to preserve the image.

"You've got style, Nartan Lupan."

For just a moment she felt a tingle of apprehension on the nape of her neck. Every little luxury could become a bar in a lavish cage. The perfectly performing staff could transform into a network of spies that would make it impossible to breathe.

You're building your own prison…

Nartan's words rose up from her mind and snapped her back into the moment.

She reached for the silver teapot that was also on the table and poured hot water into a delicate teacup. A selection of teas sat in a box alongside a small pot of honey and a miniature pitcher of cream. Celeste unwrapped a tea bag, dropped it into her cup, and took it out onto the viewing patio. She settled into the large, rocking love seat, smiling as she sunk into the thick cushion, and sipped her tea.

She refused to notice how everything was built for two people.

She wouldn't notice it because she'd made her choice to be single.

But you do still feel Nartan's kiss…

She drew another sip from her tea, letting the hot liquid override the memory.

Her choice.

And she was happy with it.

Bullshit…

She took another sip and realized how easily Nartan had become the ghost lurking in her thoughts.

Well, at least that was a step forward.

The real question was: Would she let him kiss her after dinner?

―⁓―

Celeste primped in front of the bathroom mirror.

She was avoiding thinking about what she was doing. Going with the flow; letting herself enjoy the buzz of dressing up.

Why not?

God it felt good to think like that!

She finished her makeup and loosened the soft dressing robe that had been hanging in the bathroom for her.

The matching lingerie set she had on made her pause. She looked down at one of her garter straps, almost feeling the brush of Nartan's fingers against her thigh.

Ghost. Only this one was far more welcome than the specter of her ex-husband.

Drawing in a deep breath, she walked over to where her dress was hanging. She tore off the plastic covering in which the pressing service had encased it and lifted the dress over her head.

As overwhelming as Nartan was, it was a relief to have memories of someone other than Caspian.

You're enjoying the idea of seeing him again…

Actually, she was, and she wasn't going to get her panties in a twist over it.

Nartan wasn't the only one who knew how to make an entrance. She was going to knock him off his stride tonight and enjoy every second of seeing him on edge.

Playing with fire…

Yes. And high time too.

The dress was spring green, matching her eyes, and settled just above her knees. She stepped into a pair of heels that clicked on the tile floor, and reached into the closet to pull out a wrap in case she wanted to venture outside. The Alaskan summer was packed with eighteen hours of sunlight. Maybe she'd get a look at the peak before sunset.

She tucked her room card into her bra and left her purse on the bedside table.

No cell phone.

Nope.

She was on vacation.

You're going on a date...

Date, vacation—there was no need to overthink the moment.

Whatever emergencies were brewing in the Lower 48 could be resolved without her tonight.

She was working on her to-be-dealt-with list.

She took her time walking toward the restaurant, the scent of dinner teasing her nose before she arrived. The hallway was constructed to allow for an unobstructed view of the granite peaks in front of the hotel. She heard the low rumble of conversation coming from the restaurant before she turned the last corner and arrived in front of the reception desk.

"Good evening, Ms. Connor."

The way everyone knew her name was a little unnerving. Of course, she was a guest of the boss, so everyone would be betting on just how much influence she had with Nartan. It wasn't much but no one would believe her if she claimed otherwise.

The gentleman smiled and gestured her past his desk. Instead of taking her into the spacious dining room, he led her past the floor-to-ceiling wine cellar to another more private dining area. Large tables were set into secluded dining alcoves with velvet curtains that could be closed to provide privacy. There were also small, intimate tables.

"Please mind your step."

The man took a moment to point out the first step of a staircase with the help of a small flashlight. He led her up the stairs silently, the mark of a professional butler. The stairs took a right-hand turn and rose another floor. Once she stepped onto the landing, the restaurant below and its sounds dissipated, leaving her immersed in the wide expanse of Alaskan wilderness surrounding her. Some sort of soft music was playing,

"The Denali dining room…"

The man gestured her forward but that wasn't really necessary. The table was set in a section of the restaurant that overhung the viewing patio below. Floor-to-ceiling glass created a temperature-controlled environment with a breathtaking view.

"May I take your wrap?"

"Yes, thank you…" Celeste surrendered the garment as she moved closer to the table. Another waiter had appeared while she was absorbing the grandeur of the view and now held her chair out.

He reached for a wine bottle that was nestled in a silver bucket and opened it, then poured a small measure into a glass for her approval. She swirled it once around the glass and inhaled before taking a sip.

"Perfect."

He nodded before filling her glass and a second one. The waiter finished with a twist of the bottle to keep it from dripping and set it back in the bucket. He disappeared quietly while she looked over her shoulder.

There was a little swish as doors slid shut, ensuring complete privacy. A chef was waiting beyond the glass doors to speak with the waiter. They conferred for several moments before the waiter disappeared.

Celeste turned back to look at the second wineglass.

"Your neck is tight."

She didn't jump. Nartan's voice washed over her and every muscle tightened. Her lips parted as her heart accelerated and she fought the urge to look behind her.

She lost.

She did a double take, blinking as she drank in the sight of him. He was hot. And mouthwatering. The realization sunk all the way into her brain. Nartan was watching her from beneath hooded eyes, gauging her reaction and looking like he was taking her apart like some sort of complex math equation.

At least, she felt that vulnerable.

Totally stripped down in front of him.

She was tempted to label him intimidating, but the truth was it was her own failing that made her so susceptible to him. There was some reaction brewing inside her on a cellular level that was reducing her to a bundle of responses that operated on a purely instinctual level.

She noticed every little detail about him.

Like that what he did for a suit should be bottled and sold. The gray wool was loose enough to show how fit he was, his tie the same ocean blue as his eyes. All of that rich fabric lay over him like wrapping paper made to be ripped away.

He moved closer, his fingers brushing her nape. It was just a light touch at first, gauging her acceptance. She took another sip of wine and let him rub the tense muscles in her neck for a moment.

He moved away and sat down. She watched him, feeling on edge.

"Admit it, you're impressed with me."

Maybe…

"I can always check out if you get too presumptuous," she countered softly.

One inky, dark eyebrow rose. "Only if you're willing to admit you're too chicken to be in the same room with me."

She tapped her fingernail against the pristine tablecloth. "Touché," she admitted. "Even if I think you're a bit of a cad for voicing that thought."

"Cad?" He picked up the folded napkin and gave it a snap before laying it across his lap. "I call it persistent."

"Hmmm…" She battled the urge to let her lips curl up with enjoyment. "Stalkers are persistent too."

He tossed his head back, laughing. The column of his throat snagged her attention, and the desire to lick him flared to life.

The doors behind them swished open. One waiter lit the candles on the table while two more delivered a starter to both Celeste and Nartan at precisely the same time. The waiters lifted the polished silver domes off the plates with a flourish before disappearing as quickly as they'd appeared.

"Don't I at least score points for originality?" he asked.

Celeste picked up her fork and considered the plate in front of her for a long moment. "Only if I were interested in being the point of a game."

Nartan was considering her over the rim of his wineglass. "You think I'm playing, with you as the prize?" He was hiding behind a polished business demeanor, leaning back in the chair to give the illusion of being relaxed, but she could feel how sharp his attention was. The man was sizing her up.

She lowered her fork. "I'm really not trying to be a bitch. The afternoon was amazing."

"But you're still not sure what you think about me following you?" he clarified in a smooth tone that raised the hair on her nape in warning.

"I'm not sure what I think about the fact that I had a hell of a lot of fun with you this afternoon and that I put this dress on with you in mind. Because it's possible that you just hate getting the brush-off. You didn't build all of this by being a pushover."

He raised one dark eyebrow. "You kissed me back. Whatever you want to label my appearance, make sure you allow for the fact that you're right. I don't get the brush-off very often, and if all I wanted was sex, I'd have gotten it somewhere else by now."

"Like I said, I'm not sure what I think."

She reached for her wineglass, which she regretted once she had it in her fingers. Dulling her wits wasn't a wise course of action. She had dressed for him. She *had* kissed him back.

And dreamed about him…

She drew a slow sip of the dark liquid into her mouth before setting it aside. "The lodge is impressive." It really was, and she could see how much care and excellence had gone into it. That kind of quality could only come from the top.

He finished and sat back, his lips rising into a grin. "Thank you. Changing to a safe topic?"

She fluttered her eyelashes at him. "Forgive me. I thought you wanted to actually have a conversation with me." She pushed her chair back and stood, disappointed beyond measure. "As I told you at the wedding, I'm not interested in hooking up with you."

His gaze slid down her body. "Then why are your nipples hard?"

She stepped away from the table like it was on fire. "Screw you." Her disappointment was transforming into full-out anger. Now he was just being a jerk—as if to live up to the worst of her expectations.

"That is the main point of contention, isn't it? You want to give in to me, but it clashes with your ideas of what good girls do. So you label me arrogant, when in fact, you don't want to face your own reaction."

"Facing it and jumping you before the salad arrives are two different things."

"Bull." He cut her off. "That's just an excuse for not being daring enough to take what you want from life."

"I love cupcakes too, but I don't grab one and shove the entire thing in my mouth the moment I get a craving for them. Ruins the experience."

His expression became carnal. There was a savage beauty to it that captivated her, hypnotized her.

"I could handle you shoving me into your mouth."

She pushed her chair back and turned her back on him, but there was a soft click and the window she faced frosted. It brought her up short, and she turned to find Nartan dropping a small remote control into the breast pocket of his suit jacket.

"You can't control it any better than I can." He stood up and came around the table. He had a prowl to the way he moved, something very uncivilized that sent fire to all of her logical decisions. Choice seemed to be nothing but ashes now. There was only stimulus and reaction. Honestly, she wasn't sure who was pinned in the room with whom. He might be fire, but she wanted to consume him too. She took a breath and fought for a hold on her logic.

"Just because I find you attractive doesn't mean I'll cut straight to the 'get naked' part." She faced off with him, needing to make her point. Or stand her ground. Or something else that seemed impossible to name.

Maybe she just needed…him.

He'd stopped a couple of feet in front of her and looked like he was trying to decide what to do with her about-face. Hell, she was trying to decide what to do.

They stared at each other, her heart accelerating, his eyes narrowing. Each of them becoming more aware of the other with every second.

"You have to stop running at some point." His voice had changed, deepening into something that struck her as genuine.

"You don't know what you're talking about, Nartan." She tried to deliver her brush-off softly, kindly, because it wasn't his fault he sent her sex drive into high gear.

He gave her a shrug. "Maybe, maybe not because I'm guessing I'm the first man who's kissed you since your divorce."

"Only because I want it that way."

She was such a liar.

His eyes narrowed. "Really?" There was a soft, seductive tone to his voice that sent a shiver down her spine. She'd never been so conscious of her body and the craving to have his pressed against her.

"I don't want to talk about my past." She took a step toward him.

He stepped forward, allowing her to flatten her hand against his chest. She shuddered, feeling the connection down to her toes.

"Neither do I." He locked gazes with her. "Tell me you dreamed about me pressing against your body the way I dreamed of touching every inch of you."

He cupped her chin, keeping their gazes locked. His blue orbs were full of hunger, the same sort of craving that had been gnawing at her since the wedding.

"I…did." Her lips went dry. She swept her tongue over them and watched his eyes narrow and his mouth thin with hunger.

"Good."

He sealed her mouth beneath his. She almost pulled back but he followed, licking and sucking on her mouth as every inch of her body erupted into flames.

It was so damn instantaneous.

And he was everything she craved.

The hard body she'd dreamed about was beneath her fingertips. She slid her hand up his chest and felt it vibrate with a growl. He slipped his hand around her neck to cup her nape and keep her mouth beneath his. But she wasn't content to be kissed. She moved her hand all the way up and across the warm skin of his neck until she was able to thread her fingers through his hair. She wanted to hold him, control him, just as he was doing to her.

The kiss was a battle, a meeting and merging of their mouths as well as a collision. He pressed her lips wide, his tongue boldly thrusting into her mouth. She closed her lips around it and sucked, needing to taste him, desperate for him. She pulled on his tie, loosening the knot and slipping her fingers inside his collar to touch his bare skin.

She purred with satisfaction and felt the connection ripple all the way down to her toes.

"*Shit!*"

He groaned, pulling their mouths apart long enough to grant her a glimpse of his startled expression, but it melted away, leaving her facing a level of arousal she'd never seen before. It was blunt and fierce and something inside her crackled with satisfaction.

He cupped her shoulder and swept the straps of her dress down, instantly baring her breasts and binding her arms to her sides. Her room card went fluttering to the floor as she gasped.

"I want to taste every single part of you…"

He leaned over and closed his mouth around one puckered nipple, cupping the soft globe with a grip that was just shy of too aggressive. She gasped, her eyes opening wide as she arched back, offering her breast to him. An insane spike of need tore through her, sending her hips thrusting toward him. His mouth was hot around her nipple, but his cock was rigid behind the smooth wool of his pants. She twisted, trying to reach for him, but the straps of the dress held her arms at her sides.

She must have made some sound of distress, because he lifted his head and tried to focus on her face. His eyes were dilated, sexual hunger making them bright. In some part of her brain, she was pleased to know she'd driven him just as insane as she was.

Pleased? Hell, she was proud of herself. Delighted all the way to her core to know what she did to him.

He chuckled, low and deep. "Enjoying the sight of what you do to me?"

"Yes."

He reached down and grasped the hem of her dress, pulling it up and over her head. His gaze felt like a flame as it traveled along her length, his jaw clenching. "I like the view too."

She reached for the lapels of his jacket, pushing it back and forcing him to put his arms back as he struggled out of it.

"Wait…" He grabbed the jacket before it fell to the floor and rummaged through the pocket for the remote. He was breathing heavily as he pressed another button and they heard the door lock.

Somehow, she'd forgotten about the door. Embarrassment

began to burn a hole through the desire. She glanced around, remembering where she was. She stepped back and wobbled in her heels.

Nartan caught her, pulling her close and using his body to steady her. She lifted her head, intending to tell him that they had to stop, but he sealed her protest beneath his lips. She ended up melting and reaching for what she craved. She tore at his tie until she yanked it loose and threw it aside. He reached down and cupped her bottom, slipping his fingers beneath the edge of her lace panties.

Need twisted violently through her clit.

"I can smell how wet you are…" he growled. He gripped the back of her thighs and lifted her up, spreading her wide as he carried her and set her on a service table.

She reached out and stroked his erection. He arched back with a groan, his teeth showing as his face became a tapestry of male need. He reached down and ripped open his waistband and fly, freeing his cock.

The swollen organ fell into her hand. It was hard, covered in soft, hot skin. Her clit pulsed as she stroked him from base to tip with her fingers.

"Not yet…" he ordered hoarsely. He shoved his hand into his pocket and pulled out a condom. "You're going to come with me."

He tore the packet open and looked down as he donned the latex. "Next time, I'm going to lick every inch of you before we get to the fuck."

He reached out and dipped his fingers beneath the small triangle of satin guarding her slit. "But you don't want to wait any more than I do."

She let him push her back all the way until she was lying across the table. He pulled her last garment free and pressed into her body. The acute sense of arousal had made sure she was slick and wet. His cock slid easily between the lips of her slit to the entrance of her body, and the walls of her pussy protested.

He gripped her hips and snarled something in Apache as he forced himself to ease forward. "You're so tight."

"I don't care."

She opened her eyes and locked gazes with him. She closed her legs around him, pulling him toward her.

"Not yet…" he growled, holding back with only the tip of his cock inside her. He reached down, slipping the pad of his thumb against her clit and rubbing.

She cried out, pleasure spiking through her.

"That's it… Open for me, Celeste."

He rubbed as his cock slipped deeper.

"Now," she insisted.

He gritted his teeth and surged forward, stretching her body as he impaled her. It ached, but at the same time, an intense wave of satisfaction washed through her. It was deeper, more intimate than she recalled, and she arched to take his next thrust, and the next and the next.

The blood was roaring in her ears, her heart pounding so hard that it felt like her chest couldn't hold it.

None of that mattered. All she cared about was lifting her hips for him, making sure she was straining toward him so that her clit received the maximum amount of pressure. She was racing toward the peak, and all that mattered was the climax she felt building deep inside her. Somehow, she'd forgotten how incredible the pleasure was. Every thrust sent a cry past her lips as she moved closer and closer to the moment of release. Reason melted away as instinct controlled her.

When it came, she felt like she was being ripped apart. The pleasure started as spasms in her core. She felt the crown of his cock lodging deep inside her and her body clenched around it, trying to milk it as ripple after ripple of ecstasy rolled through her.

"Look at me…" he commanded. He pinned her beneath his body, even locking her arms above her head. "Let me see."

Her eyelids were heavy, but she lifted them and felt like the last layer of personal space between them was ripped away. He commanded the rhythm completely, surging into her with motions that made her breasts bounce and the table jerk.

He was just big enough to stretch her to the limit, and it satisfied some deep instinct to feel his balls slapping against her bottom. He was growing harder, thicker as he bared his teeth and snarled. The muscles in his neck corded as he tightened his grip on her wrists.

"God damn it... Mine...mine...mine..." he growled as he drove into her.

She wanted to close her eyes but held them open as his face contorted in ecstasy. She watched it bite into his expression, stealing every last bit of composure and laying him bare. She purred with satisfaction a moment before her body erupted into a second round of rapture. It was deeper, tighter, and harder than the first release. She lost the battle to keep her eyes open and arched as sensation ruled her completely.

When it was finished, she felt like she'd been dropped onto the table. Every muscle felt strained and she was coated in perspiration. Her heart thumped so hard she thought it would burst. Nartan stroked her cheek and laid a line of tiny kisses across her bare torso. He cupped her breasts, massaging them before he pushed up and withdrew from her.

Something buzzed and she opened her eyes to see what it was.

"No rest for the owner..."

Nartan stepped back, grabbing a towel from the end of the table and wiping the condom away with an efficient motion. He closed his fly and handed her a towel before withdrawing a cell phone from his pants pocket. He read a text message before frowning and pushing a button.

"Take care of him."

Someone on the other end of the line was arguing.

"I pay you to deal with this sort of thing."

There was another round of arguing before Nartan snorted. "I'll be right there."

He dropped the phone and started buttoning his shirt as she sat up and used the towel to dry herself, feeling unbelievably exposed.

"I have a health inspector down in the galley being a dick and demanding to see the owner since he heard I'm here."

He offered her her dress before he turned and retrieved his tie. He was pulling it around his neck as he made his way toward the door.

"I've got to go deal with the guy. He shut my kitchen down saying I've got illegally harvested salmon. Asshole."

He'd already mentally withdrawn from her, his mind back on business. Celeste pulled her dress on and leaned over to pick up her room card as he unlocked the doors and left.

She felt sick.

It was everything she'd expected, but that didn't mean the experience was worth it. She stood for a long moment, letting the sting burn through her.

She should have remembered.

Should have forced herself to recall the place where men like Nartan put the women they fucked.

And that's all it had been to him.

A fuck.

So she couldn't let it mean anything else to her.

Just a check mark on the to-be-dealt-with list.

She grabbed her wrap and headed back toward her room. The majestic view held little appeal as she did the walk of shame past the staff, who knew exactly what their boss had been doing. She tore her dress off the moment she turned the bolt on her room door and then dropped the dress into the trash can, feeling filthy and cheap.

Stupid…so stupid!

She refused to cry. Absolutely forbade the tears welling up in her eyes to drop down her cheeks. She settled for getting into the shower and scrubbing her skin until every last trace of Nartan was gone.

~~~

Her cell phone was buzzing when she finally emerged from the shower. The mirror was completely obscured and steam swirled around in a lazy cloud. She picked up the phone, frowning when she read the caller ID.

"What are you doing calling me on your honeymoon?" Celeste admonished Sabra. "Your new husband's image is taking a major hit right now."

And it was far too tempting an opportunity to unload. Celeste bit her lower lip, sealing in the emotions that were trying to spill out of her. She might have made a colossal mistake, but that didn't mean she was going to top it by being a lousy friend. Only Nartan seemed to be able to strip away her standards. There was no way she was going to spill her guts while her best friend was on her honeymoon.

Sabra laughed on the other end of the line. "Hmmm, I might tell him that," she purred. "I just wanted to make sure everything is measuring up. Can't have my best friend disappointed on a trip I arranged."

"About that…" Celeste caught sight of herself in the defogging mirror. Her eyelids were heavy and her lips swollen. "Who's paying for this? You or Nartan?"

"Ummm…I'm not sure." Sabra answered. "Nartan owns the lodge, so it's possible he's just writing it off as a favor to Tarak."

"He's here."

"What?" Sabra's voice sharpened.

Celeste bit her lip to contain the tremor trying to leak into her voice. "A little warning would have been appreciated."

Sabra clicked her tongue. "Excuse me, Celeste, but I need to go kill my husband. Or at the very least impress upon him the dangers of setting up my best girlfriend."

"You do that."

Celeste snapped the phone shut and tossed it onto the bed.

Her knees were still weak.

The puddle of green satin in the trash can caught her eye and ignited her temper. She flipped open her phone and dialed the number to Nektosha Industries' private planes.

"Good evening, Ms. Connor. How may we help you?"

"I'd like to return to Southern California. Immediately."

She could hear the soft sound of keys being depressed on a terminal. "I've got a crew that can be airborne in half an hour."

"Thank you. I will be ready."

She killed the call and yanked on a pair of jeans. Within ten minutes, she had her clothing shoved back into her suitcase. She made it down to the desk as someone drove up in the all-terrain golf cart.

"Sorry to see you leave, but at least the mountain has come out to send you off."

Celeste turned around to see Mount McKinley in all its glory. The sun was just going down, casting a ruby glow over the snow-capped peak. It was a shame she hadn't had a chance to meditate with such an amazing view as inspiration, but for a moment, the sight shoved aside the massive boulder of regret sitting on her chest. She climbed into the private aircraft and sat near a window so she could watch as the plane took off. The moment she felt the aircraft leave the ground, she sunk back into the seat and felt the devastation rip into her.

She knew better. Really, really knew better.

⁓

Nartan struggled to maintain his composure. The health inspector was in the mood to draw out his visit. He ambled through the kitchen, selecting various personnel for lengthy discussions during the peak dinner rush. Orders were backing up and tempers were running short as Nartan tried to keep the man on track.

By the time the inspector left, Nartan was close to sending his fist into the man's face. Instead, he turned to find his head room steward waiting for him.

"Did you deliver the order?" he growled.

"Your guest in the Denali suite has departed. The front desk says she left in a Nektosha private jet."

Nartan checked his watch and cussed in Apache. Two fucking hours!

Of course she'd run.

What bothered him the most was how strong his impulse was to give chase.

He should have been relieved.

He turned and made his way to the suite. He pounded on the door just once before using his master key to open it. Two steps inside and he knew she was gone. The wardrobe doors were open, granting him a view of the empty interior. The bed was crisp and clean, the sheets turned down but undisturbed. A used towel was dropped on the bathroom floor, a few wet puddles remaining on the surface of the marble tile. There wasn't a personal item left.

The trash can caught his eye, the dress lying there abandoned.

Maybe he should thank her. There were certainly plenty of times he'd enjoyed knowing his liaisons didn't expect anything further from him.

Right now, that thought made him feel like shit.

Like complete shit.

⁓

Her butt really was numb by the time Celeste made it back to Southern California. She wished her feelings would join it.

She wasn't going to get that lucky, it seemed. As she made her way to the curb and flagged down a cab, she fought back a wave of bitterness.

Honestly, she'd known what sort of man Nartan was the moment she'd first set eyes on him. Dark, controlling, and impossible to resist. He was a danger zone for any woman who had even a scrap of decency. The type who played high-stakes games and went after sexual interests with the same zeal. She'd known, so there was no reason to become emotional. It was time to look on the bright side.

Caspian was no longer the last man in her bed.

Well, on her table.

She felt her cheeks burn and drew in a shaky breath. Focus, she ordered herself. At least the sex had been good.

Okay, it had been mind-blowing.

Another bright little thought.

She paid the cab driver and dug her house keys out of her bag. Everything inside her house was familiar, like a good friend welcoming her back. She locked the door behind her and reengaged the security system.

Yeah, that was familiar too.

The need to watch her back. Her ex-husband was an art collector, and she had been one of his prized possessions. He wasn't a man used to having his toys taken away. He thrived on control, and she felt the days ticking away to when he'd be free to torment her again.

She'd handle it. Because she had to.

At least Nartan had made sure she didn't need to do anything about him. That should have gone down in her book as another good thing.

But it didn't.

<center>~~~</center>

When her alarm clock went off the next morning, she decided she was pathetic.

She'd been up for the last two hours.

She rolled out of bed without even thinking about sleeping the better part of the day away.

Pathetic.

At work, her boss poked his head out of his office when she passed by on the way to hers.

"Did a grizzly bear kill you up in Alaska, and now your ghost has decided to haunt our hallways?" Marcus Flynn asked from her doorway with his usual brassy, navy yard tone. There was no hedging around the topic. When Marc wanted to know something, he went ahead full throttle right past personal boundary lines.

"No, I just came home early and decided not to burn my vacation days," Celeste answered as she tucked her purse into her desk drawer.

Her ex-JAG boss was still very fit, even if genetics had let him down when it came to hair. He'd responded to his rising hairline by shaving his head. It made him look like more of a badass, as if the tattoo on his forearm wasn't enough. Marcus crossed his arms and leaned against the doorway. "You have three months on the books. I was happy to see you taking some of it."

The hint hung in the air between them.

"Thanks for the warm welcome, boss." She put her hands on her keyboard and hoped he'd shove off.

Marcus's eyes narrowed, warning her of an incoming cross-examination.

"Don't," she warned him.

One of his eyebrows rose.

Celeste pointed a slim finger at him. "Don't put on the JAG face. You're a civilian now. Which means I can argue with you."

Marcus bared his teeth and bit the air in front of him.

"Sorry, we work together." Celeste answered his silent "bite me." As usual, Marcus had his shirtsleeves rolled up to his elbows.

His upper body was still in prime condition, despite his discharge from the Judge Advocate General's Corps. Baring his forearms was cutting loose as far as her boss went, but Celeste didn't judge him too harshly. After all, twenty years in a JAG uniform would make bare forearms pretty laid back by comparison.

"Tell me with a straight face that you have nothing you'd like to get off your desk, and I'll leave," she challenged him.

Marcus snorted. "Guilty as charged. But you shouldn't make this place your home just because I'm a sucker for hard-luck cases."

"You like the buzz of winning the fight for the underdog."

"That's what I said."

Her boss abandoned the door frame and returned to his office. His law firm wasn't in some upscale part of town because Marcus had a soft spot for servicemen who needed legal services on a budget. Sometimes, that budget was only a handshake and a promise of payment when they could scrape it together. If ever.

Celeste loved her job.

Oh, it never would have suited Caspian and his ideas of what his wife should be doing. Every aspect of her life had been expected to enhance his image. She'd taken extreme pleasure in leaving the law firm she'd worked for during her marriage. Marcus took on real problems, not petty quarrels between socialites and their husbands of the moment. She wanted to practice law where justice was served, not the whim of those who only wanted to escape retribution for their crimes and had the money to do it.

She signed into her computer and dove into her inbox. Lunch was a sandwich at her desk, and by the end of the day, she was almost feeling normal. Total immersion in her job had its uses.

"Hi-yah!" Marcus yelled from his office at four thirty. "Get your tail going before Master Lee comes calling on me."

Celeste signed off and grabbed her purse. She paused in her boss's door frame. "Master Lee doesn't even know I'm back."

Marcus looked at her over the top of his monitor. "I'm out of here in twenty myself. Can't get soft in my old age. Meeting Chunky for a run on the beach."

"You guys have the weirdest taste in names."

Marcus grinned and rubbed the top of his shaved head. His buddies had taken to calling him Whiteout.

Celeste offered him a two-finger salute before heading down the hallway. The office was neat but furnished with only the basics. She was one of eight lawyers. The office had only three assistants but she didn't care. It was satisfying work, even if she'd taken a pay cut when she signed on. She didn't miss the top-shelf life-style.

The Denali dining room flashed before her eyes, and she conceded that she did miss some things. Fine dining was one of them.

But that only soured her mood, because one of her favorite restaurants was off limits now. Angelino's was one of her favorite brunch spots too. She slid behind the wheel of her Corvette and pouted. She might need to go into full mourning for the Malibu cliff-top restaurant.

Southern California traffic was teeming as she made her way across town to the martial arts studio where she trained. Pulling around back, she parked and grabbed her gear bag before opening the back door. One of the junior masters poked his head out of the back room to see who was arriving. His eyes widened with surprise.

"Vacation got canceled," she offered before disappearing into the women's locker room.

No, you chickened out...

Maybe, but sometimes picking your battles really was the wiser course of action. When it came to Nartan, she couldn't trust herself, so engaging him was a bad idea.

The studio was full of kids in white uniforms. They all had on different-colored belts, and their parents waited in the seating area as the kids trained. As the evening progressed, more advanced students arrived. By the time Celeste made it home, she was completely exhausted. Her own training was hard, but teaching younger kids held unique challenges that mentally wiped her out.

Kids needed to be motivated, and that was a lot harder than just snapping at them to stand still. Her own classes made sure her legs felt like noodles from fatigue. The brisk pace kept her mind from having time to kick in and distract her with Nartan. Another reason why she loved her martial arts training: the focus needed to do it kept her from going insane from her memories.

She punched in her security code and was welcomed into her small townhouse by a chirp. Once through the door, she tapped in the second code and heard another chirp to let her know the perimeter was armed.

Her first stop was the kitchen for some pain reliever. But she smiled with satisfaction as she swallowed a couple of capsules. Training was her choice of drug. It gave her a high and made sure that she'd sleep through the night. She headed up the stairs. A short shower later, she collapsed on her bed in an old T-shirt and pair of sleep shorts. It was a routine that served her well, giving her little time to think about men.

Except that Nartan Lupan showed up in her dreams.

Chapter 4

Saturday arrived with too many free hours for her taste. Celeste rolled out of bed early because the summer heat was going to make housework a bitch by midday. She left her old T-shirt on and only added a bra and cutoff jeans that had several splotches on them where bleach had hit the fabric. She used a clip to hold her hair on top of her head and added a headband to keep the shorter strands out of her eyes.

August in Southern California was always blistering.

Yeah, that's why you booked an Alaskan vacation...

She indulged herself in a moment of self-pity as she imagined how cool the glacier tour would have been, both figuratively and temperature-wise.

Celeste started on the windows first. She pulled her ladder out of her garage and climbed to the second story. She fit her key into the lock on the artful but sturdy floral iron screens she had fitted over the windows to secure them. Swinging one out, she began to deal with the dirty glass. The sun was baking the back of her neck by the time she finished the corner bedroom and climbed down.

"What are you doing?"

She jumped back and blinked like a simpleton at Nartan. He looked up the ladder and back at her gloved hands. It took a moment for it to sink in that he was actually there.

"You're a lawyer, Celeste. Haven't you ever heard of a cleaning service?"

Dealing with his memory was a lot easier than facing him. He had on a pair of jeans that fit him too well for her comfort. She was already noticing details about him—how dark his hair was, how much she wanted to run her fingers through its length. Her damned hormones were kicking into overdrive at the sight of him. Her world tilting off center.

Shit! The guy was her personal form of crack.

She pulled one of her gloves off. "Excuse me. Is there any reason why you feel you have the right to make observations concerning my life choices?"

He pulled his mirrored sunglasses off, and she was instantly caught again in his powerful gaze. The way the man struck her was so bloody unfair. Awareness rippled through her, like the lights turning on in a dark warehouse. Where she had thought there was nothing but empty darkness, there were now a thousand different areas of interest.

His lips rose, just the slightest amount at the corners. "I'll be happy to remind you if you've somehow forgotten."

She hadn't.

His memory had kept her company last night. Not that she planned on admitting it to him. Dealing with her own fickle reactions was trouble enough.

"Maybe you should go check your cell phone." It was a low blow, but she needed a shortcut back to reality before she lost her head again.

His teasing demeanor vanished. "That was poor timing on my part. I'm sorry."

"Don't sweat it." She meant it as a brush-off and tried to walk by him, but he reached out and caught her elbow. The contact was jarring, snapping her back into the vortex of need and arousal that had been the cause of her downfall in Alaska. There was something about him that was sinfully hard to resist.

Celeste pulled her elbow away and faced him. "I don't need this, Nartan. It's been a week." She hadn't meant that last part to slip out and ground her teeth together after hearing it.

She sounded pathetic. Marking time like a jilted prom date.

"It might have been piss-poor timing, but I was trying to run a business. I couldn't break away until yesterday. Alaska runs on its own timetable."

"You don't owe me an explanation." She managed to soften her voice. "You didn't seduce me." She turned and walked around the corner of her house and opened the back door.

But Nartan followed her right inside her kitchen, making it shrink. "I should have."

She froze. Not because of the words he choose but because of the tone of his voice. He was sincere and it touched her deeply.

"I lost my head." He crossed his arms over his chest and leaned back against her kitchen counter, making it clear he was settling in.

She opened her mouth but a snappy retort seemed beyond her grasp. "Likewise."

Satisfaction flickered in his eyes. It warmed her insides, sending them into a soft churning that horrified her with just how intensely he affected her.

It would be so simple for him to become her habit.

"I would have called, but that would have entailed asking Sabra for your number since yours is unlisted and you didn't give a number to the lodge with your registration."

She didn't care for how much she liked hearing that he'd at least tried to reach out to her. A ridiculous amount of pleasure bubbled up inside her, forcing her to press her lips together before she ended up smiling like a simpleton.

"I didn't think you'd appreciate me asking Sabra."

"Well, we have that in common. 'Cause you know she'd tell Tarak you asked for it." She didn't need any witnesses to how much of a failure she was at ignoring him. But her lips twitched just a bit as she shared a moment of common ground with him.

He tilted his head to one side, offering her a sheepish grin. "That too. Tarak has a memory like a steel trap."

She was caught up again in how easy it was to talk to him. Like stepping into a bubble where a kindred spirit waited. Their gazes met and his grin melted as his jaw tightened. She felt the shift between them, that undeniable pull toward each other that overrode every scrap of reason she had. Celeste took a deep breath and started tugging one of her work gloves off. "But it doesn't explain how you found my address."

"You used a credit card at Angelino's in the past."

Of course, her billing address was attached to the card.

"If you want to give me the slip, better learn to cover your tracks, Celeste."

His words rose from her memory and sent a chill down her spine. She felt cornered but there was still that undeniable twinge of appreciation for his skill.

"I think that's a tad bit…illegal."

He stared straight at her, his stance unwavering. She ended up choking on a laugh.

"You've got no shame, Nartan Lupan."

"Not a scrap," he confirmed. "I left it behind when I went to Alaska. Along with those who laughed at us. I'm successful because I go after what I want and don't take much time worrying about what other people think of my methods."

In a single sentence, he'd changed the mood back to one that had her shifting away from the overwhelming stimulus he radiated. He was aggressive, but it was attractive.

"Admit it. You enjoy knowing I tracked you down."

Maybe…

Oh, who the hell was she kidding?

The air-conditioning flipped on and Celeste reached over and pushed the back door shut out of habit, grateful to have something to focus on beside her unexpected guest. She flipped the lock and tapped in her security code while still on autopilot.

When she turned around, Nartan was watching her with a frown on his face. "Sorry, guess I shouldn't have locked you in. Habit."

"I noticed." He contemplated her for another long moment. "You don't have a cleaning service because you're restricting access."

She didn't care for the way he had switched over to all-business mode. His razor-sharp gaze swept across her small kitchen, pausing on the decorative iron over every window. The key was still dangling from a bungee cord around her wrist.

"You're drawing conclusions without evidence."

His gaze narrowed before sweeping the kitchen again.

"You must have only a third of your available resources tied up in this place." He turned and looked out the kitchen window at the tiny backyard and the neighboring unit rising above the fence. "Privacy is very limited."

"It's not a big deal."

He returned his attention to her, and she found herself staring at the side of his personality that had helped him build the lodge out of a gold strike. There was directness in his gaze and a sense of focus she couldn't help but admire, as much as she wanted to hide from it.

He opened his arms and gripped the edge of her kitchen counter. She got the feeling that he was holding himself back, and her belly twisted with anticipation.

"You ran."

Two little words had never sounded so incriminating. She stiffened, determined to maintain her composure.

"You were clearly finished," she countered but flinched at how sharp the words were.

He slowly shook his head. A flicker of need in his eyes sent her body into meltdown.

"Nowhere near finished. Neither of us were. I was an idiot for taking the call." He stepped away from the counter, sending a shiver down her spine. "I might even admit that it's a habit to keep from having to deal with messy good-byes. But I am not finished with you."

Sometime during his speech, she'd forgotten to breathe. She felt like she was poised in the open doorway of an airplane, trying to decide if she really wanted to jump and trust the fragile fabric of her parachute.

"Well, I'm finished." There would be no jumping for her.

He slowly shook his head. "Not by a long shot."

She backed up, the heat in his voice scalding her. Even with the air conditioner pumping cool air into the room, she felt overheated and trapped inside her clothing. "I'm not interested."

"Yes, you are," he shot back.

That was an argument she wasn't going to win, so she switched tactics. "Is your ego really so inflated that you can't deal with the fact that I left before you decided you were ready for me to go?"

He drew in a stiff breath. "That thought crossed my mind."

"Good." Except she was disappointed. There was a ring of truth in his tone that snagged her attention.

"Which is why I'm here." He extended his hand, palm up, the invitation clear.

Celeste looked at it and shook her head. "What do you think showing up here is going to prove?"

"Maybe the same thing you're worried it will—that walking away isn't going to be easy for either of us. That there was more to what happened than either of us wants to admit. Maybe I am jaded enough to admit I keep my sex life casual, but I think there was more to the spark between us. At least, that's what's driving me insane enough to swallow my pride. Question is, are you going to let it slip away because you're too busy avoiding the issue of trusting a man?"

She stiffened, her fingers itching to take his challenge. "It might have just been the moment…" Maybe it had just been the wine and the Alaskan air that made him seem so devastating.

"That's what I want to find out…" He extended his hand a little further toward her.

Tempting.

So tempting.

She extended her hand and laid it on top of his. His skin was warm and smoother than she'd recalled. He didn't close his hand around hers. Instead, he drew his fingers over the top of her hand in a slow stroke that made her knees go weak. His eyes narrowed and his lips thinned in a purely sexual way. She remembered the look, felt like it was seared into her memory.

In fact, she was sure her face mirrored his.

Nartan smiled in victory.

He stepped back and leaned against the kitchen counter once more, looking like the effort cost him a lot.

"Have dinner with me," he said.

Her composure was cracking, threatening to desert her in a shower of broken glass at any second. "I don't think that's wise."

"You're selling us both short, Celeste. I want the chance to make my argument."

She liked hearing that. There was no way to deny it. It seeped into the cracks in her shell. "Last time I was at Angelino's, there was no shortage of attractive women clustered around you."

"None of them give me the same charge I get when I touch you." He challenged her with a hard look. "At least I'm honest enough to admit it."

"Only because you want me to throw caution to the wind," she answered. "You're daring me."

He shrugged and replaced his shades. "True but you didn't strike me as a woman who'd let fear paralyze her. Maybe I misjudged you." He pulled a business card from his wallet and placed it on the kitchen counter. "If you don't burn this one, maybe you could let me know before five."

He reached over and punched in the code to her security system and it chirped. Her eyes widened with horror at just how keen his sight was. He touched his fingers to his lips in a silent kiss before disappearing onto her back patio. She caught a glimpse of him as he passed the side of her townhome, and heard the side gate open and close.

She cut through the house and peeked out the front door as he slid behind the wheel of a recently polished Jeep with the top down. The sun glistened off his black hair, and he grinned as he grasped the gear shift and put it into drive.

Her mouth went dry as she watched him disappear down the short cul-de-sac she lived on. That Jeep was sexier than any sports car. It fit the image she had of him, one supported by the memory of him in that low crouch, halfway down a rock incline in Alaska. Strong, hands on. Competent. She closed the door and found herself caught in a vivid memory of the way he'd stroked her clit.

He was arrogant, but his attitude left her craving more.

And he had a point. A very valid one that stung more than she'd realized it would.

She was letting herself be paralyzed.

Caspian shouldn't be able to do that to her.

She wasn't sure when she'd stopped getting back to doing what she wanted. But the hard truth was that Sabra had been her sole friend for the past few years. Sure, there were business functions and mild flirtations that she'd never allowed to grow into anything more.

She stopped in the kitchen and stared at the personal card he'd left.

To be dealt with…

Nartan had a more…direct way of asking.

Well, he wasn't the only one who enjoyed a challenge.

And sometimes, it was a case of now or never.

He had things to do.

Lots of important matters that would increase his profit margin. But Nartan found himself waiting for his cell phone to buzz.

More to the point, he was waiting for it to buzz with a message from Celeste. The little piece of technology lit up and buzzed, but he sent the incoming calls to his voice mail. He was only interested in hearing from one person.

He hit the interstate at seventy-five, but the wind in his face wasn't strong enough to carry away the delicate scent of her skin. His cock twitched, hardening as he recalled just how green her eyes were.

He'd wanted to know if a week would make a difference, and he had that answer now. It had made a difference.

She was worming her way even deeper beneath his skin.

It was both a balm and an irritant, leaving him poised on the edge. He didn't want to admit how infatuated he was with her.

He took the cutoff toward the ocean. The air became thick with the scent of water and salt. In the distance, he could see the glitter of the sunlight on the water. Inside his pocket, his phone vibrated and he dug it out in defiance of the law. A surge of primal enjoyment went through him when he found a text message from her.

Touché. I have been hiding. What time do you want to connect?

Chapter 5

I'll drive myself.

Celeste waited for a reply. It didn't take long.

Making sure you have an escape plan?

She glared at the screen of her smartphone but didn't hesitate when she punched in yes. If he didn't like her terms, too bad.

One step at a time, she added.

Wear jeans, was his response.

Nartan's Italian restaurant was located on the Southern California coastline, overlooking a stretch of the beach. It was definitely not the place for jeans. She felt odd getting into her car wearing denim, even if she'd dug out her best pair of jeans.

Caspian had demanded designer dresses at all times.

Fuck Caspian.

That made her smile, so she mouthed the words a second time as she smoothed a hand over her thigh.

Denim was perfect.

She headed toward Malibu. The freeway became crowded and expensive cars were more common as she neared the coastline. Drivers talked on their cell phones in spite of the hands-free law, watching the road through designer shades. Angelino's boasted a clientele that enjoyed the best. Sunset was still an hour away when she pulled up in front of the posh establishment. A valet jogged around the hood of her Corvette and pulled open the door for her. She gave him a five and a sweet smile.

"No scratches."

"Yes, ma'am," he answered before sliding behind the wheel with a grin.

"Somehow, I never pictured you driving a cherry-red Corvette."

Nartan appeared from one of the elegantly landscaped areas off to the right of the main entrance. He wasn't wearing the suit she normally associated with his five-star establishment. Instead, he had on a pair of jeans and a button-down, brushed-denim shirt. He was shaking his head.

"I'm divorced, not dead."

His lips split into a grin as his gaze swept her from top to bottom. "Nice choice."

"You said jeans." Hers were forest green, and she had on a flowing, goddess-type tunic in a soft ivory that complemented her fair skin. She hadn't realized how turn-of-the-century it looked until she was facing Nartan. With his long hair and bronzed skin, it was hard to remember just what year it was.

"We tried the dinner-table thing, so I thought we might try something a little less private to begin with."

He offered her his hand. Reaching for him took more effort than she anticipated. But the moment her fingers connected with his, he pulled her against him, slipping his arm around her back and clasping her hip. The grip sent a ripple of excitement through her pelvis.

Damn. Hard and primal and instantaneous.

"Less private?" Her voice had turned husky, her heart hammering away inside her chest. Every inch of him was enticing. She flattened her hands against his chest, unable to resist the temptation to touch what had been filling her dreams.

His breath teased her jawline before he pressed a soft kiss over the same spot. "Trust me, half a dozen of my employees are peeking out the windows at us."

"What?" She arched back, but he held her at the waist.

"One kiss," he demanded, one of his hands beginning a smooth slide up her back to press her more tightly against him.

"Is that a ransom demand?"

He'd reached the center of her back and pressed her forward so that her breasts yielded to the hard planes of his chest.

"Yes," he breathed through his teeth. "I think it is."

He was forceful and demanding, which pressed a button inside her that sent her core into meltdown. Nothing mattered except the surge of anticipation lifting her up toward his kiss. The phantom memory that had kept her company in her dreams wasn't enough anymore.

But she pressed one finger against his lips to stop him from taking what he wanted.

"If it's a demand, then you have to wait for me to give it to you."

There was something about teasing him, making him wait on her whim, that sent a charge through her. His eyes darkened, dilating as she stood her ground and refused to bend. He bit her finger gently and she pulled it back.

"I'm waiting…"

She tapped the center of his chest. "That's half the fun."

He didn't agree. His expression tightened as she sent him a challenging look and pushed against his chest. It was both triumph and torment when his arms opened, because moving away from him left a dull ache between her thighs.

But the surge of control was enough to make her smile.

"Bitch," he accused softly.

"Arrogant," she countered.

He laughed and offered her his hand again. "Only because you make me crazy."

"Right. Like I believe you don't enjoy all the benefits of being rich."

"Financially solvent," he corrected briskly. "A rich man has a loving family who stays with him no matter how few possessions he owns. I'm not rich."

His words surprised her. He was dead serious, and for just a moment, she felt like she had gotten a glimpse at his unguarded personal feelings. He covered the opening quickly, closing his hand around hers and leading her along the side of the restaurant. It was already filling up, the staff uncorking expensive bottles of wine as people prepared to enjoy Saturday night with a view of the sunset over the ocean.

A soft nicker reached her ears. They turned around the edge of the building and stepped onto a perfectly manicured lawn. A pair of Appaloosa horses stood there with two grooms holding their bridles. One swished its tail and tossed its head when it spied Nartan.

"Ever been on a horse?" he asked as he released her hand and stroked the horse's neck. The animal nuzzled him, earning a chuckle from Nartan.

"Sure. Caspian—" She shut her mouth. "Yes, I see why you told me no dress tonight."

Nartan's eyes narrowed just a touch before he gestured her forward. "I grew up with horses. My grandfather bred these two and the two he brought up to Alaska for the wedding."

"It must cost you a fortune to keep them here." But the animals were majestic. White with brown spots and light-colored manes. They watched her with large, dark eyes.

He shrugged, enjoyment clear in his eyes. "What's the point of being financially solvent if I can't have the lifestyle I enjoy?"

"That's very true," she muttered as a memory rose up from her past. She tried to cover her lapse by running her hand over the horse's mane.

"Your ex had a taste for expensive art." Nartan refused to let her shut him out.

She set her teeth into her lip and considered avoiding the topic. Oh well, might as well air some of the dirty laundry. Maybe she could finally put it behind her.

"He enjoyed possessions he could arrange into collections for his friends to view and be impressed by," she answered. "I was just another one of those."

She shot him a hard look. Nartan stared back at her for a long minute before he pointed at the stirrup. She lifted her foot and slipped it in before gripping the saddle. Nartan helped boost her up and she swung her leg over the back of the animal. It snorted softly as it adjusted to her weight.

Nartan took the opportunity to stroke her from hip to knee before withdrawing his hand with a naughty grin.

He mounted the second horse, and the groom tossed the reins up to him. He turned the animal around with a confidence that was undeniable. She had to think about how to keep her knees pressed in and her weight slightly forward, but Nartan did it with a natural ease that spoke of a long history with riding.

He started down a path that wove through the scrub brush on its way to the shoreline. Angelino's was above them, but they soon left it behind and the sound of the surf drowned out everything else. Nartan didn't stop until they reached the sand. He looked back at her before easing his command on the reins. His horse flung its head back and raced into the water.

Her horse snorted and let out a shrill sound as she pawed at the sand. Nartan turned around and watched to see what Celeste would do. She surrendered to the look of mischief in his eyes, and a moment later she was wet from ankle to hip.

But she laughed. The horses began running through the breakers, Celeste's horse following Nartan's. The frothy water splashed up in her hair and her face.

She didn't care. It was pure fun, and by the time they reached a point where the coastline curved around a rocky point, she was sure she looked like a drowned rat.

"You should have said to bring a change of clothes," she admonished her host when she managed to pull up beside him. She reached down, scooped up a handful of water, and threw it at him.

He leaned away, proving how powerful his legs were. The wave rushed out and then another one rolled in to cover them to the bottom of the horses' bellies. Nartan scooped up a handful and returned fire.

Celeste turned her horse around and leaned down over its neck as she charged back the way they'd come. Nartan let out a savage cry behind her. She looked back and squealed as she caught sight of him bearing down on her. His horse was bigger, with a wider leg span, and closed the distance as she urged her mount faster. He let out a yell before slapping her butt as he surged past her.

She ended up choking on her laughter. Nartan tossed his hair back from his face and turned around to gauge her reaction.

He led her back the way they'd come as the sun began to kiss the horizon. The grooms had come down to the water's edge, waiting as Nartan rode up to them and dismounted. He caught the bridle of her horse and spoke a few words in Apache to the animal as he rubbed her muzzle, his fingers sliding over her soft hair.

Memory rippled through Celeste, her skin recalling exactly how good Nartan's touch felt.

"We're going to miss the sunset if you stay up there."

He reached up for her and she was sorry to slide off the horse. Celeste reached back up and patted the animal before one of the grooms led her away, then turned to a golf cart fitted with huge tires to travel over the sand.

"We're not missing it," she said as she gestured to the expanse of private beach. The city was all around them, but the stretch of sand and breakers was completely secluded by the curve of the coastline.

The grooms had already disappeared with the horses, the landscaping hiding them.

"I know a better viewing location."

Nartan jumped behind the wheel of the cart and waited while she slid in. The evening breeze was whipping across her wet clothing, chilling her as Nartan headed for a dock at the opposite end of the beach.

"Do you own all this land?"

He nodded, satisfaction glittering in his eyes. "The only reason I own a restaurant named Angelino's is because of the property it sits on." He cut her a sidelong glance full of arrogant satisfaction. "I rent the beach out for weddings, but every now and again, I get to have some fun on it too."

He drove off the sand and right up onto the dock. She hooked her hand into the rail as the cart rocked. The coast thrust out into the ocean in a rocky point. On the other side, the water was calmer, the breakers kept back by a natural breakwater rock formation. A silver and black yacht bobbed on the surface of the water, its mirrored windows reflecting the setting sunlight. It was a sleek, modern vessel with at least three decks. Small outdoor lights were strung from the bow and over the bridge to the back, where the light strings branched out into a fan. Nartan put the cart in park and swung out.

"And what beach wedding is complete without a sunset cruise?" she asked as she joined him.

"Exactly." He offered her a hand as two uniformed crew members stood by to fold up the ramp that connected the yacht to the dock.

They entered on the back deck of the vessel, where the cheery little lights made the deck feel festive. There was comfortable seating all around the exterior of the craft and a bar open to the deck, with another deck above it. Nartan pulled her inside the vessel.

"There's a shower and dry clothes in there for you. Meet you up on the promenade deck in fifteen."

"Is this your way of ensuring I can't make an escape?" she teased.

He grinned and shrugged, turning to lean over her in the tight companionway. "You got that right. I'm also making sure I can't be called away."

The engine revved up as the captain began to push away from the dock. Nartan pulled his cell phone from his pocket. "They don't work well at sea."

He tucked it back in his shirt pocket and eyed her as he braced himself against the motion of the ship. "I'm all yours, Celeste."

Oh…hell yes.

She could feel her insides twisting, her body melting as anticipation began to mount inside her. The logical side of her brain was quickly abandoning its post, and she could feel the need to press up against him chipping away at everything she thought.

What she wanted, desperately, was to respond to his nearness, his appeal, his sheer animal magnetism. He wasn't like any man she'd ever encountered, and it was about time, too.

She was heating up, her breasts feeling tender and heavy. He leaned down, curving over her as he propped his arm against the wood paneling of the hallway.

"Are you ready to give me that kiss?" His breath brushed her lips.

She reached up and toyed with some of his hair. She couldn't recall ever seeing such truly black hair before. It suited his bronzed complexion. He was darker than Tarak and she realized it was because he spent more time outdoors.

"We'll get distracted," she decided.

His eyebrows lowered. "I hope so."

He pressed a kiss against her lips, licking and sucking on them as she reached up to slide her hand along his neck. For a moment, she let the pleasure boil up inside her and pull her nipples tight behind the wet fabric of her blouse. She slid her hand into his hair and tightened her fist.

He offered her a little groan as she pulled his head away from hers. She indulged in a long look at his eyes. They were flickering with need and promise.

"We'll see," she purred suggestively. "But the sunset won't wait."

She slipped through the small doorway and shut him in the hallway. There was the distinct sound of male amusement before she heard him walk down the hallway. She twisted the little lock on the door handle until it clicked. It was a pathetic barrier.

She froze when she turned around and found her green dress hanging from a hook next to the door to the bathroom. It had been cleaned and pressed, but what she discovered herself dwelling on was the fact that he'd found it.

The staff might have given it to him.

No.

She felt sure of that as she looked at it. He'd gone looking for her, and it warmed her in a way she'd never felt before. This was a man worth wanting, and he wanted her back just as much, she was beginning to admit.

She ducked into the bathroom. It was a generous bathroom for a yacht, but still compact. She rinsed off quickly before wrapping a towel around herself and going back into the bedroom. Sitting on the bed were a pair of loose, drawstring pants and a pullover made of a windbreaker material that would no doubt be comfortable up on deck. She tugged the tags off and stepped into the clothes. The top was soft and comfortable, and once she had it on, she noticed the matching hair clip and shoes.

He had thought of every detail.

She shook her head and put the shoes on the floor. They were a sensible pair for a moving vessel, outfitted with gripping soles. She took a last moment to gather her hair up and clip it on the back of her head before opening the door and heading out of the sleeping area.

The yacht had three stories. Four if you counted the bridge, which was perched highest up on the vessel. The bedrooms were downstairs to afford the passengers the smoothest sleeping accommodations. Once she climbed up to the second story, there was more of a roll.

Soft music, some sort of tribal mixture of flutes and drums, touched her ears and she followed it around the edge of the vessel until she came to the front. There was a seating area and a sundeck.

"Come on up."

Nartan was another deck above her. She found the narrow stairs and climbed up. He was wearing a similar sportswear outfit, but he'd left his shoes at the top of the stairs. They were heading out to sea, the wind whipping his hair back. He looked at ease and even wiggled his bare toes, turning around to judge her reaction.

She climbed the last step and kicked her shoes off to join his. His lips twitched before he offered her a glass of wine. The deck was super smooth beneath her bare feet, and the wine had a soft bite that made her smile.

"Best seat in the house is up here."

He pushed open an access gate in the chrome railing that went around the deck, and climbed out onto the front of the boat. He left his wineglass behind on the table.

"Come on."

He offered her a hand as he sat down on the front of the boat. There was a smooth area for sitting, where the lights came down at the nose of the vessel. She put her wineglass down, climbed out, and took hold of his hand. He pulled her closer and studied her as she folded her legs and sat down. The wind was hitting her full in the face, and she pulled the collar of her top up to her chin.

"Too cold?" he asked.

She shook her head and enjoyed the scent of the sea. They were heading out toward Catalina, while a steady line of boats made their way in on the other side of the waterway. The California coastline was ruby from the sunset, and as she looked further out to sea, there was only darkness. The lights on the deck behind her were out, making sure they'd have a good view of the evening.

"Don't spoil a perfectly good setup, Celeste…"

She looked back at him, trying to decide what he meant as he scooted up behind her.

"Setup, huh?"

"Planned down to the last detail," he confirmed as he settled against her back. "I've been plotting just how to get you back in my arms. I had to send the personal shopper over to your studio to size you up. Apparently, martial arts uniforms are very bulky."

She laughed softly. "True, but that's just a tad creepy."

He nuzzled against her neck as his body heat surrounded her. The motion of the vessel made it impossible not to lean on him, and he draped an arm around her to complete the embrace.

"I plead insanity."

"What detail does the dress represent?"

He cupped her jaw and turned her face so that their gazes met. "That I enjoy a challenge."

He pressed a kiss against her lips, pushing through her hair and cupping her head to keep her in place as he took the deep kiss she'd denied him earlier. The passion rose between them like a fire catching hold of a stack of dry wood. His tongue dipped between her lips, seeking hers and stroking them in a long lap that sent her turning toward him and plunging her hand into the neck of his shirt because she needed to touch his skin so badly. She wasn't close enough, couldn't seem to kiss him back hard enough to satisfy the craving gnawing at her.

Someone bellowed at them from a passing boat. "Wooo-hooo! Score, buddy!"

Celeste jerked her face away, turning forward in an awkward

jumble of limbs. The boat was just passing, the two guys on it waving beer bottles at them.

She heard Nartan mutter something in Apache as his arms tightened around her. She felt his heart hammering into her back and a distinct tremor running down his arms that matched the one making her tremble.

"I don't think I need a translation for that."

He pulled in a stiff breath. "You're driving me insane."

His tone was gruff and so low that she had to strain to distinguish the words. Part of the problem was that her brain was shutting down. She didn't want to absorb conversation; she wanted to sink into a pool of responses and let him satisfy every last impulse she had.

"The feeling is mutual…" She reached behind her, laying her hand on his thigh because she just couldn't resist the urge to touch him, reach for him.

He made her shameless.

He shifted, moving forward until the very distinct bulge of his erection was pressing into her back.

"I've been hard for you every night. I think I might have resorted to singing under your window if you hadn't agreed to come out with me."

She snorted. "Oh right." She disengaged herself and crawled back through the open gate. "You'd have cruised through the bar at Angelino's and found someone to enjoy Saturday night with."

She wasn't trying to be bitchy, just attempting to grasp reality. "I mean…you're a total hunk."

Nartan had turned around and sat watching her. A tingle touched her nape as she caught the look in his eyes. The night was closing in behind him, adding to the power radiating from him. He was so sure of himself, so confidently in control that it fanned the lust simmering inside her until it rose to a full boil.

"I left everyone behind." He unfolded his legs and stood up.

Her belly fluttered, her passage feeling empty. Her lips were dry and she rolled her lower one in to moisten it. His keen gaze targeted the little motion, narrowing as he prowled closer to her.

"I promised myself we'd have dinner…chat…enjoy the view…"

Celeste started retreating, moving back out of pure instinct as he bore down on her with a steady pace. She bumped into the wall behind her and Nartan pressed his hand on it, caging her.

"But all I want to do now is explore your sweet body…"

He leaned down and inhaled the scent of her hair. Arousal prickled along her skin, raising goose bumps and heightening her sensitivity.

"The way I didn't take the time to in Alaska…"

His voice had turned rough with hunger. She could see it glittering in his eyes and felt her breath catch as anticipation nearly drove her insane. "Yeah, it was…rushed…" Somehow, her voice had gone sultry. She'd never been so conscious of her need to have sex, nor had she ever discussed it so openly. It opened a door to a side of her personality she'd never experimented with. The part of her that didn't give a shit what anyone thought.

"I never got a look at you, Nartan…" She reached out and touched his hip, trailing her fingers along the hard edge before she ventured onto the tight plane of his abdomen. The sports pants were made of soft fabric that did little to disguise what was beneath. "You just stripped me…"

"And took what I craved," he finished. He toyed with a lock of her hair that had been pulled free by the wind. "What you didn't want to admit you craved…"

Her fingers found his cock. He twitched, his face tightening as she teased the hard bulge with only two fingertips.

"I want more this time…"

He sucked a breath through his teeth, the sound harsh and somehow perfect for the moment. She teased his cock, trailing her fingers down to the softer sacs of his balls and back up to the top. Need clawed through her, settling in her clit as she absorbed just how hard he was.

It was dark now, the overhang from the bridge above them encasing them in darkness. The slap of the waves joined with the soft music, but what Celeste really heard was the steady beat of the drum in the Native American melody.

It echoed the demand pounding through her. She pushed off the wall and stretched up to kiss his neck. He cupped her nape, and something inside her rebelled. The scent of his skin was an aphrodisiac. She stretched up onto her toes to kiss more of his neck and bared her teeth when she felt his grip tighten on her nape.

She bit him in reprimand. A controlled nip that surprised her as much as it did him. He pulled her head back, growling softly at her.

"I want more than to be taken," she informed him and thrust her hand into the front of his pants.

"Christ!" he snarled, his neck cording as she wrapped her fingers around his length.

There was nothing beneath the soft jersey but hard flesh. She purred with victory and slid her closed hand all the way down to the base.

"I'm not going to be your plaything," she promised him.

He opened his eyes, just to a slit, and angled her face up to look at him. "Yes. You. Are."

They were like two forces clashing. She was fascinated by the friction, agitated by it, completely engulfed by it. She pumped her hand up and down his thick staff, keeping her eyes on his face as she did it, He stiffened again, fighting to keep his eyes open, but surrendering when she found the sensitive spot just beneath the crown and thumbed it.

"Pump it…again…"

She sent her hand down to the base of his cock, not because he'd told her to, but because she wanted to see him lose control.

She wanted to make him lose it just as insanely as he'd made her. The sound he made was so erotic that she trembled and twisted free of the grip on her nape so she could slip to kneel on her knees in front of him.

"Shit…" He flattened his hand against the wall and opened his eyes. "I wanted to…"

She pulled the waistband down, freeing his cock. For a moment she just enjoyed the sight of it, stroking it once, twice, and a third time from base to tip as she absorbed its size. She didn't want him in control. The need pounded through her, and she leaned forward, sticking her tongue out for her first taste of him.

"Celeste," he growled, the strain in his voice delighting her.

"Hmmm?" she answered as she slid her thumb through the wet trail she'd left around the crown of his cock. He'd opened his eyes but his fingers curled into a fist as she stroked that sensitive ridge of flesh.

"I don't give up control…well…"

She closed her hand around his cock and pumped it hard several times. He shuddered, sucking in his breath as a word of profanity escaped.

"I hope not."

She had no idea where the urge to push him came from. His eyes widened and his nostrils flared with savage need. She cupped his balls with her other hand, rolling them. Indecision held him for a moment before his features contorted with pleasure.

"Lick me again." His tone was as hard as his cock.

He was surrendering but still holding on to command. She lowered her attention to his cock, feeling the bite of arousal burning up through her pussy. But she reached out with her tongue and swept it along the ridge of the crown before closing her mouth completely over the head.

There was something about the scent of his skin that drove

her crazy. It was heady and spicy, and tasting him seemed to intensify it.

"God…yes…like that…"

He was growling at her, his commands sharp and short, but it delighted her to hear what she did to him. She pumped her hands up and down, rising onto her knees so that she could push her mouth down and take more of his length inside. She hollowed her cheeks and rubbed the underside of his cock with her tongue, twisting and working her hands along the part that she couldn't get into her mouth.

"Shit!" He hit the wall above her head, his hips beginning to thrust toward her. "You're going to make me come…"

She wanted to. In fact, she wasn't sure she'd ever wanted anything more. It was pulsing through her veins, the blood roaring past her ears as she bobbed and sucked. She needed victory over him, over the pure abundance of need that he unleashed inside her. But it was happening too fast. She wanted to slow it down, but he was thrusting toward her and she met every jerk of his hips, opening her lips and taking more of him as she sucked harder, tightening her mouth around him to squeeze.

"Oh God…like that!"

He reached down and caught a handful of her hair. The grip was hard and she discovered she loved knowing she was driving him to the edge. She cupped his balls, fluttered her tongue across the slit, and hummed when she closed her mouth around him again.

He jerked and the first spurt of his come hit her tongue. It was thick and hot. She pressed her head down, straining to take more of his length, and purred with delight as he pumped more of the salty fluid into her mouth.

"Yeah…just like that…"

He was past knowing what he said, his hand holding tight to her hair as he jerked back and forth, fucking her mouth through the orgasm. Everything stripped away except for the need to come. That soul-shattering quest for release had the power to completely wipe away everything else.

She felt him shudder as the last wave traveled through him and relaxed her cheeks as she drew her mouth away. His hand shook and his fingers sprang open as he snarled under his breath.

"No one…does that…to me…" The ragged sound of his voice made her belly quiver with anticipation.

"No one's ever sucked you off?" she asked incredulously as she stood up.

He cupped her face, his eyes widening as he leaned toward her and only stopped when their foreheads were an inch apart.

"Not before I've done it to them first." His voice was full of pride.

Realization dawned on her and she stroked his member a few teasing times. He was always in control, always setting the pace, always the decision maker.

"I warned you, I'm not going to be a pet…"

He pushed his hand into her hair and tightened his grip to keep her from moving away. "I want you to be." His gaze was sharpening again and control was shifting between them. She drew in a sharp breath because she could feel him taking back command, feel his frustration rippling across her skin. Denial was shooting through her, and she curled her lips back to bare her teeth. He smashed his mouth against hers. It was a hard, demanding kiss that she resisted. The hand he had in her hair fisted, holding her in place. The kiss was a ravishment, a hard claiming that she wanted to refute.

But she was melting, her resistance crumbling. He kissed her like he was starving for the taste of her, and she found herself just as famished. She needed him, craved the taste of him more than her next breath. Arousal was twisting, tightening in her core. He just felt so right against her, so perfect that she had to reach for him and tug him closer. Her nipples were hard little points that jabbed into his chest. His scent filled her head, completing the intoxication and making her his slave.

"You're undermining me, Celeste, making me break my promises to myself…"

A tingle of apprehension broke through the haze of arousal clouding her thoughts. There was something in his tone that struck a chord deep inside her where she'd stashed all of her own concern over just how deeply he'd affected her.

Nartan held tight. "Look at me."

His control was back in place, his tone commanding and impossible to ignore. When she locked gazes with him, she felt her mouth go dry.

"I'm going to break another promise I made to myself now."

She licked her lower lip before being able to ask him, "And what is that?"

"I'm going to fuck you before dinner again."

———

Celeste gasped, but she hadn't really finished before he bent over and tugged her forward. She tumbled over his shoulder and he straightened up, sending her head spinning. She grabbed his waist to steady herself as he pulled open the door and dove down into the stairwell. It was a tight fit and she pulled her elbows in as he turned and headed down the hallway past the bedroom she'd changed in.

The master suite was larger and they fit through the doorway together. Nartan sent the door shut with a kick and tossed her onto the large master bed.

"I promised myself I would sit through dinner like a gentleman…" He tugged his shirt off and chucked it aside as he watched her on the bed like a starving man. A moment later, his sports pants joined his shirt, giving her an unobstructed view of his body.

"You're magnificent." The words just tumbled out of her lips.

Every muscle was sculpted and covered in bronze skin. His groin was only slightly lighter than the rest of his body, proving that he liked being bare.

"And still hard," he confirmed as her attention fastened onto his cock. "I can't recall ever being so hard after shooting my load off."

She settled back onto her knees and slowly smiled. "What a silver-tongued devil you are."

One dark eyebrow rose. "You like the fact that I don't treat you like a trophy. You don't want seduction. You want to be pushed until you respond. You like the fact that I get a charge out of trying to handle your reactions."

She wanted to be offended, but she choked out a dry laugh instead. "We're a pair...aren't we? You like me for all the same reasons."

She swept her gaze from head to toe, enjoying every last succulent inch of his bared body. "We're a volatile combination. We should probably be way more wary of this than we are."

He nodded and turned the lights down. They had come on instantly when he and Celeste entered the cabin, blindingly bright after the darkness of the deck. As the room became darker, the tension shifted to something far more sexual.

"Strip for me."

His tone had deepened, his expression turning hungry.

"Bare yourself for me."

His eyes brightened with a need that sent a coil of anticipation through her. Her own hunger had only been set on the back burner, and now he was tugging it forward toward the front of the stove where the flames would lick her.

"Show me those tits. I've fucking dreamed about seeing them."

And she'd dreamed about the way he sucked them.

She let her knees part and rolled the hem of her top between her fingers. His attention dropped to her fingertips, his lips thinning with anticipation. It was a different form of power, a more vulnerable sort. He waited on her whim, but with his body on display, it was clear his strength was greater.

She craved that strength. In some dark corner of her mind, she wanted him to take her, possess her. It was a base, hard need that burned away every idea of what she thought she was. There was only need and the desire to satisfy it with him.

As long as she was willing to submit.

And to trust.

"Do it," he rasped. "Prove I'm your choice as much as you're mine…"

She pulled the garment up, feeling like time had suddenly slowed down so that every second was an eternity. The air was refreshingly cool against her bare skin, like freedom from an airless room. She tossed her top aside and watched his face as he viewed her.

"Mouthwatering tits…"

He climbed onto the bed, reaching for her breasts. She moaned softly as he cupped them, massaging them with a groan of enjoyment. He toyed with her nipples but pushed her back until she was lying on the bed.

The dominant look on his face was undeniably pleasure. She expected her memories to rise up, but all that happened was a twist of enjoyment that shocked her. He grabbed the waistband of her pants and tugged them down. Her bottom rose off the bed, the garment slid down her hips, and she dropped back down as he dragged the pants off.

"This shouldn't feel so good…" She didn't intend to let her thoughts pass her lips.

Nartan planted his hands on either side of her shoulders, pressing her legs wide with his body. For a moment she saw agreement flash in his eyes. But it was only a glimpse before he moved down her body and hovered over her spread sex.

"Nartan…"

Her protest came too late. He'd already trapped her thighs open. But he looked up her body, his expression hard and unyielding.

"Give and take is what makes a great relationship." His breath teased her open slit, drawing her body tight. "You gave. Now it's time to receive."

She twisted, unable to stay still. He chuckled darkly before teasing the curls on top of her mons. She kept them clipped back and the rest of her body shaved.

"Nice and smooth…" he observed as he trailed one fingertip along the side of her sex.

She stiffened and a tiny sound that she was powerless to contain made it past her lips. Her skin was so sensitive, her clit throbbing so hard, that she was sure she'd climax at the first touch.

But Nartan wasn't willing to satisfy her so easily. He teased her slit, stroking it and rimming her opening with his finger while she strained to lift her hips up and press against his finger. When he licked her at last, she cried out, on the edge of reason. The ripples of sensation were so strong she tried to recoil, but he held her down and returned to lap and tease her clit until she was sobbing with the need to climax.

It was insane and undeniable. He made her shameless and reduced her to a pile of cravings. Her core was tensing, twisting as her clit throbbed and twisted. She was lifting her hips, undulating up toward his mouth, desperate for the attention of his tongue.

She came so hard that she lost track of everything. She must have closed her eyes, because she didn't remember anything except the burst of pleasure deep in her core. It spasmed through her belly, contorting her with pleasure so sharp that she felt poised on the edge of pain. He growled as she climaxed, the vibrations prolonging the moment of satisfaction and keeping her straining against his mouth.

She ended up gasping and clawing at the bedspread beneath her. Nartan was watching her, satisfaction sharpening his features.

But there was also hunger. A deep, uncontrollable need burning in his eyes. His nostrils flared as he rose, supported by his powerful arms, and moved up her body. There was no protest from her, the ability to deny what she craved strangled long ago. She reached for his biceps and dug her nails into his skin.

"Hard," she demanded as she finally succeeded in sucking in enough breath to speak. "Do it hard."

He pressed forward in answer, his cock slipping easily into the opening of her body. She stretched to accommodate him, his girth pressing her just a fraction past what was comfortable. She groaned, the tingle of pain sharpening her senses.

"You're so perfectly tight," he growled, pressing forward until she felt his balls smack against her bottom.

"Perfect little cunt."

They were blunt words but she purred with approval. She wanted it hard, wanted him to possess her. She was wild for it, lifting her hips to take each plunge as she clawed at his arms.

He rose up, leveling himself above her to give himself space to pound her. The bed shook, her breasts bounced, and perspiration coated both their bodies before she felt another climax tingling through her. It was deeper, centered in the spot he hit with each hard penetration of his cock. Another thrust, and another, and she was spiraling out of control again, twisting her legs around him to hold him against that spot inside her.

"Yes!" he snarled. "Squeeze my dick…*milk it*!"

She tightened, the walls of her passage doing as he commanded as pleasure dulled her wits completely. The hot spurt of his release was the final thing needed to push her over the edge into oblivion.

He'd come inside her.

Nartan had no idea how long he'd been out, but his eyes snapped open and his brain turned on.

Shit!

He looked down his body and his cock was still half-hard, lying against his belly, wearing nothing but a sheen from being inside Celeste's body.

The tension tried to ball up in his gut, but Celeste shifted, making a soft sound, and he rolled toward her, folding her in his arms as the scent of her skin filled his senses. The ship rocked softly, the engine only a dim sound in the distance. Then what filled his senses was the breathing of his partner. Her heart throbbed slowly against his forearm as he cupped one of her breasts and snuggled closer against her body.

Sleep was suddenly easier to slip into than it had been for a while. Whatever thoughts had been chewing on his brain, they dissipated as he moved closer to Celeste.

Chapter 6

HER BED WAS ROCKING gently.

There was a cool breeze teasing her bare toes but she was toasty warm. In fact, her blankets were wrapped around her.

A blare of a horn somewhere in the distance intruded and Celeste opened her eyes, trying to identify the odd sound. She found herself looking into a full-length mirror mounted on a closet door. Her eyes widened when she took in Nartan's body tangled with hers. His skin was darker, making it easy to see where he had an arm draped across her waist, cupping one of her breasts. Her head was tucked under his chin and her ankles were trapped between his legs.

It wasn't blankets keeping her warm.

"The fog must be coming in," Nartan muttered as he shifted and massaged her breasts before rolling away.

The bed shifted even more as he got up. There was a soft chirp before a set of window shades lowered with a muffled electronic sound and the soft gray light of dawn filtered in.

"We slept all night?" Celeste tried to sit up, but her body still felt heavy. She rubbed her eyes and watched Nartan pick up a slim phone mounted by the door.

But he stopped and replaced it. "I have a high-profile wedding this afternoon I need to be on hand for."

He was waiting on her. Surprise burned away the remains of sleep still clinging to her brain.

He was actually waiting for her to approve of his actions.

"I understand. I've got a brief to get on top of."

He reached for the phone again and held it to his ear for a moment. "Take us in."

She found her pants and shook them out. Her top was in a different corner of the room. She was mentally focused on the fact that he'd put that phone down the first time. A small thing, and yet a rather large one for a man who ran a multimillion-dollar business.

The engine fired up and the yacht turned around.

"Let's go up top… The trip in is beautiful in the morning."

He opened the door to the room as Celeste was pushing her fingers through her hair. There was a lazy expression on his face that warmed her insides. He made it through the hallway and looked behind to see if she was following. The morning air was crisp, turning her nose cold when they hit the deck. Nartan didn't stop until he'd reach the spot where they'd started their evening. Everything was spotless, the crew having cleaned away their wineglasses efficiently. They never had eaten their dinner. To Celeste's surprise, she wasn't even hungry this morning. Another appetite had been so thoroughly sated. She smiled to herself. She should be ravenous, but she found herself suffused with a sense of joy and well-being.

"Come on," Nartan urged her. He was back on the bow of the yacht, holding his hand out to her.

She found herself actually blushing as she put her hand into his. He closed his fingers around hers and pulled her gently toward him. She knelt and felt him fold around her. He nuzzled her hair and warmed her with his body heat. They had entered the traffic pattern of boats going back into the harbor. Most of them were going west to the yacht club. Their captain headed east, into the morning sun, for the pier where they'd boarded the vessel.

"I want to see you again."

He rubbed his hands along her arms, sending tremors through her.

"Have lunch with me tomorrow," he pressed.

"I have to work."

"You don't eat lunch?"

She offered him a shrug. "I tend to keep my lunch break short so I can make it to the studio early. So lunch is normally a sandwich at my desk."

"Dinner," he insisted as the dock came closer. "I swear I'm going to turn this boat around if you don't agree to a date."

"I can swim."

He nipped the side of her neck in reprimand.

She laughed, the sound surprising her. But he chuckled behind her and she found herself fighting off the sting of tears. She must have made some sound or motion of distress because he trailed his fingers gently across her cheeks and captured one of the salt droplets.

"I'm fine," she defended herself quickly. "Just salt spray."

He pressed her back against him when she tried to move away, her emotions crumbling because of the tenderness of his hold.

"Liar," he accused roughly. "Dinner. Monday."

"Don't you have a restaurant to run?"

"A million-dollar wedding needs personal attention," he countered as they slowed down to pull up next to the dock. "Monday dinner service can do without me, or I need a new manager."

"We should probably take a break."

The crew was out on the lower deck, securing the vessel.

"I am taking a break by not dragging you down to the cabin now." He pressed up against her, proving that his cock was hard and eager. "You've infected me with some form of addiction or turned back time, because I feel like I'm about eighteen with the need to get back inside you."

She laughed and stood up. "You struck me as a rogue the first time I met you, Nartan Lupan. Don't think for a second I am going to buy that line. You like women and indulge often."

He lifted one dark brow before standing up. The pure power

in his body struck her full force as he braced himself against the slight motion of the ocean. "Don't devalue yourself, Celeste. We've been over this ground before, but you're right. I don't have to share my rather limited private time with anyone if all I want is a fuck. You're more."

His words were clipped and tight, but they struck her as one of the sincerest compliments she'd ever received. "Dinner, Monday. But it will be late. I have tae kwon do class until seven," she warned. "And I'll probably limp in. Master Lee likes to do power practice on Mondays."

"An excuse to rub you down. It's a date."

He nodded and jumped back onto the deck. Then he turned around and offered her a hand. Once she'd joined him, he pulled her close.

"And you'll tell me about Caspian."

She pulled back, but he slid his arm around her waist and bound her to him.

"Caspian is my past," she said. "He doesn't deserve any more of my time."

Nartan's expression didn't soften. There was only a momentary flicker of compassion in his eyes. "His memory stands between us. I want to know what I'm fighting."

Her anger deserted her as she struggled to handle what he was saying. "Look, Nartan, I'm not sure I'm ready—"

"You already chose me." He held her in place when she tried to push back again. "And I swear I'll pull out to sea again right now, no matter how asinine a business decision it is, if that's the only way I'm going to learn who the ghost is between us."

The word "us" was bouncing around inside her skull, sinking in amazingly fast.

"I'm not sure what we're doing. And I really do need to work."

The crew was extending the loading ramp, the sound of metal harsh against the concrete of the dock.

"You're making an excuse, but I guess this is the part where I have to give a little."

He grunted and let her put some space between them. Maintaining a grip on her hand, he started pulling her behind him down the stairs to the lower deck. The crew was lined up, ready to bid them farewell. Heat burst in her cheeks as she realized they all knew exactly what she and Nartan had been doing.

Nartan touched two fingers to his temple in a half salute as he passed the captain before striding confidently down the gangway and onto the pier. He held her hand the entire way, his fingers threaded between her own. The sand-buggy-style golf cart was waiting for them.

He slid behind the wheel and pulled a pair of sunglasses from the dash as she climbed in beside him.

"Show up Monday and we'll discuss what we're doing, because I'm a bit of a novice at this myself," he confessed.

She snorted at him. "You're throwing your weight around a lot for someone who admits he's a novice."

He flashed her a grin that showed off all his teeth. "For the record, I'm countering your reactions. It's part of my charm."

She tried to hold back her laughter and ended up choking.

But she couldn't have agreed with him more. The man had charm.

—⁓—

Sunday dragged on.

Celeste tried to work, but all she wanted to do was nap. She finally surrendered and crawled onto her sofa.

Nartan was waiting for her in her thoughts. The memory of him was even stronger now, and she smiled as she settled into a deep sleep. A ring on her front doorbell startled her in the afternoon. She rubbed her eyes and ran a hand through her hair before trudging to the door and looking through the security lens.

A fresh-faced kid in a florist delivery uniform stood there with a huge basket of flowers. She opened the door and the scent of them rushed in. It was a colorful arrangement that looked like wildflowers. There were daisies and small sunflowers and paper whites. It lacked the sophisticated edge Caspian had demanded of everything and reminded her of Alaska with its natural beauty.

It was perfect.

She set it on her small kitchen table and pulled the little card off.

Monday is too far away…N.

It suddenly felt that way for her too. Afternoon was wearing on, but it felt like the hours were dragging by. She took a last look at the flowers before diving back into work.

Even with the hours she put in on Sunday, Monday arrived like a freight train. Marcus had a court appearance, so the office was quiet as long as she didn't look at the way her emails kept breeding in her inbox.

By the time she made it to the studio, her brain was beginning to fry with anticipation. Her focus wandered, earning her a few curious looks from Master Lee when she made mistakes in simple things, like forms she'd been practicing for years. But that was nothing compared to the look she received when she appeared from the shower room in a dress. It wasn't a formal dress or anything grand, but she'd redone her makeup and styled her hair. Two of the younger instructors did a double take. She bowed and slipped out the back door before Master Lee found a break in the class he was teaching and could question her.

Since she didn't know what she was doing herself, there was no way she would be able to explain it.

You're going on a date. Big deal.

Only it was a big deal. At least to her it was. It was far more than an item on her to-be-dealt-with list. She discovered herself shamed by the idea that she'd ever consider Nartan as fling material. It didn't make any sense, but there was still no controlling her reaction to him. Sense wasn't making any impact on the way she was practically shivering with anticipation.

Her heart was beating faster as she turned off the highway and began climbing the twisting road that led to Angelino's. The Corvette hugged the road like a dream, and normally she would have enjoyed using some of the vehicle's supreme engineering.

Instead she was caught in a rush of anticipation, her breath bated as she got closer and closer to Nartan. The valet was efficient and she found herself standing in front of the doors before she really sorted out what she was feeling.

She took a deep breath and walked confidently toward the door. Both sides opened as uniformed personnel greeted her. She smiled at them on her way in. The host looked up, but the sound of Nartan's laughter drifted to her.

She recognized it instantly. The deep, slightly rough sound was branded into her memory. She was already beaming and moving toward him when her brain made sense of the scene in front of her.

A dark-haired beauty, in a dress that hugged her ass and was slit up to her thigh, was pressed up against Nartan as he leaned on the elaborately carved bar. His lips were curved in sensual enjoyment.

An expression she had branded into her memory as well.

Only this time he wasn't looking at her. He had his arm looped around the woman, his hand resting intimately on the small of her back, just slightly low enough so that his fingers brushed the curve of her bottom. She stretched up and said something to him that made him nod. She flattened one hand on his chest, her fingers dipping inside his shirt while her body connected with his from knee to shoulder.

"May I help you, madam?" The maître d' had come around from his desk to stand near her.

"Yes. Tell your boss he's an asshole."

The man's eyebrows rose, shock registering on his face. Celeste turned around and yanked open the front door herself. By some freak chance, her car was still sitting outside, the valet who'd taken her keys engaged in a conversation with another patron who had pulled up behind her.

"My plans have changed." She fumbled with her purse and shoved some folded bills into his hand while reclaiming her keys. She slid back behind the wheel and tore out of the driveway with every bit of power the Corvette had under its hood.

She refused to cry.

It wasn't anything she hadn't expected, so there was no reason to be upset.

Okay, no reason to be so upset that she cried.

She was a confident, modern woman.

But that didn't stop the hot tears from spilling over and down her cheeks.

Asshole.

⸺⁓⸺

Nartan's flowers were waiting when she got home. She snarled something profane and carried them out to the trash can. At least fuming beat crying. At times like this, she was sorry that tae kwon do had taught her so much discipline, because she would have loved to smash the vase against the wall.

When she came back in, the first thing she saw was the card lying on the table where it had fallen.

Great, she couldn't even clear him out of her house on the first try.

She reached for it but jumped as someone laid their fist on the front door.

"Open the door, Celeste!"

She turned around, welcoming the surge of temper that made her see red.

He wouldn't be calling her a chicken tonight—that was for damned sure!

She wrenched the door open. "There is nothing to talk about!"

"You can bet there is." He swept her off her feet and carried her over the threshold and back into her house.

"You've got some nerve, Nartan!"

He tossed her onto the love seat she had in the small entry room and propped his hands on his hips. "So you've noticed before. I think you like it."

Celeste bounded off the love seat and faced off with him. "Go back to your restaurant. You seemed to be having plenty of fun without me."

She was jealous and it hurt too much without him making fun of her.

Nartan bared his teeth at her. "You misunderstood what you saw."

"She was practically lying on top of you," Celeste countered. "I'm sure whoever she is, her name is on your 'list with benefits.' There is no misunderstanding the fact that she knows you really fucking well."

He bit back a word in Apache, but lifted one hand and pointed a thick finger at her.

"Not that well. Laura is a family friend."

"She wants more."

"She hasn't gotten it," Nartan said.

Celeste didn't care for the way his words sliced through her anger. With the flare of rage, she was left doubting her own motives for arguing with him. He was watching her and nodded slowly, reading her thoughts off her face.

"Maybe I've been enjoying bachelorhood, but it's no more of a sin than you refusing to take a chance on living."

"I took a chance on you tonight," she insisted. "And found you with your harem girl." She whispered, feeling like they were so far apart that the distance was impassable. It tore something inside her, stunning her with the rush of hot pain that filled her.

How long had it been since she'd cared?

"I never promised any of them more than the moment."

Celeste opened her hands wide. "You haven't promised me anything either." She gasped when she realized the opening she'd just given him. "I'm not asking—"

He jumped forward and flattened his hand against her lips, pushing her back against the wall until his hard body was flush with hers. In the semi-darkness, his face was cast in silver and shadow, making him look like part of the night.

"I want you to ask me for everything." His tone was husky and hard. "I wanted you to tell Laura I belong to you. It pissed me off when you didn't."

He closed his eyes, slid his hand along her jaw, and buried his nose in her hair and inhaled.

"You could have told her, but you didn't." All the hurt she'd ordered herself not to feel was bleeding out. "You invited me over. She should have never been that close to you."

He opened his eyes, and even in the dark, she felt his gaze. "It's been a long time since I was in anything that might even be close to a committed relationship. I wasn't thinking when she slid up to me. I screwed up." His lips curled back from his teeth with raw emotion. "When I saw you leaving, all I wanted was for you to turn around and claim me right there in public and fucking tell her I was yours."

She was stunned and the last of her resolve crumbed. "How was I supposed to know that?" She shoved at his chest, growling when he didn't give even an inch.

"You felt something for me." He growled softly, menacingly as he leaned down, curving over her. She shivered, the sheer size of his body causing a reaction inside her. She was softening, surrendering as passion began to take control. Her flesh was so needy, so weak.

"But you ran from it…again." He stroked her cheek with his fingers, his expression tightening. She felt the change in him, a charge of determination that sent a prickle of sensation across her skin.

"And you chased me."

The word again lay unspoken between them.

He made a low sound, a rumble of male satisfaction. It was a declaration of victory, one she rebelled against. She reached forward, flattening her hand against his groin. Behind the smooth Italian wool of his trousers, his cock was swollen and hard. Her lips went dry with anticipation and she rolled them in, drawing his attention.

"I'm not going to let you off that easily."

Her breath caught. "Excuse me?"

He smiled slowly and her belly twisted with anticipation.

"I'm going to make sure you see me here in your safety zone." He slid his hand into her hair and fisted a handful of it. "So that you run to me…"

He pressed his lips against hers, kissing her hard. She wiggled away but he followed her, claiming her mouth with a dominance that should have pissed her off. Instead she was caught in a crazy spiral of excitement that was wringing her like a wet dishcloth. It was impossible to pull in enough breath, and she panted when he left off kissing her and set fire to her neck with a series of hard kisses.

She arched, offering her tender skin to him, the savage hold in her hair turning her on in a brutal fashion. Her breasts were suddenly heavy and full, straining against the cups of her bra.

But he backed away, allowing the night air to sweep over her. She shivered, moaning softly at the loss.

"Not here," he snarled.

He bent over, and before her passion-intoxicated mind processed what he was doing, she was hanging over his shoulder.

"Nartan…" She pressed her hands into his lower back, rising slightly as she tried to regain her dignity.

He reached right up and swatted her bottom. The breath rushed out of her lungs as she fell back down, mostly from surprise. The smack was loud in the silent house, and the soft pain snaked through her pelvis to twist with crazy intensity in her clit.

He bounded up the stairs, carrying her into her bedroom and tossing her onto her bed. She rolled over and found him watching her. The drapes allowed enough of her neighbors' lights through to illuminate him in a soft golden glow.

"Right here, Celeste…" He reached up, yanked his tie off, and shrugged out of his coat. "Where you won't be able to erase the memory."

Determination flashed in his eyes. "You're being an arrogant prick. This is my house."

He shrugged out of his shirt, distracting her with the perfection of his body. His face was gorgeous and harsh in the shadows, stunning her with just how much she enjoyed seeing him there at the foot of her bed. The dominant, demanding arrogance transformed into a compliment that made her feel like she was glowing inside.

"And you're my woman." He opened his pants and stepped out of them. She licked her lips as she waited for him to remove that final barrier covering the part of him she craved.

"I didn't agree to that."

"Good." He slipped his last garment free, allowing his cock to spring into view. Something inside her tightened, sharpening with need so intense that she thought she might climax the moment he touched her.

"That offers me the challenge of proving my worth to you."

She shivered, but flattened her hands on top of her comforter and crawled down to where her mattress ended. Her bed frame was simple, with no footboard, and tonight she was sure it was one of the best design decisions she'd ever made, because she was able move right up to his cock.

She smelled his skin as she got closer, purring with satisfaction as she opened up her mouth and leaned forward to lick through the slit on top of his cock. He slid his hand into her hair, but pulled her up so that she was on her knees and facing him.

"Tonight, you'll scream first."

He reached down and grabbed the sides of her dress. It was made of a soft jersey that allowed him to tug it up and over her head with ease.

"Perfection," he growled as he soaked up the sight of her garter belt and matching bra. "Almost…"

He leaned over and caught the thin strap of her G-string. With a twist, he snapped it, startling her with how much strength was in him. He chuckled darkly and snapped the other side before pulling the little triangle of silk away from her mons.

"Now it's perfect."

"I agree," she offered as she reached for his cock once more. She closed her fingers around it, enjoying the satin-smooth texture. His eyes closed to slits but he kept their gazes locked as she fisted him, pumping her hand from the crown to the base with a firm, slow motion.

"Do you like doing that, Celeste?"

She pulled her hand up and teased the slit, wiping away the first drop of his cum before pumping her hand down to the base again. "Yes." She felt the power shift between them.

"Why?" he asked softly.

He was asking for a confession that she wasn't sure she'd even made to herself. She pumped her hand up and down his cock. "What does it matter?"

She tried to lower her head and suck him, but he kept her in place.

"Did Caspian order you to suck him off?"

She stilled, tightening her grip without realizing it. His cheek twitched and she opened her fingers. But the truth was already out, even unspoken. Reactions always were the truest.

"All the time," she whispered.

"Did he ever repay the favor?"

She slowly shook her head and reached for his cock again. It suddenly made more sense to her and she twisted her head to loosen his grip on her hair. He released her and she smiled with victory.

"I like sucking you off because it's the only time you aren't pressing in on me."

Instead, she was pushing him to extremes. The idea shimmered with promise, and she opened her mouth and closed her lips around him. He jerked, thrusting forward out of instinct. She felt an anxiety tonight, a pulsing need to wring him out like the sight of him holding another woman had done to her.

"Keep your eyes open, Nartan."

She was cradling his balls, toying with the soft sack as she looked back up at him. "Make sure you see who is here with you…"

His jaw tightened.

She rolled over onto her back and his eyes widened with surprise. Her breasts moved out of the little lace-edged cups, allowing her nipples to slip into view.

"I see the merits of you following directions…"

He stepped forward and she leaned her head back so that she could lick his balls. She began to work moisture up his stiff penis until it was slick and easy to pump. She closed both of her hands around the stiff length. His breathing was heavy, his body tense as he began to fuck her hands.

"Open your legs…"

His tone was raspy but hard with demand.

"Show me your slit…"

She shuddered with the erotic thrill his command sent through her. She was crazy with need, her clit pulsing. It was a relief to open her thighs and allow it space. But her motions faltered as she watched him look at her spread sex.

"Don't you think I enjoy looking at you as much as you like looking at me?"

He leaned over, instantly flipping the power between them as he trapped her arms against her chest and kept her thighs spread with his shoulders.

"I've become obsessed by being in contact with this pretty… pink…pussy…"

She squirmed, his breath hitting her wet sex and unleashing a powerful twist of sensation. It was so sharp that she whimpered.

"There are so many things I want to do with it, but you make me feel like a teenager again, unable to control my lust long enough to taste your cream."

"Nartan—"

He touched her and she arched, fighting to buck his weight off her. Whatever she'd been about to voice, it died in a sizzle as he rimmed the opening of her body with his fingertip.

"Hmmm?"

His cock was pressed between her breasts, mocking her with how hard and thick it was. She craved it. She moved her fingers on it, just a small amount because of how tight the space was.

"I always keep my promises, Celeste. Which is why I'm careful about making them."

He placed his knee on the bed and rolled over, coming up between her spread thighs. There was a glimmer in his eyes.

"You're going to scream first."

His expression was unyielding. He settled over her, his shoulders once more bracing her thighs apart. She watched in stunned fascination as he leaned down and drew his tongue along the edge of her slit.

That was the last thing she saw. Her eyes closed and she arched up in a crazy need to press herself against his mouth. There was no reason, no thought process, only the need to satisfy her craving. Desperation controlled her.

He didn't disappoint her. Nartan leaned forward and sealed his lips around her clit. Her hands fisted in the comforter. His tongue was velvet soft, stroking, licking her slit and swirling around the pulsing nub of her clit. She was withering, working her hips up against his mouth. He pulled her folds away from the center so that he could tease her clit with his tongue.

He had no mercy, licking and sucking on her until she was ready to scream with frustration. He groaned against her, the vibration sending her over the edge into a climax that threatened to tear her apart. Her body contorted, caught in the grip of it, the wave cresting higher and crashing down to flood her with a pulsing satisfaction.

She felt like she'd been flung onto the bed, her body feeling too heavy to move for moments that felt like hours. Nartan lapped across her swollen clit a final time before sitting back. When she opened her eyes, he was sitting back against the pillows in the center of her bed. He had his arms resting on top of those pillows as he looked down at her.

He was making his mark.

Carving his persona into her bedroom.

It was deeply personal and she rolled over, feeling threatened. The moment she moved, he stretched his legs out straight, taking up more of the center of her bed. Her eyes narrowed.

"Are you staking your claim?" she asked.

"Yes," he bit back.

"You're so arrogant."

He curled his lips back and grinned at her. "So take me in hand."

"Like you wanted me to at Angelino's?" She sat back on her

haunches and watched his gaze travel to her breasts. She teased the swells of her cleavage with her fingertips before finding the little clasp that held the garment closed.

"I like the way you try to dominate a conversation."

His eyes were on her breasts as she let the bra slip down her arms. Hunger was glittering in his eyes again, filling her with confidence. He locked gazes with her.

"I can't wait to see what your tactics are going to be during this debate, counselor."

She crawled toward him. "Since you just tried to pin me down during your opening statement—"

"I did pin you down," he countered. "Flat on your back."

She lifted her leg and straddled him, holding herself above his cock as she settled her hands on his shoulders. "Which makes it imperative that I get on top of you immediately."

"I couldn't agree more." He cupped her hips, smoothing his hands over her bottom before returning to grip them again.

But she held herself above him, letting only the head of his cock nestle between the wet folds of her sex. "Maybe I should make you rise to my bait…"

"Maybe I plan to hold out and count on my ability to resist your barbs."

She rotated her hips and watched him grind his teeth. "In that case, I'd have to plunge straight on to my hardest point."

She was drenched from the orgasm he'd sent ripping through her. When she pressed down on him, his cock penetrated with a smooth, hard thrust that filled her to bursting. But she stopped once she'd sheathed him and tightened her internal muscles, squeezing him as hard as she could.

He gasped, his expression losing focus. He was dissolving into the same pit of savage hunger that she'd been mindlessly mired in only minutes before.

"I wonder who is getting more of the point, you or me?" he rasped out.

She lifted herself off him, unable to stay still. A new craving was pounding through her, one that was rooted deeper and only satisfied by the hard flesh she was riding.

"Maybe I like it," she growled, perspiration coating her skin as her heart began pounding.

He cupped her hips and shoved her down as he thrust up into her body. "You *love* it."

Yes, she did, if she told herself the truth, but that was too much to absorb right now. For the moment it was enough that she craved him with the same insanity as an addict.

She was fascinated by his face. His eyes dilated, his lips thin as he worked beneath her, commanding the tempo even as she tried to control it from above. It was a battle between them, a challenge both of them rose to. Her hands curled into talons on his shoulders as she dug in for the hardest part of the ride. He was slamming his cock up into her, fucking her with a ferocity that made her snarl at him.

He yanked her back down onto him as he grew harder and thicker inside her. The need to close her eyes was strong, but she wanted to watch him crumble at the moment of release, needed to see him ripped apart by what was between them.

But her own body was tightening, release only a few more thrusts away.

"That's right… Come on my cock, Celeste… Squeeze me again…"

She tumbled into climax, crying out as she felt him give up the first spurt of cum. It was hot and scoring, and he hammered himself up into her as his cock jerked and emptied its load.

"That's it… *Squeeze me*…yes!

Pleasure was ripping through her but she clamped her muscles down, the rapture in his voice demanding action. He shoved deep and shuddered as his cock let lose its last jerk. For a moment, he was frozen, rigid as he lifted his body off the bed to make sure he was buried inside her.

But he relaxed at last, the bed rocking as it took both their weight. She rolled over in a jumble of uncoordinated limbs that felt too weary to control. He followed her, cradling her and curving around her body.

It was tender.

So tender she shifted away.

He blew out a long breath and followed her. He cupped her shoulder and stroked her arm. "I was being an asshole. The art of being in a relationship is going to take some practice."

He kissed her shoulder before getting up. She sat up, startled by his exit. She didn't care for how exposed it made her feel. He found his jacket and fished his cell phone out of his pocket. He tapped something into it before dropping it on her dresser.

"We've got enough time for a shower." He offered her a hand.

"Before what?"

"Dinner." He grasped her hand and pulled her out of the bed. "Third time's the charm. One of the boys will be over with it in about half an hour."

He strode right into her bathroom and opened the shower door to turn on the water. Celeste hesitated in the doorway, soaking up the sight of him. He turned and lifted an eyebrow in question.

"Like what you see?" he asked.

"Do you like your current position?" she countered. "This is hardly what you're accustomed to."

He turned and caught her in a gaze that mesmerized her.

"From my vantage point, it's perfect."

He crooked his finger, beckoning her forward. She was moving before she thought. Placing her hand into his without hesitation as something new moved through her. A familiar sensation that she hadn't had any experience with in a long time.

It was happiness.

Chapter 7

"YOU THREW OUT MY flowers?"

Nartan had picked up the card that came with the basket and was fingering the edge while he looked at the few petals that had fallen onto her table. Celeste considered him over the rim of her coffee cup the next morning.

"I was a bit…passionate when I got home last night."

His expression didn't relax.

"Let's examine the facts." She put her coffee aside. "I think this calls for a reenactment of the crime scene."

She moved toward him and pressed up against him. "Your hand goes on the top of my butt…"

"It was her lower back."

"Eyewitness account says the fingertips were definitely on the swells of the gluteus maximus."

His expression gave little away as he complied, slipping his hand down until he was cupping her bottom. "Satisfied?"

"Hardly."

His eyes narrowed. "Liar."

Heat teased her cheeks as the memory of the night before rolled through her mind with a vividness that started to turn her on. Which was astounding with the lack of caffeine in her system. She was not a morning person.

"You're redirecting," she accused before pressing her body against his and slipping one fingertip beneath his tie.

"Just as I suspected…" His cock was thickening behind the fly of his trousers. "I knew she could feel your cock."

"Except that I wasn't hard."

His words astounded her. She was frozen for several moments before breaking away from him to return to her coffee.

"Which was a real game changer for Laura," he finished. The card landed on the counter next to her.

"Have you slept with her?" She probably shouldn't have asked, but she really couldn't stop herself.

He shook his head.

"That was too fast."

He pressed his lips into a tight line. "Laura is Apache."

"Why is that a problem?"

He was gripping the tile lip of her countertop so tightly that his fingertips were white. "When I left with Tarak to go up to Alaska, we were the joke of the reservation. The girl I was stupidly in love with drew a line in the sand when I told her I was going. I crossed it and never looked back."

Satisfaction glittered in his eyes.

"Was that Laura?"

"Her cousin. Laura showed up about six months ago with a head full of personal knowledge about me, and she's been cozying up to my grandparents for the last year."

"Gold-digger land mine."

His lips twitched.

"But it proves I wasn't overreacting."

"It proves you don't trust me."

His words hit her hard. She took another slow sip of her coffee.

"You're a stunning woman, Celeste. I expect men will hit on you. What matters is our commitment to each other. Trust is what makes a relationship solid."

"True," she answered. "But Laura is a special case."

"How so?" he questioned gruffly.

"She's the approved, pure-blooded bride being sent after the wayward son. Bet she's already got a list of baby names picked out."

He made a low sound in the back of his throat and eyed her for a long moment before lifting his hands in surrender. But his lips twitched with a very familiar arrogance.

"I think I love the fact that you're jealous."

She had been. Even after the night they'd shared together, it was still smarting. "What are we doing, Nartan?" she blurted out. "I think I really need to know the boundaries of this thing between us."

He settled back against the other counter and took a long draw off his coffee before answering. "The short answer is, you're making me crazy."

She choked back a dry laugh. "I told a perfect stranger to insult you in your own restaurant. I win points for insanity."

"I chased you out of there, in front of a member of my tribe, and left a business I built from the ground up. Game point."

She picked the card up and pressed it against her chest. Another long pause stretched out between them. It was awkward, but that was fine by her. There was one thing about Nartan she was pretty sure she couldn't handle, and that was a polished brush-off.

She didn't doubt he was accomplished at them.

"Why are you still here?" The question sounded pathetic, unmasking her uncertainty completely.

He drew in a deep breath and moved toward her. He didn't stop until he was curled over her, his body pinning her against the counter.

But today, there was a difference. She felt sheltered instead of cornered.

"I need to be." His words were rough, his jaw tight. "I can't explain it, but the idea of leaving before I get a commitment out of you for tonight is unacceptable."

"I have class Monday through Thursday."

He smoothed his hands down her sides. "That's important to you."

"Essential," she confessed. "It's the only way I got past the nightmares."

He stiffened and she laid her hand over his lips when he started to ask more questions. "Small steps. No one, not even Sabra, knows everything about my marriage. I was very much a typical victim of spousal abuse. I thought it was just a rough patch. Made excuses, avoided the truth."

"Now you doubt your judgment."

She slid her hand down his chest and locked gazes with him. "Logically, no."

"Emotionally…yes," he confirmed before pressing a kiss against her lips. He squeezed her in a quick hug.

"Go now, or all bets are off and I'm keeping you home. In bed."

"Ha." She turned off the coffeemaker and grabbed her purse and cell phone. "Like you don't have a business day to get to. No one enjoys the sort of success you do by being lazy. You're a workaholic too."

"But that doesn't mean I'm not interested in keeping you in bed all day."

She scoffed at him before heading for the garage. The workday was suddenly not her haven. The piles of work waiting for her were no longer a welcome relief from being alone with her memories. It was like some great burden had been lifted from her shoulders. Nartan caught her before she made it to her car and claimed a last kiss before he headed for his Jeep with that sexy prowl of his. The sensual way he moved sent a tingle through her as she slid behind the wheel of her car. His collar was open, his tie stuffed in the pocket of his designer suit jacket that he had slung over one arm. She was seeing a private side of him. Something she doubted anyone else had witnessed.

Yeah, she doubted her choices but there was no way she was going to stay away from him.

Even if she was headed for a crash-and-burn.

Chapter 8

Nartan sent flowers to her work this time.

A rather amused secretary carried the large vase filled with star lilies and roses into Celeste's office.

"This smells divine," Sandy commented before flashing Celeste a smile and disappearing.

The arrangement was colorful and the star lilies, with their pink and cream colors, did have an amazing fragrance. Celeste reached for the card with a happy little smile on her lips.

Is it quitting time?

Her smile grew brighter and it felt like a bubble of happiness was lodged in her chest.

"That's a new look for you," Marcus said from the doorway, his expression pensive as he contemplated the flowers and the look on her face. "Who's the guy?"

Celeste lifted one eyebrow and went back toward her desk with the card clasped securely in her hand. "Maybe it's a girl."

Her boss's lips twitched before he pegged her with a hard look. She knew from experience that there was no escape. Marcus would keep at her until he gained what he wanted.

"Nartan Lupan," she supplied.

"As in the owner of Angelino's and the adjacent spa?"

Celeste lost a little of her composure. "I didn't realize he owned the spa."

"And golf course, as well as all those new condos along that stretch of coastline," Marcus fired back. "Some women would be ecstatic over how loaded he is."

Celeste shrugged and looked at her laptop. But she realized she was avoiding the topic. She looked up at her boss. "I met him up at Sabra's wedding. He's Tarak Nektosha's buddy."

The moment the words were out of her mouth, she realized she'd made an error. Marcus's face tightened.

"Did you come back early to be with him?"

Marcus was always direct and nosy.

"Jury is still out," she said, settling on something that wasn't a flat-out lie. Marcus would see through one anyway.

Marcus also knew when she avoided giving him a direct answer. He looked back at the flowers and nodded. "Just be careful. If you need him out of your life, you know who to ask. But your timing is good. Your ex is out of prison."

A tingle touched her nape as she saw the hard glitter in Marcus's eyes. He left silently, leaving her with the unshakable knowledge that he knew exactly what was in the police files concerning her and Caspian.

Of course he did.

Who was she kidding?

She drew in a deep breath and blew it out. Marcus was likely more comfortable looking at classified documents than he was working with civilian ones. What on earth had made her think he wasn't fully aware of her past?

She was holding the little card so tightly that the corners were cutting into her. She released it and looked at the card again.

She tapped the interoffice button on her computer screen and selected Marcus's icon.

So what else do you know about Nartan Lupan?

Class was hard.

But she liked it that way.

There was no way to get stuck dwelling on her personal demons. If she wasn't fully focused, she was likely to get dumped on her butt. Celeste wiped the sweat on her sleeve, and before the night was finished, her uniform was wet. She plopped down on a bench near the back door, grateful for a moment of rest while she drained her water bottle. Master Lee was locking up the front of the studio and starting to flip off the lights.

She took another drink as the light above her went dark. It was suddenly easier to see through the open back door into the parking lot. They left the door open most of the time to air out the studio. Most of the lowlifes in the area had the sense not to wander too close. Curious people would stop near the front windows when class was in session, but the back door was attached to a short hallway that made it hard to see into the studio.

Celeste lowered her water bottle, looking out into the night because someone was watching her. He stood just far enough away to make her strain to see his features. She stood up and pushed her feet into her shoes, but the guy didn't move.

"Good night, Instructor Connor," Master Lee said.

"Good night, sir."

She reached for her gear bag and fished her car keys out. Her car was parked just outside the door, but her belly knotted with tension as the man continued to watch her. She slipped behind the wheel and pushed the key into the ignition. Putting the car in reverse, she tried to ignore the urge to look over at the guy. But she lost and turned her head.

A street lamp was casting light down on him through the branches of a tree, illuminating a face that was thinner than she recalled, but still just as chilling.

He was watching her, his lips curving with satisfaction, before she pushed down on the accelerator. She hadn't quite made out his features, so she couldn't be absolutely sure who it was.

Her heart was pounding as hard as it had been during class, but the sweat coating her skin felt cold. Icy dread gripped her as she drove through the streets while checking the rearview mirror.

You're overreacting.

She'd only taken a quick look at him. There was no reason to think it had been Caspian.

But it might have been. He was out of prison.

Still, the back parking lot of the strip mall where the studio was located was hardly his sort of place.

You're making excuses.

When it came to Caspian, she was good at that. But there was something calming about telling herself it might not have been him. A sort of victory against letting him control her.

And if it had been?

There was nothing to do. She'd given up that right when she refused to testify against him. She didn't have a restraining order.

There were times when she was a fool.

———

"Finished at last?"

The driver closed the door with a soft touch that sent only the briefest sounds through the limousine. Caspian settled himself before looking toward the female sharing the ride with him. She was scantily clad, showing off her sculpted figure.

"Your body gives me pleasure. Make sure your personality doesn't dilute it. You are here because I desire it. I am the master. Never forget it."

She stopped working the emery board along the edge of one fingernail. Her lips pressed into a pout as a temper snapped in her eyes, but she remained silent and slowly worked the file along her nail again as she smiled at him.

Disappointing. She had no spirit.

Caspian drew a smartphone out of his pocket and made a notation. The driver pulled the car onto the city street and began the journey back toward the exclusive mansions nestled in the Hollywood Hills. It would be a good hour before they made the distance.

He'd have to make sure Celeste understood how little he liked having his precious time wasted. The state had already robbed him of too much of it. Now that he was free, he didn't intend to let a moment go unused. That was the only reason he was sharing his limo.

"Take your dress off."

There was another snap of temper in his companion's eyes, but it lasted only a moment before she uncrossed her legs and pulled her dress up and over her head. That was a shame. But then again, Celeste was one of a kind. A creature with a rare spirit, the sort that renewed no matter how far he bent her. The creature crawling across the limo toward him was nothing compared to his wife. She would be amusing on the ride home but that was all. She reached him and slid her hands along his thighs to his groin, rubbing his cock and purring as it hardened behind the fine wool of his pants.

He leaned his head back as she began to open his fly. As the night air touched his cock, he closed his eyes and let Celeste's face fill his mind. He'd gotten very good at imagination while in prison. When a pair of lips closed around his cock, all he saw was Celeste.

Ah yes. His wife.

His.

─∾∾─

Nartan was waiting for her when she got home.

She recognized the Jeep, but didn't see him until she made the turn into her driveway and found him sitting on her porch. She wrinkled her nose because she reeked from two hours at the studio.

"Thanks," he remarked.

"I'm not at my best," she offered as she disarmed the security system.

Nartan followed her into the house and surprised her by wrapping his arms around her and pulling her back against him, wet uniform and all.

"You smell hot," he said next to her ear.

"Yuck." She squirmed.

He buried his head in her half-wet hair and inhaled.

"Double yuck!" she insisted. "I need a shower, Nartan."

He chuckled and released her. "Since you put it that way…"

She looked over her shoulder at him and found him grinning. "What way?"

"If your plan is to get naked, I'm happy to let you go."

"Ha, ha." She started up the stairs, her legs complaining. She peeled her uniform off and stepped into the shower. It was the oddest feeling, knowing Nartan was near.

It made her feel secure.

Relief swept through her. She hadn't realized until that moment just how tense and knotted her insides were after that non-encounter in the tae kwon do studio's parking lot.

Nartan appeared in the doorway carrying a large candle, which he set on the bathroom vanity. A moment later he killed the lights, leaving Celeste and himself in only the yellow glow of the single flame. She forgot what she was doing as he stripped down, revealing the hard body she'd found impossible to forget during the day.

He pulled open the shower and stepped in. The candlelight made the water golden. Her imagination was running rampant with ideas of how his ancestors would have looked by firelight. It was suddenly very easy for her to understand how captive women had fallen in love with their warriors.

"Your thoughts are racing." He captured the bar of soap and began to rub it along her arm.

"Yes."

He made a low sound of male disapproval. She shrugged. "I keep trying to understand why I've let you into my life so quickly."

"Starting a relationship wasn't on my calendar either." He lathered up her torso, cupping her breasts and smoothing the soap along her skin. "I'm not complaining." He turned her so that the water washed the soap down her body, and pressed a kiss against her neck. "I feel more alive than I have in years."

It was an admission, one that sounded like it came from the deepest part of his soul. She reached for him, splaying her fingers out on top of his hard thighs, leaning back against him, surrendering completely.

"Me too."

She shivered, the intimacy of the moment shaking her to her foundation. But he was just there, folding around her, surrounding her until she didn't want to know where either of them ended. She couldn't stop touching him, didn't want to move away. He forced the breath from her body with a climax that made her scream.

He provided dinner again. She hummed with enjoyment as they sat on her bed with only the candle and some music from his smartphone going. Eating five-star cuisine while they sat cross-legged.

"I'm going to need double workouts if you keep feeding me like this." She savored a last bite before reaching for a glass of dark wine that reflected the candle flame.

"You're addicted to your workouts," he accused. "And if I never eat another blackened excuse for food again, I'll die happy."

He popped something in his mouth, and his eyes closed with enjoyment. "But my shower is bigger."

She looked around the master bedroom. "I know it's small."

"You could afford more."

"It's plenty big enough for me."

"That's not the whole reason."

She used the excuse of biting into a breadstick to avoid answering immediately. Nartan continued to watch her, his expression giving her no hint of backing off. He was just so *there* in her life. It was unsettling, but in a way that made her giddy.

"Okay, I didn't want to have all my assets tied up. In case I needed to leave quickly."

Nathan's face tightened. "You think he might come back for you?"

She reached for her wine and took a sip, gathering her courage. "That's not Caspian's way."

Nartan straightened up. "Meaning what?"

She bit her lower lip as she swallowed the first thing she wanted to say. Running wasn't the answer.

"He has a fascination with submission. That's the only reason I ended up married to him. I was the girl who wouldn't chase him. Somehow, I became a challenge to him. The ultimate challenge." She watched his eyes narrow. "He'd find a way to force me to bend to his will if he wanted me back."

A chill touched her nape. The man in the parking lot flashed through her mind.

"He was convicted of assault." She frowned, but Nartan wasn't repentant. "Yes, I checked into it."

"You and Marc, it would seem."

Nartan didn't even offer her a shrug. "Why don't you have a restraining order?"

"Because a bondage date night gone too far landed him in prison, not a domestic dispute turned violent."

Nartan's eyes narrowed. "You're saying he didn't hit you?" His tone told her he didn't believe it.

"I already told you I'd convinced myself it was a rough patch." She drew in a deep breath. "I was young and stupid and thought I wasn't sophisticated enough to understand mature sexual games."

"Bullshit," Nartan cut in. "He was a predator looking to exploit you."

"I married him when I was fresh out of law school. Who knows what they want at that age? By the time my marriage was sinking, I had too much pride to admit what sort of colossal mistake I'd made."

Nartan had the good grace to nod in agreement. "Pride is tough to swallow. Tell me how he landed in prison if it wasn't you who turned him in."

"Caspian expects the world to jump at his command, or suffer his wrath." She reached for her wineglass again, needing something to cover how dry her mouth had become. "Whenever I had my period, he'd spend that week with someone else. I cried about it for the first few months, but it turned out to be my saving grace, because he went too far once with one of his liaisons and she went to the police. Sabra's father was largely responsible for talking some sense into me and introducing me to Marcus, who handled the divorce while Caspian was in prison."

But now he was out...

The man outside the studio filled her mind. Her heart started hammering. Something touched her elbow and she jumped. "What?" she squeaked.

Nartan was watching her through narrowed eyes. "What's wrong, Celeste?"

"Nothing." Her voice squeaked.

He reached out and pressed his thumb against her chin gently to make her release the lower lip that she'd set her teeth into.

Shit.

"Why do you notice things like that?"

He chuckled softly. "Because you're my drug of choice. Like any addict, I focus on my fix. Now tell me what you're hiding."

"Nothing, really. It's just the nature of the topic."

He wasn't buying. Nartan watched her, pegging her with a hard look that sliced right through what she thought she wanted.

"Just some guy that was watching me outside the studio tonight as I left. My oversensitive emotions tried to make me think it was Caspian, and this conversation has me connecting dots that aren't in the same line."

His expression hardened.

"But you didn't get a close enough look to know for sure?"

She shook her head.

She stood up, unable to sit still. "He wouldn't waste his time looking for me. I was nothing more than a wound to his pride. Caspian needs challenges."

He made a low sound before unfolding his legs and standing up. "Like getting you to put his ring back on your finger of your own free will?"

Her throat felt like it was tightening, her mind working frantically to recall the features of the man outside the studio. He'd been looking at her; there was no way to ignore it.

"You're jumping to conclusions." She felt so exposed that it was almost impossible to resist the urge to hug herself.

"You know in your gut that he might come back for you. That's why you've walled yourself off."

"I'm not walled off."

Nartan picked up his pants and stepped into them. "Sabra is your only friend. You work for an ex-JAG officer who was a Navy sniper before earning his law degree. The sort of guy who would welcome anyone who wanted to start something, because he'd have the legal excuse to kick his ass."

"I have other friends," she defended as he put on his shirt and buttoned it.

"All masters of martial arts and well connected with lots of other black belts." He zipped his fly and killed the music. "In short, not the sort of people you want to start something with, or one of their numerous relations will finish in the event you get the best of them. Get dressed and pack a bag."

"Excuse me?"

He tapped a text message into his phone before answering her.

"Pack a bag, Celeste. I don't want to sleep with one eye open. We're going to my place."

"I'm not sure that's necessary."

"You said yourself he wants submission from you."

She nodded. The topic was too uncomfortable to keep talking about. "I doubt it was him."

"I don't. You have sharp senses but are still in denial about being a victim. If I set eyes on him, Marcus is going to have a tough time getting me out of a murder charge because I won't wait for him to start something new."

Her eyes widened with horror. Nartan held her gaze for a long moment before he walked across her bathroom into her closet and flipped the light on. He grabbed a duffel bag that was on the closet shelf and tossed it onto the vanity.

He walked back to her, stepping up close and draping an arm around her body. She shuddered, the smell of his body filling her with a need that was more than sexual. She craved him.

"I'm sorry… I didn't think about what he might do to you."

"Shhh…" He pressed a kiss against her mouth, sealing her words beneath his lips. "I should apologize for taking advantage of the situation to get you home with me, but the truth is, I don't care how I take you home with me."

"Maybe you should just go," she whispered. "It would be safer. Marcus told me Caspian is out."

Nartan went deadly still, his expression tightening. Something glittered in his eyes that convinced her without a spoken word that he was contemplating murder.

"Marcus told you he's out?"

She was rolling her lower lip in again but stopped.

"When?" Nartan demanded.

"Today."

"You can pack the bag or I'm going to stay here with you."

"No." The word barreled out of her mouth without hesitation. It was an intense feeling, a complete rejection of him being in the line of fire because of her.

"Pack the bag or not. I'll just have what you need brought in."

He started to release her but she curled her fingers into his shirt, holding him. "Caspian has a lot of friends, Nartan. He could make trouble for you, for Angelino's."

He stroked her back as his eyes darkened. "I hope he tries. Marcus isn't the only one who would welcome the excuse to beat Caspian senseless."

Part of her wanted to rebel against the idea of being protected. Nartan read it in her face, and for a long moment he stared her down. But his arms tightened and he lowered his forehead to hers.

"You're not alone, Celeste. Don't push me away. I don't think I can handle it."

She was shaking, or maybe it was him.

"I've never asked another woman to come home with me," he whispered against her ear.

"I kept one of the condos for my hookups. I'm not taking you there," he told her bluntly. "My home is for the woman who makes me feel rich." He pulled in a stiff breath. "You make me feel that way. So deeply, it scares me."

His tone was rough and edged with emotion. Her throat was tightening up, her eyes itching with unshed tears. But he kissed her forehead and moved away.

"Pack. I need to make a call."

—∾—

She wasn't sure what she was doing.

But she filled the bag and grabbed a suit. Nartan was waiting at the foot of her stairs, pacing back and forth as he spoke on the phone in Apache. When he turned back around and saw her, he finished up.

"I'll have you know, I just lost a bet with Tarak."

He was trying to lighten the mood and avoid the emotional high they'd just encountered so unexpectedly.

"He's been on me for the last year to beef up my personal security." Nartan grabbed her bag and opened her front door for her.

"Nektosha deals with Defense Department contracts. I remember Sabra waiting for her background check to come back."

Celeste was already across the threshold when she stopped to fish her car keys out of her purse. "I'll follow—"

"You won't." He dropped her bag and grabbed her keys.

She held out her hand for her keys. "I'll need my car tomorrow."

"I'm getting you a driver, one who carries a gun."

She opened her mouth to argue.

"And I'll discuss it with your boss if you don't see the wisdom."

"You're overreacting," Celeste agreed. "You're right. He'll go after you first."

"My second call will be to Master Lee."

"That's not fair." She propped her hands on her hips.

"Caspian has had a lot of time to stew in prison." Nartan scooped up her bag and carried it to his Jeep. He tossed it in the back and turned around to face her. "He wouldn't be the first man who planned retaliation. Until I get a private detective to verify his whereabouts, I'm not going to let you be exposed."

"You are overreacting," she repeated. "And you're the one walling me off now."

"So indulge me until I gather some information on the prick." He cut through her argument. "You're important to me, Celeste. I have no idea what that means, only that right now, the thought of you spending even one more night away from me hurts."

There was an intensity in his voice and in his eyes. Her pride still balked but she turned around and went back to her open front door and armed the security system. She pulled the door shut and he locked it.

When he slid behind the wheel of the Jeep, he paused for a moment with his hands on the steering wheel.

"I'm glad you feel the same way I do," he muttered.

"I didn't say—"

"You're sitting there." He cut her off. "Trusting me. From you, that's an admission."

For a moment, she felt horribly exposed, unmasked, but a moment later, a little bubble of happiness rose up inside her and lodged in her chest. It filled a void she hadn't realized ached so much. She was closer to achieving the true balance she had been seeking.

"I have no idea what it means, Nartan, but I'm ready to go."

He flashed her a grin before pulling out of her driveway.

Chapter 9

NARTAN DROVE PAST ANGELINO'S and further back into the exclusive Malibu hills. Condos were perched on the hillsides, looking out over the ocean. Many of the condos were three-story units to maximize the million-dollar view. Even the roofs were viewing patios, furnished with expensive iron patio sets. Smoke rose from a couple of them as residents made use of barbecues and the balmy Southern California weather.

Nartan drove past them, leaving artificial light behind. Moonlight showed Celeste the single-lane private road that led further out onto the cliff. The wind was whipping in from the ocean, chilling her nose. She crossed her arms over her chest as the wind hit them full-on in the open Jeep.

"Sorry, I didn't think about the weather."

"You don't feel it," she countered.

He shrugged but reached behind her seat and pulled a parka forward, dropping it in her lap while keeping his eyes on the road. "I do sometimes."

She opened the jacket and just laid it across the front of her body, tucking her chin so that her nose was behind the collar.

Nartan looked at her and laughed. He turned a bend, coming to the point in the coastline that they had ridden up to on horseback. There was a single house here, the road dark except for the lights from the Jeep. A light came on when he opened one door of the six-car garage. He drove inside and punched the controller so that the door slid shut behind them.

"Come on, I want to show you the deck."

There was a playful quality in his voice now that she hadn't heard before. He held open the door linking the garage with the house and lights came on, nice muted ones. Mood lighting.

"I don't like to kill my night vision." He pointed to the wall. "You can fix the controls however you want."

He captured her hand and was off again. The house, a sprawling complex with open arches that let her look into all the rooms, passed in a blur as he headed toward the back of it. Most of the entire back of the house was floor-to-ceiling glass. She stood for a moment, marveling. Support beams were set in, of course, but the amount of glass was still impressive.

"The best part is outside." He reached over and captured her hand, clasping it in a firm grip. He opened one door and pulled her outside.

"You don't have an alarm?"

"Tarak has been busting my balls about it," Nartan answered. "This is a private road, so I never worried about it much. The closest neighbors are the condos, and anyone who can afford the price isn't into petty theft. An expensive private patrol is paid to keep undesirables out of the condos, so I've never had to worry about anyone getting this far."

Off to their left, they could see Angelino's. They were about fifty feet higher. An eternity pool reflected the night sky like a polished sheet of black glass, and a glass weather wall marked the end of the property. Nartan pulled her to the edge of the pool before turning and scooping her off her feet.

"Nartan…it's too cold to go swimming…"

He chuckled and carried her straight into the water. She wrapped her arms around his neck, bracing herself for a drenching.

All that happened was that his amusement doubled. She looked down to see him walking through only a foot of water. He had left his shoes back on the patio.

"You might have shared that tidbit," she groused, slapping his chest.

"And give up my moment of carrying you off to my fire?"

He crossed onto an island. The pool surrounded it, lapping gently across a lip that was covered in thousands of weather-rounded stones.

"Wow…that's an amazing sound…"

He lowered her onto a double-wide lounge bed next to a fire pit. The sound of the surf breaking was just loud enough to be soothing. Nartan opened a small chest and pulled out a blanket. He tossed it to her before striking a match and lighting the wood that was already positioned in the fire pit.

"No gas?"

"I want the real thing."

The wood popped and cast a yellow and red glow across him, illuminating his face as he worked and granting her a glimpse at his relaxed expression. The impressive house hadn't brought that look on; it was the simple act of being able to set fire to wood beneath the night sky. There was an ease settling over his body and she felt privileged to witness it. He was letting his guard down completely.

"Gas doesn't smell right," he offered as he moved toward her. Awareness prickled along her limbs as her lips went dry. She was so in tune with him, which really was a marvel when she took time to think about it.

The lounge was raised up at the back so she could recline. He pulled off his shirt as the fire licked across the dry wood and sent sparks drifting up into the air. He stretched and looked at her, studying her with an expression that was unreadable.

"Trying to decide if bringing me here was a wise idea?" she asked.

The fire was going strong, the scent of the burning wood touching her nose as tiny sparks floated up before they died.

"Do you regret coming?"

He was dead serious and almost sounded like he might be vulnerable. He looked so powerful, so majestic in that moment that she ached with how much she wanted to be right there.

She shook her head, her throat too tight to force words past. It felt like they were linked with one another and a million miles from the rest of the world. She lifted one side of the blanket in invitation.

He stood and stripped down to his skin before moving toward her. His cock stood up, hard and promising. Hunger was growing inside her again, as though they hadn't already satisfied one another. She wanted more than sex, though. The desire gnawing at her was for intimacy.

He walked around behind her, gripped the back of the chaise lounge, and lowered it. Celeste propped her elbow against the padded surface before rolling up to her knees and reaching for his erection. The fire bathed him in crimson and gold, casting a feeling of endlessness over her. They might have been almost anywhere in time. All that mattered was that they were together.

She drew her fingers along his staff, marveling at the silken smoothness of his skin. His cock jerked and she scooted forward so that she could fit her lips around it. Her sex clenched with demand, but she was determined to enjoy the moment. She licked around the crown as she pumped her closed hand down his length once, twice, and a few more times before opening her lips to suck the head of his cock inside her mouth.

It was her turn to make memories in his private space. She hollowed her cheeks and sucked him hard, working her hands along his staff as he groaned. He fisted his hand in her hair.

"I love fucking your mouth…almost as much as your pussy… almost…" He pulled away from her and reached down to grab the sides of the jersey top she'd put on. He pulled it up and she raised her arms so that it slid up her body, but he didn't pull it free. He kept her wrists caught in it and twisted the fabric tight.

For a moment, she tensed.

"Look at me, Celeste."

She lifted her gaze to his, not out of obedience, but because she recognized the voice of the man she trusted.

"What am I to you?"

The firelight allowed her to see the hard, demanding expression on his face. He pulled her up, until she was all the way on her knees. But she didn't feel overwhelmed. She was exposed, but the hunger in his eyes promised her satisfaction, and that made her bold.

"You're my lover," she replied in a husky voice. She twisted her hands and slipped free. Reaching around behind her, she unhooked her bra and tossed it aside. "The only man I have ever called by that word."

She scooted back and stood up. The cushion kept her slightly off balance as she pushed her pants down and stripped.

"You're the only woman I've ever brought here. I wanted to share this spot with you."

She could see how significant it was to him. He put his knee down on the padded surface and crawled toward her.

Her belly tightened, her insides quivering, because it felt like he was stalking her. She sat down and scooted back, instinct taking over.

"But right now…all I want to do is claim you."

He reached out and caught her ankle. She giggled before flipping over and sending her foot onto the other side of his hand to break his grip. His fingers opened and she heard him cuss in Apache before the chaise lounge vibrated and he lunged after her.

He tackled her, pressing her down into the cushion. She snorted, partially laughing as he growled against her neck and nuzzled the mess her hair had become. But her amusement died as she felt every last hard inch of him pressing against her. It was erotic in a way she'd never imagined. The cold air blowing in from the ocean while his body surrounded her with heat. There was a strength in his arms that made her shiver with anticipation, her nipples tightening with growing arousal.

Her hunger was explosive, shooting flames up inside her as he kissed her neck. She wanted more from him, craved something hard and primal, like their setting. She pushed her bottom against his cock, purring as he pressed between the halves of her bottom.

So close.

Yet not close enough.

She wiggled and he lifted his hips so that his member could straighten. When he lowered back down on top of her, his cock was pressing between her thighs.

She growled at him. "Stop teasing me." She flattened her hands against the cushion, intending to rise.

He captured her wrists and held her down. "I want to claim you."

His voice was muffled in her hair, but she heard him suck a breath in through his gritted teeth and her sex clenched. It was the most delicious torment, feeling his length so close to where she craved it.

"Then do it," she snarled.

He lifted his lower body. "Offer yourself to me, Celeste…"

She never hesitated but lifted up and tucked her knees beneath her.

"Spread for me…"

It wasn't easy but she wiggled her knees further apart, panting with the need to have him inside her. He released her wrists and straightened up, claiming her hips in a solid grip as he pulled her back and thrust forward in one, powerful motion.

"Christ!" She gasped, not even sure of what she was saying, only that it was impossible to keep silent. He pulled free and sent his penis back into her, and all she could do was moan with rapture.

"Yes…" he growled behind her. "Let me hear how much you enjoy your lover."

She responded by lifting her leg and swinging it up and over his head. The action broke his grip on her hip and she landed on her back. Nartan was on her in a second, pinning her down and thrusting back into her body.

"I want to watch you come, Nartan…"

She clamped him between her thighs, perspiration coating her skin as they both worked at a frantic pace to feed their desire. Her heart pounded so hard that she wasn't sure she could catch her breath, but she didn't care. She sunk her fingernails into his shoulders, purring when she heard him snarl.

"You…first…" he ordered through a clenched jaw. His expression was dark and possessive, but also determined. "Always…first."

She wanted to hold out, but her body was too famished, too needy to be denied. He was hammering into her, stretching her sex with his girth. His balls slapped against her bottom, the wet sound of their flesh meeting mixing with the surf and the water surrounding them.

She arched up, everything inside her tightening voraciously before it burst into a show of red-hot sparks. She cried out, trying to pull him closer as the walls of her sex tightened around him.

"That's it's… Milk me…" He began to come, his cock pumping a thick, hot spurt of seed into her. She twisted and strained toward him, pleasure whipping her around as she felt him pumping her through the waves of his own climax. It tore through them both, wringing them out and then dropping them back to earth.

He caught his weight before he smashed her and rolled over onto his back. For a long moment, Celeste could only gasp. She felt red hot, the wind a cooling relief. It blew across her body, lifting the heat away as her heart slowed.

Nartan moved first. Rolling over and lifting her up, he cradled her for a moment before turning her around and settling her on the chaise lounge so that they could gaze out to sea. He retrieved the blanket and held her close as the night air drove her into his embrace.

He lay on his back and she placed her head on his chest, unsure if she had ever felt so wonderful in her entire life.

"I used to lie under the stars with my cousins at night and listen to my grandfather tell legends. When I built this house, this was the spot I wanted to be my place of peace."

He stroked her hair back from her face and pulled the blanket up to cover her shoulder.

"It's amazing." She spoke in a low tone, not wanting to mask the sounds of nature.

"You make it complete."

He pressed a finger against her lips when she tried to respond.

"Just let it sink in, Celeste. That's what I'm doing."

She kissed his finger and stroked his chest. The scent of his skin filled her senses, and she gazed at the stars as he held her.

Yeah, just let it sink in, because no matter how much she wanted to resist the idea, it felt very, very right.

His bedroom had a glass ceiling.

Celeste groaned and rubbed her eyes as dawn brightened the master bedroom. She had a dim memory of stumbling into the house behind Nartan sometime after falling asleep in the yard. All that had mattered at that time was burrowing deep beneath the thick blankets on his bed. It might have been a dingy hotel room for all she cared.

It certainly wasn't dingy.

The master bedroom was built in a circular fashion. Above the bed was a glass roof with panes fitted together like pie pieces, held together by copper, which made it look like a giant star.

She turned her head and found Nartan still sleeping beside her. The bed was huge, fitting him. The sheets were a warm honey color, and the frame set had decorative ironwork. Posh but still comfortable. All of the furniture was wood or iron. Wood beams that ran from floor to ceiling were set into the walls of the bedroom at regular intervals, lining up with the edges of the glass ceiling star. There wasn't an ultramodern line in sight, and she decided she liked it. There was an earthy feeling, like she was in contact with the planet, with life.

She'd never felt so at home before.

Shock held her still for a moment. She sat up and hugged a pillow as she tried to decipher why there were tears stinging her eyes. He took her breath away with the way he lived. The house wasn't built to impress his friends; instead, she got the impression that he'd designed it because he wanted to enjoy time with them. She could easily see the two younger cousins who had attended Tarak's wedding running across the back deck and jumping into the pool.

The house she'd shared with Caspian had been cold and devoid of life. Its sleek lines and polished marble floors had dampened any burst of playfulness before it got the chance to get started.

"You're thinking about Caspian." Nartan had all the covers kicked off and was lying on his back with one arm flung above his head.

He opened his eyes, displaying an unmistakable glitter.

She nodded. "I like your house."

He reached up and stroked her cheek.

"And I can totally see your cousins making s'mores at the fire pit." She shifted her attention to the deck. "It's really great."

"With you here, I think it can be." He sat up and snuggled behind her. "But it takes two to make a home."

Doubt intruded, dampening her enjoyment. "I've never lived in a home. I'm not sure I know how to make one."

He placed a kiss on her shoulder. "Hmmmm…" He reached around to cup one of her breasts. "We can start with the s'mores, but if you get chocolate on me, I'm going to make you lick it off."

She swung a pillow at him, turning around and settling on

her knees. He choked on his laughter as he put up his hands to shield himself. The bed rocked as he reached for her and rolled her beneath him.

"I have to get to work," she reminded him.

He nuzzled her neck, sweeping her hair aside so he could press a line of kisses against her throat.

"We need to adjust your hours…to allow for mornings in bed," he purred against her neck.

"I like my job."

He rubbed himself against her, sending a rush of excitement through her that escaped her lips in a little sigh.

"You'll like mornings in bed, too," he promised wickedly.

"Maybe." She slid her hands up his arms, enjoying the feeling of how hard he was. Her fingertips seemed more sensitive when they were in contact with him. All of her senses were heightened. The world beyond his bed lost its meaning as he sealed her lips beneath his in a slow, hard kiss that drove her insane. He pressed into her, riding her as passion built, and then hammering hard through both their climaxes.

It was a while later before Celeste opened her eyes again. "I see uses for that ceiling," she muttered after glancing at the clock. She still wasn't late.

Nartan stretched and rolled out of bed. "I was raised in the desert, so I sleep right through dawn."

He pulled on a pair of sweat shorts and winked at her. "How do you like your eggs?"

"Poached," she answered before yawning.

He disappeared, leaving her with another look at his master bedroom. The bed was on a raised portion of it. The colors were maroons and golds, the floor covered in warm brown wood. Stretching out around her were windows from floor to ceiling that looked out over the ocean and a corral. She walked down the two steps from the bed and moved closer to the one that faced the corral. The two horses they'd ridden were slowly grazing.

"Horses and ocean." Nartan reappeared with her bag and suit. "The two things I swore I'd have views of if Tarak and I ever struck gold up on that frozen claim. These all open up." He indicated the panels. "To let the breeze in."

"It's amazing."

"Caspian lived in high style, so that's a compliment."

"Not really." She shuddered and turned around to take her bag. "It might have been high style, but it was cold. I never pictured anyone making s'mores in the backyard fire pit. I'm not sure I ever walked barefoot through the marble hallways."

So cold and devoid of life, it had been like a giant office building. She looked back at the bed and the morning light washing over it. She smiled, joy lifting the corners of her lips. It was just there, the feeling warming her from the inside.

"Make yourself at home." His tone held a wealth of meaning—rich, deep, and full of promise that set off a little ripple of excitement. She shied away from it, fearing the loss when reality smashed in on her.

They hadn't known each other long enough.

It made sense, good sense, but the thought slipped right out of her mind because she felt like she was glowing with happiness.

She wandered toward the bathroom. Just like the master suite, it was lavish but tastefully designed. The shower looked out over the cliff. A huge wall along the side of the yard made sure no one could see in from the road. But instead of concrete blocks, the wall was made of cobblestones. She should have felt exposed, but she realized Nartan didn't like to be caged.

That was something she could understand.

The master suite was connected to the main section of the house through a hallway. She passed an office and another room set up as a home gym. The scent of coffee teased her nose so she moved on into the main living area.

But she froze when she got a look at Nartan.

"What?" he questioned, proving that he'd heard her. He turned to look at her while holding a spatula in one hand and wearing a chef's apron. "No confidence in my cooking ability?"

She moved across the spacious great room to a barstool tucked under the edge of a kitchen island with a granite countertop.

"No, I guess I didn't expect you to be cooking." He slid a cup of coffee toward her. She lifted it and inhaled its rich aroma before taking a sip. When she opened her eyes, Nartan was absorbed in what he had sizzling on the stove. It was a massive eight-burner range with a stainless-steel hood above it. "Guess it makes sense that you'd have a culinary degree."

He shrugged and brandished his spatula in the air. "No degree. After I bought Angelino's, I had the chefs teach me. Perk of being the new owner. They had to tutor me. How did you manage to get through Harvard Law without financial support from family?"

She smiled above the rim of the mug. "Checked me out?"

"I like to see it as reading up on something I'm fascinated by."

"Ha!" She put the coffee down and pointed at him. "You were looking for a way to track me."

He pulled a plate from a warming rack and began to load it. "Guilty. But you redirected, and honestly, you should be proud. Getting to where you are with no support is an achievement."

He delivered a plate that had an array of breakfast foods. Ham, potatoes, toast, and a perfectly poached egg. Steam rose from it and her belly rumbled.

Nartan was pouring himself a cup of coffee when he heard the sound of her belly growling. He sent her one of his deadly gorgeous grins. "You seem to have worked up an appetite."

"I did." She took a bite of the egg and hummed with delight.

"You know, a man with your mad skills in the kitchen might just be worth keeping."

"Where...wrapped around your finger?" He sat down with a plate of his own. "How did you manage to get accepted to Harvard?"

She laughed and finished off the egg. "Your report should have told you I had one of the top scores in the nation on the SAT. Harvard gave me a scholarship for my undergrad work. Without it, there is no way I could have gotten a degree from an Ivy League school, much less gone on to attend their law school. My foster family made it clear I was on my own the moment the state checks stopped coming. I made sure I stayed at the top of my class so I'd have a shot at a scholarship for law school too. Spent my summers working for a very notable law firm to help that dream come true. The firm's lawyers helped me get into law school."

"How did you get the SAT score?" he questioned bluntly. "It sounds like there wasn't much support on the home front and you went to a public high school with minimal resources."

She smiled with satisfaction. "The school library had a computer program heralded to be one hundred percent effective in raising SAT scores. It was free because of that minimal achievement record the school had. They needed some guinea pigs, and I had nothing to go home to anyway. Used to stay until they kicked me out, just working through those questions until I had that information memorized. I understand I'm one of their prize marketing-poster children." But a memory stirred and she sipped at her coffee, hoping it would dissipate.

"Spill it, Celeste."

She looked up and found Nartan watching her with his blue eyes.

"You always roll your lower lip in when you are thinking about holding something back."

"Maybe," she answered, suddenly feeling tired. "But I promised myself that I wouldn't spend my life talking about Caspian. He loved the fact that I was the library mouse and that he could brag to all his buddies who grew up just as rich and entitled as he did about how he rescued me. He liked to tell me how grateful I should be for his rescue." She tapped the granite countertop with her fingernail. "I earned everything I am."

A tingle touched her nape. She slid off the barstool, but Nartan came around the kitchen island before she could take a single step away from him. He caught her, pulling her against him.

"The difference between him and me is that I see the value in earning your affection." He smoothed his hands down her back. "Give me the chance to do that."

Part of her wanted to say yes so badly that she bit her lower lip to contain it. He reached up and pressed his thumb against her chin and pulled it down. She ended up smiling, another one of those bubbles of happiness lodged in her chest. It was a ridiculous sort of elation, one that made no sense and didn't need to. She just felt ecstatic.

"Relationships require give and take, Nartan." She eased herself from his embrace and grabbed her coffee to finish it off.

He folded his arms across his chest and leaned against the countertop in complete business mode. "Meaning what?"

"No driver."

He contemplated her for a moment.

"You said it yourself. Marcus would enjoy anyone showing up to mess with me, and the only other place I go is the studio."

"Which I made the same argument about," he finished.

She nodded.

"You move in here."

Her mouth went dry, "Are you sure?" She sounded lame, or at the least in need of a dose of self-confidence. "I mean, this relationship is sort of new. We might crowd each other."

"We can't keep our hands off each other. Worry more about me driving recklessly because I'm in such a hurry to get to your place."

Her cheeks turned pink. "I'm going to work," she warned him as she stepped back.

"Would it freak you out if I told you I want you to work for me?"

"Yes." And thrill her, but she wasn't going to admit it.

He slowly smiled. "We could enjoy nooners."

She had to choke back a half laugh. "Cute."

"There's nothing cute about me."

"On that we agree," she answered. "You're hard and dangerous to the core. But I'm late for work and you made me leave my car behind."

His teasing demeanor vanished, leaving her facing the business side of his persona again. "You keep me in the loop on where you are."

"You don't forget to tell your 'friends' that you're in a relationship, starting with Laura," she countered.

"Done."

He moved past her and headed across the great room. Her purse was sitting on a small table by the garage door. He pushed the door open and flipped on a light. The Jeep was parked next to a full-size truck complete with snorkel, which was next to a BMW sedan, which was next to a Lamborghini in the same blue as Nartan's eyes.

"Take your pick." He pointed at a row of hooks inside the entry-way door with keys hanging from them.

She looked back at the Lamborghini. "You really need a security system with that thing parked in here."

"Tarak is sending one of his people over this morning to deal with it." He grabbed the keys to the Lamborghini and tossed them to her. "Enjoy. But I know your weak spots now. Sports cars and s'mores. I plan to exploit my new knowledge."

"That was your cousins making s'mores."

He licked his lower lip. "I'm altering the idea to suit my mood."

She backed away with her hands up in surrender. "I'm leaving."

He pushed his lip out in a pout.

"And you have things to do too," she instructed. "Or we'll be too broke to afford s'mores."

He bit the air, his expression tightening. "Right here…seven thirty sharp."

"It's a date."

So simple.

And it felt so right.

Turning around took more effort than was logical.

She should have taken the sedan, but she just couldn't force herself to give up the chance to drive the sapphire-blue Lamborghini. The key was already in her hand, tempting her beyond her control. Her cell phone started ringing, shaking her back into the real world.

"Got to go."

He punched the garage door opener, and the double garage door behind the sleek sports car started sliding up. He watched her slip behind the wheel and adjust the seat and mirrors. The engine turned over and purred like a kitten.

Tiger kitten, that was.

It suited him.

That was the thought that stuck as she pulled out of the garage and watched him walk over to the corral. Both horses perked up and came to the rail. He reached out to stroke their necks. She was barely moving, unwilling to leave while he was allowing her to see the personal side of him. It felt like a privilege, one she enjoyed deep inside her heart. There was suddenly less enticement from the rest of the world, less of a pull to get out into it.

There were suddenly a lot more reasons to stay.

"Were my instructions somehow unclear?" Caspian Devitt drawled. "I am sure I can find a florist who is more competent in their duties for the price I am paying."

"Your instructions were clear." The man on the other end of the phone responded with the soft, practiced tones of someone used to serving. "However, the intended party left in the company of a gentleman before your order was delivered, and you specified that the delivery had to be done in person."

"I want his name."

"I'm sorry, I don't have that information."

Caspian killed the call with a quick jab of his index finger. He took a moment to admire the manicured nail as his lips curled with disgust over the conditions he'd been forced to live in during his sentence. He tapped in a number and waited for the call to connect.

"Yes?"

"I want to know the name of the man my wife is seeing. His details."

The call ended but Caspian slowly smiled. He liked Gabon. The man didn't talk unless he had something useful to say. He also followed directions very well.

Caspian looked across his desk at a recent photo of Celeste. This one was of her in a martial arts uniform. He didn't care for the look at all. But it represented the beginning of his quest to bring her back to heel. It would be a fine "before" picture. He'd enjoy showing it to her when he'd groomed her once more into a polished persona.

There really was nothing like the challenge she presented.

Nothing.

Chapter 10

"NEED YOUR CELL PHONE."

Celeste hadn't even finished closing her desk drawer when Marcus appeared in her office doorway with his hand out. One look at his face, and she realized she didn't know her boss as well as she thought she did. There was a glint in his eyes that chilled her. A hardness she'd never seen.

She tightened her hand on her purse as she stared at his outstretched hand.

"I'm going to bug it," he confirmed.

"Nartan called you." She was stating the obvious.

"Caspian was released three days ago. If he's already making contact with you—"

"It wasn't contact," she interrupted. "I'm not even sure it was him."

Marcus covered the distance between the doorway and her desk, and held his open palm in front of her face. The look on his face offered her no hope of convincing him. She forced her hand to open and pulled her cell phone out of her purse. But she still hesitated about handing it over.

"Look at it as one of the perks of working for me."

She made a low sound.

"Security net against your new relationship turning sour?"

She let out a grunt and handed over the phone.

"I liked number one better myself," Marcus informed her.

"Because I'd have had to chew you out for not telling me Caspian made contact with you."

"I'm not sure it was him."

Marcus pegged her with a hard look. "Yes you are."

She was.

He made a crisp turn and she tried not to feel like she was being suffocated as he left with her cell phone in hand.

She was making excuses again. Hiding from the facts.

But there was still one hard truth she couldn't ignore. Her training had taught her the self-respect she had sorely needed. She wasn't sure if she could deal with being anyone's possession.

Even Nartan's.

The muscles in her neck started tightening as she drove back to Nartan's. Her emotions were roiling in spite of her attempts to keep everything in perspective.

Nartan was waiting for her. He was leaning against the kitchen counter, watching the door to the garage when she came in. His tie was tossed on the counter beside him, the collar of his dress shirt open.

He was ready for a fight.

It irked the hell out of her that he knew her so well.

"Nartan, I know you're feeling fiercely protective of me, but you had no business calling Marcus or Master Lee." She dropped her purse on the kitchen table. "It's my life. I should have been the one to share personal details. When and if I wanted to. I'm struggling enough with whatever this is between us. I really don't want to be treated like a child or caged in or have someone else controlling my life. Been there, done that. It didn't really work out so well for me."

He hadn't moved. Hadn't shifted, hadn't even narrowed his eyes.

"Aren't you going to say anything?"

He shook his head slowly. Menacingly.

There was a promise etched into his expression and something dangerous flickering in his eyes. The sight should have sent her temper over the edge. Instead, all it did was make her feel hot and cold at the same time. She wanted to crawl into his skin somehow and be consumed by the fire they were both feeling.

He brought out something in her that she had never known was there. Some part of her that defied logic and thought. It was pure response, pure reaction.

He nodded before pushing away from the counter.

"Now do you have something to add?" she demanded.

His lips twitched, curving up arrogantly. She felt him closing the distance, awareness of him rippling along her skin.

She backed up.

It just happened, pure response to the animal bearing down on her.

He was hard and powerful, strength radiating off him. He reached out and cupped her hips, the hold sending a bolt of hunger through her pelvis.

"When it comes to your safety, Celeste, there is no discussion."

He lifted her and she ended up slung over his shoulder. A sound escaped from her that was half scream, half squeal as he carried her down the hallway to his bedroom.

"Nartan, put me down, you caveman!" She couldn't help it. She was on the verge of laughter, completely exasperated, and as turned on as she'd ever been, all at once. She really, really needed to get a grip. She was going to have to even out the power balance in this relationship somehow.

Her words bounced off the walls of the hallway but he never slackened his pace. He carried her through the double doors and deposited her on the huge bed.

"Did you hear me?"

He reached over and caught the bottom of her pants, pulling the loose martial-arts wear down her legs with one swift motion.

"I might ask you the same question, Celeste."

She rolled away from him, ending up near the headboard as he tossed her pants aside and worked the buttons loose on his shirt before shrugging out of it. The sight of his body was distracting and amped up the heat licking its way through her insides.

"You didn't ask me how I want to handle things."

He opened his waistband and shucked his pants. "That's right. I didn't ask and I'm not apologizing."

He was being as hard and razor sharp as she'd always suspected he might be. Completely in command of his world.

"You don't have a shred of remorse for how controlling you're being. You can't just plan my life like an expansion of your empire."

"Yes I can." He put a knee down on the surface of the bed. She wanted to ignore his cock, but the rigid length drew her attention as he moved toward her. He crawled across the surface of the bed until he loomed over her, his heat warping around her as his scent filled her senses.

Intoxicating…

"And I will, Celeste."

"Over my dead body," she snarled, reaching out to close her hand around a fistful of his chest hair.

"Acceptable." He scooped her up and hugged her to him as he rolled over and flattened her onto her back. "The 'over your body' part, that is."

He hooked her underwear and pulled it off with one swift motion.

"Damn it, Nartan. This is important to me."

He lowered himself onto her, capturing her wrists and pinning them above her head. "I assure you, it's far more important to me. You aren't part of my world, you're the very heart of it. There is no life without you. Only a vessel without a pulse."

His tone was fierce and his words more tender than any flowery compliment she'd ever heard. For a moment, she stared into his eyes, watching the way they glittered with emotion so deep that tears flooded hers. He nodded and leaned over to kiss away one tear that escaped to slide down her cheek.

She twisted her hands, trying to break free because she needed to touch him. Needed to hold him. He tore her top from her, earning a satisfied purr from her before she pressed back against him, eager and desperate to connect with him.

Desperate.

An hour later, Celeste rolled over in his bed and looked at him.

"Sex maniac," she accused, in a teasing tone.

"Demanding bitch," he countered.

She laughed and rolled over and onto her feet. "I still haven't seen the entire house."

"Another excellent reason for you to work for me. All the commuting time could be put to better use."

"We'd never get out of bed." She walked into the bathroom and turned on the shower. Nartan was across the hall, pulling on a pair of loose jeans.

After her shower, he met her in the hallway and walked with her out into the kitchen. "Dinner will be here in a few. Someone is driving it over."

He took a moment to adjust the lighting, keeping it nice and low. The patio doors were pushed all the way open, letting the ocean air in. "Did Marcus notice the Lambo?"

"I think that's a test of manhood. If he didn't, he'll have to turn in one of his tattoos." She curled up in a large leather recliner.

Nartan settled into another one and grinned at her. She was still tingling from the mind-blowing sex they'd just shared. "I still wish you had talked to me first about calling Marcus."

"Would you have told him yourself?"

It was a hard question. She wanted to say yes, but a glitter in Nartan's eyes made her hesitate.

"Most likely not."

One dark eyebrow rose. "You refused to testify against Caspian."

"That was then."

"And now I'm a part of your life," Nartan said. "Which just might tip the scales inside Caspian's head. He thinks of you as a possession, and when he learns you have another man in your life, he could turn violent. He wouldn't be the first man to do that."

She opened her mouth to argue but realized she didn't have any valid points. His logic was sound.

He offered her a smug look. "But if you'd like to…discuss my position in your life again…I will be happy to make time."

She took on as disapproving a look as she could, considering she was still buzzing from afterglow. "Using sex to settle differences of opinion isn't very healthy."

"More fun than therapy." His lips curved into a wolfish smile. "Much, much, more fun."

Celeste snorted.

"I spent a fortune on a security package today," Nartan informed her. "By the end of the month, there will be a full gate on the road."

She didn't care for the resigned look that took possession of his face.

"You don't have to do—"

"Yes I do," he cut her off. "And Tarak is right. I should have done it sooner. I'm not living in a shack on a worthless piece of dirt anymore. It will be tasteful and mostly out of sight."

"You like your open spaces."

He nodded and glanced at the way the sections of wall were slid back like French doors to allow the boundary of the house to blend seamlessly with the environment. "You're not the only one who needs to make mental adjustments. I can't keep sleeping with half the house wide open and an open road leading to it. Besides you and me, I need to think of my horses. Some drunken idiots could get the idea to take a moonlight ride and injure them."

"We'll do it for the horses," she teased softly, grateful because it gave her a chance to sidestep feeling trapped.

"Life is the only thing that can't be replaced." He offered her a hand and led her out into the main house. "The rest of it is just stuff that can be replaced."

Their dinner arrived with the addition of a fresh, raw salmon head with bone still attached. Nartan set it aside and laughed when she stared at it.

"It's an offering," he explained.

"Excuse me?"

He slid their dinner into the oven and punched a few buttons. "Indian bird feeder and mouse trap."

He jerked his head toward the door and she followed him, taking a moment to slip her shoes on before following him across the yard toward the corral.

He pointed up to the barn's eaves. "I had nesting spots built in for hawks or eagles, maybe owls. They'd have just used the eaves, but I don't want the nests falling."

A few feet below where the roof peaked, there were three boxes with round poles extending from them. Nartan took the fish and laid it on a six-foot-high pole that had a small flat board nailed to the top of it, just long enough for the fish to fit without hanging over the edges.

"The horse feed will attract rodents, no matter how well kept the corral is. So I'm encouraging some raptors to claim this as their territory."

He clasped her hand and turned her back toward the house.

"I think that might be illegal."

"Better than putting out poison." Nartan kicked off his shoes when they reached the open back of the house. "Hawks die all the time from eating poisoned rodents. Look at it as a housewarming gift. I won't feed them every day. They'd get weak. And I can't have rats in my barn."

He pulled their dinner from the oven and slid a plate toward her.

"The horses are important to you."

He sat down across from her and started attacking his dinner. "Horses represent wealth and strength." He wiggled his eyebrows. "I'll need a few if I ever convince you to marry me."

Celeste smiled. "With a horse?"

He nodded. "Disappointed I'm not the diamond-ring-on-bended-knee sort?"

She toyed with her wineglass. "No. Caspian made the grand display." She worried her lower lip as she imagined Nartan offering a horse. "I think I like your idea better. I know I enjoyed the ending to Sabra's wedding reception."

"Why?"

She drew in a deep breath. "It seemed…honest. Like it really reflected who Tarak was as a person."

The topic felt too serious. They ate in silence for the next few minutes. Nartan glanced up, looking past her before pointing.

She turned her head and stared at where they'd left the fish. There was a flutter of wings as a bird of prey landed on it.

"Wow," she muttered. The raptor looked around before lowering its hooked beak to tear into the flesh of the fish.

"That's a chick," Nartan informed her. They eased closer to the door, moving slowly. "You can tell by the feathers. Chicks have to find their own territory."

"Looks like your housewarming present is being received well."

He draped an arm across her back as they watched the raptor eating. "If the bird stays, it's an omen of good luck. A sign of life wanting to be here."

He leaned over and kissed her, pulling her tightly against him.

They spent the last hours of the evening laughing and talking and ended up back in bed before long. Their need for each other was only growing deeper and harder to resist. Even Celeste's will to question it was crumbling.

And she found herself rather pleased about it all.

⁓

"You know, it's killing me not to know about the Lambo." Marcus finally broke down a week later.

"It's Nartan's."

"No kidding," her boss responded dryly. But he pegged her with a hard look. "And here I was thinking that your boss is a hell of a guy for giving you a bonus."

"I'm okay, boss man."

He nodded. "Let me know if that changes."

"I will."

A little tingle stroked her nape, but it had to be because Nartan had been right. Marcus was her crutch. She'd taken the job because she knew he would help keep her safe, and he was safe himself.

After class she sent a text to Nartan.

Need to pick up mail and more clothes.

A moment later he responded.

Get the mail, forget the clothes.

She laughed and drove toward her townhome. It looked silent and lonely. When she walked through the door, the feeling of welcome was missing.

You're absolutely insane, Celeste.

She'd known Nartan for only the better part of a month. But her feelings were real. She had no desire to stay in the townhome, and not because of the luxury waiting at Nartan's home. It was the fact that he was there. Her phone vibrated with an incoming text.

Stop at Angelino's.

She smiled, feeling giddy and excited. She raced up the stairs and showered. When she returned to the driveway, she had her mail in a bag and several more suits. She slid behind the wheel of the sleek sports car and swung out of the driveway without a second thought.

Traffic had eased, but in Southern California, the roads were never empty. She pulled up in front of Angelino's and grinned when the valet jumped. Another car pulled in behind her, but she didn't pay it any attention. She walked toward the entry doors and inside. Nartan was in his element, watching the half-full dining room as one of his senior staff members leaned close to him to ask a question.

What the man did for a suit should be outlawed.

Or patented and bottled.

Tonight it was a slate-black wool that complemented his dark hair. His tie was the same shade of ocean blue as his eyes. He caught sight of her, and his business face cracked with a smile. He held out his hand to her. Behind him, two women looked over to see what had gained his attention. Their makeup was perfect and their hair looked salon fresh. With ample, obviously enhanced cleavage and ultra slim thighs, they clearly spent their days ensuring that their assets were in prime condition.

The diamonds sparkling around their necks made it plain that they were also very good at getting top dollar for their efforts. They narrowed their eyes as she drew closer and it became evident that Nartan was waiting for her. She shot them a hard look that caught Nartan's attention. He turned his head and they instantly smiled at him.

Celeste slid her hand along his forearm and reclaimed his attention. He raised his eyebrows at her before escorting her across the restaurant toward the private section. The maître d' standing there opened one of the sliding sections of wall for them. Inside was a smaller number of guests, every one of them having paid well in excess of fifty grand for a membership. They were celebrities and high-profile business professionals. Nartan took her through to the most exclusive dining rooms his establishment had to offer, the private rooms that overlooked the Southern California coastline.

He pulled her into his embrace the moment they entered one of the private rooms. "Damned professional image," he complained before sealing her mouth beneath a hard kiss. She indulged herself in the moment, stroking her hands beneath his tie. Her need for him never seemed to diminish. It peaked and flowed, as constant as the tide.

"I missed you," she whispered before disengaging herself from his embrace. He pulled out a chair for her. "Are we actually going to make it through dinner?"

His eyes narrowed. "Don't bet on it."

She drew her finger across her collarbone, and his gaze settled on the path she was tracing. "I think I might," she purred. "Anticipation does sweeten the climax..."

He bared his teeth at her. "I'm not the one who has to get up early tomorrow."

"You're up early every morning," she replied as the door opened and a waiter entered to begin serving dinner. Nartan's eyes glittered, sparking an answering hunger in her. The meal was splendid, but her attention was focused on the man sitting across from her.

Tension tightened as the moments went by. She felt the intensity growing, the insatiable need beginning to block out everything else. The moment she finished her entrée, she wiped her lips with the napkin and tossed it onto the table.

Nartan's eyes narrowed, her challenge pleasing him. She had a moment to watch his pupils dilate before he was out of his chair and rounding the table to pull hers back. He clasped his hand around hers and pulled her through the private section of the restaurant and out into the night. His valet scrambled to bring the Lamborghini around.

Nartan took them down the private section of road far faster than she'd ever driven it. His hands locked on the wheel, controlling the precision automobile with a confidence that sent a jolt of excitement through her. The sensation was sharp and hard, and she liked it that way.

The civilized ceremony of dinner had tapped out her patience too.

She didn't wait for him to pull into the garage, but got out of the Lambo while the garage door was rising. Nartan pulled it inside as she followed him, feeling her hips swaying.

She pulled her dress off, enjoying the way his lips thinned at the sight of her garter belt and matching bra.

"They can't put that damned gate in soon enough… I want you stripping in the garage every night."

The garage door slid shut as they connected. They actually lunged at each other, reaching for what they craved. He fisted a handful of her hair and turned her so she was backed against the smooth, sapphire blue of the Lamborghini. Her senses were overloaded, the feel of his hard body, the scent of his skin all combining to intoxicate her.

She reached for his belt and had it open before she unzipped his pants and pulled his erection free. It was hard and promising in her hand. But he caught her hands and pressed them back on the car.

"I want dessert," he growled. He hovered over her mouth for a moment, teasing her with the softest of kisses while he stroked the swells of her breasts. He followed his fingers with his mouth, kissing the tops of her breasts and sending her arching up to offer them to him.

Clasping her hips, he held her in place with a grip that sent a twist of need through her sex. He licked and kissed his way to her navel as he lowered himself.

"This smells delicious…" he rasped as he found the short curls. Her clit was pulsing, pounding with the same tempo as her heart.

"I'm not sure…I can take that… Fuck me, Nartan. That's what I want."

She tried to shift but he had her locked in place with his hands on her hips. He lifted her up, perching her on the edge of the car.

"Dessert first." He pressed his head between her thighs.

She gasped, the feeling of his hair against her inner thighs a rush of sensation that she hadn't anticipated. She fell back and caught herself with her hands as he pulled her folds away from her clit and exposed it completely.

The first lap made her cry out. By the next one, the only sound she had left was a moan. It bounced around the garage as he licked and sucked on her clit. Her pussy contracted, desperate for his cock, but he was driving her insane with his tongue, sweeping across her clit again and again before returning to suck on it.

She was on the edge, straining toward him as an orgasm began to burst inside her. She locked him in place with a leg over his shoulder, raising her hips toward his mouth as he sucked her through the wrenching climax. It was hard and sharp and snapped like a whip.

And it wasn't enough. "More," she demanded. "Fuck me."

He teased her swollen clit with a soft lap before rising. His face was hard, his eyes reflecting how close to the edge he was. She reached out and fisted her hands in his shirt, popping one of the buttons free as she pulled him to her.

"Fuck me hard!"

He thrust forward, forcing a whimper out of her as her body stretched to accommodate him. But she was drenched from her climax, making it easy for him to penetrate her until his balls smacked against her bottom.

"Like that?" he demanded.

"Harder!"

He didn't disappoint. There was a savage glint in his eyes that pleased her greatly. Knowing that she'd driven him to the edge set fire to something deep inside her. He was breathing hard, thrusting into her with purpose while he held her in position for every hard penetration.

"More!" she sobbed, her eyes closing as everything centered on the hard pounding he was giving her. She fought his grip, wanting to meet him, but he kept her prisoner, using her and pleasing her as he satisfied his appetite.

His breath left him in hard grunts, a snarl warning her that he was losing control. She opened her eyes and watched the muscles in his neck cord. His lips curled back as he worked faster and slammed himself harder into her. He cried out, the sound savage as he began to come. She was already melting, but the first spurt of his cum was molten. She shuddered, clenching around him, and another burst of pleasure exploded inside her.

He slid his arms around her, pulling her into an embrace as they both panted. She had no sense of time, only a heightened awareness of him surrounding her with his strength. Euphoria engulfed her, keeping her warm when her heart had slowed enough for her to feel the night air.

"Come on…let's soak."

He cradled her against him as he walked through the house and off to the left where an indoor Jacuzzi waited. He set her down and she wobbled before kicking off the heels she'd put on for dinner. After turning on the glass fireplace, he unlocked the sections of French doors and slid them open. The night air rushed in. He turned on the jets and the water began to bubble as Celeste unhooked her bra and garter belt before she got in.

She gave a little sigh as the water started to work on her sore muscles. She heard his clothing hitting the floor and opened her eyes to enjoy watching him bare himself.

"Like what you see?"

He pulled off his socks and dropped them.

"Hmmm…if stripping for you in your garage wasn't compliment enough, I guess I could resort to words."

He joined her and pulled her in front of him. "Stripping works for me."

"A man of action you are."

"As often as you like," he promised next to her ear. "But at this rate, we're going to end up with a nest full."

"I'm taking birth control." He locked her in his embrace and settled his chin on her shoulder.

"Nature has a way of making her own plans."

"Like making you so irresistible?"

He chuckled and scooped up water to dump over her shoulders. "I could charge you with the same crime." He stroked her breasts and lower until he was fingering her clit. "You've become an addiction."

"Still not happy about it?" She rubbed her back against him, feeling his cock hardening as he rubbed her.

"Still want to run away from it?"

She turned around, climbing up to straddle him. "I like being here."

Four little words. She had resisted him so much, but in the end, the words weren't that hard to say. She bit her lip as she lowered herself onto his length. He cupped her hips, holding her down on him as he angled his head and kissed her.

"I'm desperate to have you here, Celeste."

They weren't flowery words, but they struck her as some of the most deeply felt she'd ever heard spoken. They reflected her own need for him, both sexually and emotionally. She couldn't separate the two hungers. At some point, they had merged into one craving.

Just one craving for him.

~~~

"I got his name."

Caspian smiled as he sat back and crossed his legs. "It took you longer than I expected."

"I double-check my facts before delivering."

Caspian didn't care for the tone of the man's voice, but he wanted the information badly enough to overlook it. "Who is he?"

"Nartan Lupan, owner of Angelino's in Malibu. He's got a private house on the property."

"She went there with him?"

"Got naked the minute they pulled into the garage. He doesn't have shit for security. No street lighting on the road. Piece of cake walking up on them. Got the photo evidence if you want it."

"Send it." Caspian tightened his hand into a fist. "Your fee will be transferred."

He killed the line. For a moment, he sat still, staring at the picture of Celeste on his desk. He curled his fingers into a fist and slammed it down on the desk. His door opened a moment later as his bodyguard looked in on him. Caspian didn't give the man a single glance. He was a servant; his job was to perform.

Caspian contemplated the picture a while longer before standing up. He punched the intercom and opened a line to his assistant.

"Bring the car up. I have business."

~~~

"Let's take the yacht out tomorrow night," Nartan suggested.

Celeste stretched her toes out to where one of the jets was set into the side of the Jacuzzi. Nartan smoothed a hand over her bare shoulder as she leaned against him.

"Can't. I promised to referee a tournament in Oceanside," she answered.

She ended up holding her breath, waiting to see what he'd do when faced with the fact that her life wasn't just fitting neatly into his.

He shifted, tracing her neck with his fingertips. "What's wrong, Celeste?"

"Nothing."

He closed his arms around her when she tried to sit up. "You're as tight as a bowstring. Why? Worried I can't accept that you enjoy your martial arts because I need you to be focused on me a hundred percent?"

He placed a tender kiss on her neck and she quivered.

"I guess…maybe a little…"

The admission was a crack in the dam that she hadn't realized was holding back her feelings. She felt them surging to be free and washing through her like a flash flood.

"Invite me."

"Where?"

He nipped her shoulder. "To watch you referee." He smoothed his hand over her shoulder, down her arm, and through the bubbling water until he cupped her breast. "To be part of something import-ant to you."

"You can't waste that kind of time."

"Spending time with you is never a waste." He cut through her argument. "If it's important to you, I'll make time."

"I do it to support the sport maintaining its Olympic stand-ing. There have to be a set number of tournaments yearly. But it's not necessary for you to come. I won't be able to spend any time with you."

But she was touched.

Deeply.

She turned around and straddled him, lifting up and sheathing him in a soft motion that was more about connecting than satisfying lust. She just needed to be closer to him.

Completely intimate.

He closed his eyes, pleasure drawing his neck tight. She lifted and he guided her back down with a hand on each hip.

"Oceanside has a harbor…" His eyes opened, showing her the glitter of anticipation. "What time should I pick you up?"

A black sedan was waiting outside the gymnasium for her. Celeste paused for a moment but chided herself for hesitating.

Nartan wasn't being controlling.

Just demanding.

And there was a huge difference between the two.

Excitement was brewing inside her as the driver took her toward the marina. It was full of expensive yachts, but she was looking for the man waiting for her. He was standing on the pier, his dress shirtsleeves rolled up to his bare his forearms and his collar was open again.

Yeah…demanding.

And she had every intention of being his match when it came to demanding.

Chapter 11

HER PHONE RANG JUST before quitting time on the following Friday. Nartan's number flashed across the screen, making her smile. Friday was the one night she didn't go to the studio to train. She'd been giddy as the afternoon wore on and she anticipated having more than a few hours with Nartan. As she was picking up the phone, Sandy came through the door again with flowers in her hands.

"Just getting ready to leave," Celeste told Nartan.

"I'll be late tonight." He was agitated; she could hear the stress in his voice.

"What's wrong?"

"One of my horses is sick. We're loading her up to take her to the vet. I need to be with her," he informed Celeste gruffly.

"I'm sorry, Nartan," she answered quietly, hearing the raw emotion in his voice. "You didn't have to send flowers because of that."

"I didn't." His tone immediately changed to territorial.

"Oh, just an assumption."

"Who's sending you flowers?" he demanded.

"Probably one of our clients who can't pay," she said. "Marcus has an open door for ex-military, no matter their circumstances. Sandy just brought them in. I haven't looked at the card."

"I'll be home when I can."

"Call me if you want me to come to you." She left the invitation hanging between them. The silence on the other end of the phone told her he was considering letting her into the private part of himself. "I'll keep my phone handy."

"Thank you, Celeste."

He killed the line, leaving her with that last sample of the pain in his voice. She was suddenly too far away from him, the work in front of her meaningless as the sound of his voice echoed in her head. All that mattered was being there for him.

She stood up, restless. She wandered over to the flowers, fingering their cool, fresh petals. But when she got in front of them, she saw the crystal butterflies woven into the arrangement. Her mouth went dry as she scanned it and realized it was a bouquet.

An exact replica of her wedding flowers.

She recoiled from them like they had suddenly revealed a tarantula. It took all her strength to reach for the little white envelope stuck into them. Nausea was twisting her insides.

> *You are not a Connor. Resume your place or this will*
> *be only the first cut.*

She gasped, stepping back as horror gagged her.

Oh God, it had been Caspian outside the studio.

First cut?

Nartan's horse. It was one of the few living creatures he cared about. His grandfather had bred it. Celeste was reeling and staggered back, hitting her desk and sending a sorting tray crashing to the floor. She didn't even look down at it.

Her heart was racing, sweat trickling down her sides as she tried to get control of the rising tide of terror in her. It was all encompassing, threatening her like a tsunami.

"Celeste?"

She jumped and a tiny sound came out of her mouth before she realized Marcus was standing in the doorway. Her normally easygoing boss had a look on his face that she'd only seen a few times. It was raw, hard anger. The side of him you never wanted to mess with.

"What's wrong?" he demanded.

"I'm fine." Her thoughts were frozen. She looked back at the flowers and shuddered, unable to control her reactions.

Marcus stepped into the office and plucked the card from her stiff fingers. His expression tightened as he read it. Celeste took a deep breath to still her racing heart.

"Who's he threatening?" Marcus demanded with the card between his fingers.

"I think…Nartan said there was something wrong with one of his horses." She covered her mouth with her hand, trying to scrape together her wits. "They're a replica of my wedding bouquet."

"I knew that prick would come back after you." Marcus looked at the flowers. His lips twitched up in a very menacing grin. "He's leaving an evidence trail this time."

He disappeared and came back with a cell phone. He snapped pictures of the flowers before picking them up. "I'm going to see if I can find out who paid for these. Give Nartan a call and give him a heads-up."

Celeste sat down at her desk, feeling like she was moving in slow motion.

She'd known.

Oh God…she'd known!

Memories of the way Nartan went to greet those horses sent tears to her eyes. Caspian always knew who to hire to find out what was important to his enemies. He was absolutely ruthless in the way he went after what he wanted.

Her fingers were still shaking as she hit the redial button on her phone. She drew in a deep breath, trying to still her racing heart as the phone began to ring.

But the call went to voice mail. She hung up and typed a quick text message. Tucking her phone back in her purse, she turned off her computer system.

"Where are you going from here?"

Marcus was back in her office doorway.

"No class tonight. I was going up to Nartan's."

Marcus took a moment to dwell on what she'd said. "Go straight there."

"I will."

She hesitated once she slid behind the wheel of the Lamborghini.

Her gut was starting to twist with a sick fear she recognized.

Like fucking hell!

She swallowed the bitter taste and watched her knuckles turning white on the steering wheel.

Like fucking hell she'd let Caspian punch her buttons.

She pulled out of the parking lot, merging into traffic as she searched her memory for the location of a spa she hadn't been to in a long time.

No one questioned her when she pulled into the private parking area in the Lamborghini. Once she was out of the car, her less-than-designer suit caught a few looks. Celeste hit the meandering entry-way sidewalk with a pace that didn't give anyone time to question her. A pair of Asian receptionists smiled when she entered the spa.

"Caspian Devitt."

There was only a flicker of recognition in one of the girls' eyes before they both shook their heads.

"Mr. Devitt does not wish to be disturbed."

Celeste dug into her purse and pulled out a hundred-dollar bill. She folded it up and passed it to one of the women through a handshake. She muttered a few words in Korean. The woman's lips twitched before she answered in a single word of Korean.

Celeste took off down the gleaming cream-colored hallway, past the inside fountain that was filling the place with soothing water sounds to the private massage suite marked with a number six.

She pushed open the door, startling a young girl who was rubbing the shoulders of her client in nothing but a G-string. But it was Caspian Celeste was interested in. He hadn't really changed. Maybe he was a little leaner, but he still looked at her with an expression she recognized.

Like she was a possession.

She forced down the bitter taste in her mouth.

"I see you haven't changed." But she had and that gave her enough confidence to stare him down.

Caspian lifted his head and sent the girl away with a flick of his fingers. His bodyguard had moved into view, watching Celeste through mirrored shades.

"Leave us," Caspian ordered.

He sat up and surveyed Celeste from head to toe.

"Lupan doesn't know how to dress you."

"I dress myself." She stepped forward, making sure she looked at her ex-husband just as thoroughly as he'd studied her. "And I'm here to tell you one thing. Leave me alone."

Caspian's eyes narrowed. He stood up, a towel staying around his waist. It was a damned good thing because she was fighting off nausea with just his chest on display.

He reached out and slapped her. She jerked and responded without thinking. His hand had barely connected with her cheek before she slid toward him and kicked out his knee with a low roundhouse kick. He folded with a hiss, grabbing the massage table to break his fall.

"I don't take your shit anymore, Caspian," she hissed. "I know the little games you like to play, so I won't bother trying to get security footage from this place, but touch me again and I'll find a way to prosecute you."

"Shut up," he snapped as he regained his feet. "You belong to me and I will enjoy teaching you your place again."

"Just try it," she warned.

He started toward her but his bodyguard had reentered the room. Caspian gestured him away, but the man shook his head.

"Get out," Caspian snarled.

"I'm the one leaving," Celeste declared. "Before I have to kick his ass for having poor taste in clients. I'd really rather not have to explain myself to Master Lee."

"You will come back to me, Celeste," Caspian crowed. "You crave my strength in your life. You're really quite lost without my presence." He chuckled, turning her stomach. "That's the reason you're here. Deep down inside you need me."

"Stay away from me." She looked past him to the bodyguard. "Next time he touches me, I'll put him down hard."

She turned around and grasped the door.

"Don't you dare turn your back on me!"

Caspian lunged after her. His fingers made the briefest contact with her shoulder, curling and just starting to dig in before she turned and grabbed his hand. She twisted it and flipped him over. He landed in a heap and ended up facedown on the marble floor with her knee lodged between his shoulder blades and his arm bent up behind his back at just the right angle to send pain shooting through his shoulder.

"Don't...ever...touch...me...again."

She jumped away from him as the bodyguard closed in on her. She locked eyes with the guy before opening the door and leaving. There was a scuffle and the slam of the door behind her.

"Let go of me..." Caspian's muffled words came through the door, but it never opened.

Celeste made it back to the Lamborghini and pulled out of the parking lot.

She was shaking.

A new sensation was flooding her, and this time it was from victory.

———

"How dare you stop me?" Caspian growled at his bodyguard.

"The security cameras are still on in the hallway."

He kept his hand flat on the door, infuriating Caspian.

"You'll end up back in jail."

Caspian snarled. "Shut up. You don't tell me what to do. I pay you."

He stomped back into the dressing room and grabbed his phone. Control was something he knew how to get.

Celeste obviously needed a lesson in just how good he was at getting what he wanted.

———

Traffic was moving slowly. She kept her cell phone on the passenger seat, but it never rang. The drive up to Malibu was the longest, most tedious one she'd ever endured. She drove past Angelino's and on to the house. A large construction vehicle with a huge earth-drilling attachment was sitting near the road. New holes had been dug along the perimeter of Nartan's property for the fence. The crew had left for the day.

There was a touch of chill in the air as September brought the change of season. She pulled into the garage and smiled as she heard the chirp from the new house security system. It continued to chirp, warning her to enter a code within two minutes or it would go off. She climbed out of the seat of the Lamborghini and pulled the door down.

Something shifted in her peripheral vision. A blur of motion that sent her whirling around, her purse dropping to the ground. She jerked back as she came face to face with someone a lot bigger than herself. He was already swinging at her. She shifted to the side, hours of training kicking in without hesitation.

Time slowed down. The guy stumbled past her with the momentum of his punch but recovered quickly. She brought her hands up, turned, and used a back kick against him. He grunted as her foot connected with his belly.

But turning around gave her a glimpse of a second man. He reached out and clamped his arms around her, trapping her arms against her sides.

"You going to stop whining?" the man holding her asked his partner.

Celeste took the moment to lower her body into a wide horse stance and use her elbows and a good twist from her waist to disable the man holding her. He yelped and cussed when she turned and sent a tiger-claw hand at his throat.

"She's a real pushover…ain't she?" The man behind her mocked his companion as he gasped.

The second man lunged toward her. With the car beside her, she didn't have enough room to get out of his way. He tackled her into his partner.

"Enough of this Bruce Lee crap," he choked out. "Hold her."

She was sandwiched between them, and this time, the man behind her yanked her arms back.

"This would have been a lot easier without all the rules," the man in front of her complained before smacking her across her face. Her head twisted with the blow, pain exploding in her eye from the force he used.

"Yeah…well, it's got to look right. Right in the face, but don't break her nose."

She tried to duck her head but her assailant followed her, delivering a string of blows that made her vision darken. Consciousness began to drift away from her. She heard the connection of the last couple of blows but didn't feel them. There was no way to fend off the darkness. It just dragged her down.

His phone was ringing again.

Nartan cursed and yanked it out of his pocket. His fucking restaurant had better be on fire or his manager could find a new job.

But the message flashing across the screen came from his new home security system. He jabbed his finger onto the button to stop the alarm, which left the text message from Celeste on the screen. He read it twice before he cursed again.

The vet looked up. "I'll be back," Nartan said.

He only caught a fraction of the vet's surprise before he was pushing through the doors of the office. He hit the hallway at a run and yanked open the door of his truck.

<hr />

"Mr. Lupan?"

Celeste heard the voice and tried to wake up. For some reason, she wanted to go back to sleep. In fact, the urge was so strong, it was almost impossible to resist. She felt like she was slowly twisting around in a circle while floating. Around and around and around…

"Mr. Lupan, do you need assistance?"

She blinked and wished she hadn't. Pain shot through her face. She moaned, completely awake, and rolled over as she balled up and tried to endure the agony burning in her abdomen. Her face was throbbing, and she could feel her right eye swelling shut.

"Help!" she called out, but her lips were stiff. She took a deep breath. "Police!" she yelled at the security system.

Why the hell hadn't the security company already called them?

She shivered, trying to master the pain so she could look around. Her right eye was completely swollen shut but she got a look at the garage, sweeping it twice to make sure her assailants were gone.

"Did you say 'Police'?" the person on the other end of the security system inquired.

Celeste cursed under her breath and struggled to her feet. She stumbled to the control panel and hit the panic button.

"Idiot," she grumbled at the control panel. She started to go into the house but froze. Since she was unsure where her attackers were, the house wasn't the haven she longed for.

"Police and fire services have been summoned."

Her thoughts began to clear with the help of the pain. She straightened, relieved to find that only her face was battered. She punched the garage door and it began to open. At least it was an option for escape if they came back. But there was nothing outside but the corral. No one to appeal to for help. She sagged against the doorjamb, her knees feeling weak and her body shaking. Her vision swam in blurry waves and she lost track of time.

Light flashed and she blinked, trying to decide if she was passing out again.

"Celeste?"

Nartan was still stuffing his keys in his pocket when he came into the garage. She opened her mouth, but pain shot through her jaw and all she managed was a moan.

"Holy shit!"

She made a little sound of relief as he ran the last few steps to her. Then he held himself back, his eyes wide as he searched her face. She couldn't stand the separation and huddled into his arms. He hesitated to embrace her, giving in at last and holding her shoulders gently.

"What the fuck happened?" He gently cupped the sides of her face and pushed her back against the car. Then he lifted one hand away from the bruise forming around her eye, letting his hand hover in indecision as he studied her.

"They…might still be here," she managed to get past her swollen lips.

"I hope to fuck they are," he snarled.

The cops pulled in without sirens and skidded to a stop.

"Get your hands up!"

"This is my house," Nartan snarled.

"Do it, Nartan," she advised as she struggled to lift her hands. She was shaking so badly, it cost a lot of effort.

Nartan cursed and lifted his hands as two more black-and-whites skidded to a halt in the driveway.

"Listen up. Put your hands on your head and walk toward me," the officer commanded.

Nartan looked back at her, then lowered his hands to his head and locked his fingers. He started back through the garage while one officer kept a gun trained on him from behind the open door of the police cruiser. When Nartan reached the driveway, he was ordered to stop.

"Turn around and put your hands behind your back. Do it now."

She watched in a haze as Nartan was handcuffed and pulled back toward one of the cars. "She needs medical help," he growled at the officers.

"Now you." The officers were containing the scene before listening to anyone.

Celeste took a deep breath before stepping away from the doorjamb. Her knees held her and she made her way toward the driveway. As she stepped into the light, she watched the cop lift his head above his gun. He was holstering it a moment later as he came around the open door.

An ambulance pulled up, and she lost track of who blinded her with flashlights while examining her face. She ended up sitting on a gurney as a paramedic checked her vital signs.

"Who did this to you?" the police officer asked.

She looked up, pushing away the paramedic who was trying to tape a gauze pad over her swollen eyes. "I don't know. Two men were in the garage when I got home. I didn't get a good look at them."

He grunted. "I don't need you to name him. Your blood is all over his shirt and hands. I can take you in because of the physical evidence. There isn't a mark on him, so you're safe. Help me, help you."

"No." She sprang up off the gurney. "There were two men in the garage when I got home."

"Why didn't you mention them before?"

"I did," she argued.

His face was set in stone. Behind him, another officer was facing Nartan and reading him his rights.

"He didn't do it." She tried to control the emotion coursing through her.

The first cut…

"You crave my strength in your life. You're really quite lost without my presence."

Caspian would never come for her. He'd force her to come back to him. It was a game to him, and he never played anything but high-stakes games. Nartan was her weak spot.

Nartan was shouting at the officer in front of him, resisting as two others tried to put him in the back of the cruiser.

"Marcus Flynn," she insisted. "Make them call Marcus, Nartan!"

He made eye contact with her for a brief moment before he was shoved into the back of the police car. It was a nightmare, watching him through the barred windows. The legal realities were flooding her brain, terrorizing her with just how dire the circumstances were.

She wasn't going to be Caspian's Trojan horse.

"I refuse treatment."

She pulled the blood pressure cuff off her arm with a rip of Velcro and stood up.

"Ma'am…you really need X-rays."

The paramedic tried to get her to sit back down. She brushed past him and ducked around the cop trying to get her to go back.

"I need my purse."

"You need to get back on the gurney."

Celeste made it back into the garage before the cop hauled her to a stop with a hand on her bicep.

"Lady, you need treatment."

"I need my lawyer." She ducked down, but with her eye swollen shut, her balance faltered. She ended up bumping her head on the side of the Lamborghini before landing on the hard concrete.

"Lady—"

The cop tried to haul her up, but she caught a glimpse of her purse and grabbed it before he got hold of her. He pulled her up and she ended up leaning against the side of the Lamborghini. She only spared a momentary thought for the paint job on the car before fumbling in her purse for her cell phone.

"Lady, you need—"

"To call my lawyer." She punched the speed-dial button. "You're arresting the wrong man."

The cop only hooked his hands in his belt and regarded her with a stony expression that he'd perfected through countless domestic violence calls where he saw the same people over and over, heard the same lies again and again. It had hardened him until he wasn't able to sift through the damning evidence Caspian had made sure was on hand.

This was exactly what her ex wanted. All of the pressure would be on her. He'd keep increasing it until she bent. She had the bitter memories to remind her just how determined Caspian could be.

Marcus answered on the second ring.

"What's happening, Celeste?"

"Lupan."

Nartan stood up and walked to the booking desk. The officer behind it checked the mug shot of him against his face. "You're being released. Sign here to acknowledge your court date."

Nartan scribbled his name across the line before the cop slid an envelope across the desk to him. He didn't bother to open it before making his way through the sliding door to the outside.

Marcus Flynn was standing on the other side. He held his index finger to his lips and jerked his head toward a large sign posted on the wall warning that the area was under video and voice surveillance.

Nartan fell into step beside Marcus as they walked through the dingy halls of the jail on their way to the parking garage. The moment Marcus drove them out of the building, he turned.

"Where is Celeste?" Nartan asked.

"Hospital." Marcus had his eyes on the road. "I insisted. One of my guys is with her."

"Good." Nartan rubbed his eyes. "Thanks."

"Don't thank me yet." Marcus cut him a hard look.

"You don't think I did it?" His temper was a hairsbreadth from exploding.

"Wouldn't be here if I did." Marcus cut him a side look. "I just don't need to wake my buddies this time of night to help me hide a body."

Nartan was digging his fingers into the seat. "What the hell do you mean?"

"I'm about to get free with my opinions. You might not feel so thankful when I'm finished." He made a left turn and pulled into the hospital parking lot. "Your security is shit. I never would have let Celeste leave the office today if I knew how open your house was."

"I'm working on that." But it wasn't good enough. The sight of the emergency room sign turned his insides as he realized Celeste had paid a huge price for his lapse.

"And you have a big problem, because I think her ex is coming after you. He's got a lot of resources. He sent a replica of her wedding bouquet to the office." Marcus pulled the card from his shirt pocket and offered it to Nartan.

"You should have called and told me about this," Nartan growled.

Marcus parked the car and turned off the engine. When he turned to look at Nartan, the man was deadly serious. Nartan felt everything inside him shift to something hard and deadly.

"I fully intended to, but I was going to give Celeste the chance to do it first. I don't want her pissed at me because I didn't give her a chance to handle her own affairs."

"Shit! I didn't let her get a word in edgewise because I was dealing with my horse. Just about the only thing that could distract me from Celeste."

Marcus grunted. "He's good, or at least he hires people who are good, because I let her go and you were distracted. My guess is he's watching both of you, and your horse's untimely illness was no accident. We got lucky this time. He's planning to use you to break her."

"I'm not waiting for him to make the next move. He isn't the only one with resources."

One side of Marcus's mouth rose. "I'm beginning to like you."

———

"Nothing broken."

Celeste breathed a sigh of relief as the doctor searched through the results being fed to the mobile computer parked in the corner of the emergency-room bay she was in.

"But you're going to be in a fair amount of pain for a while."

"I can deal with it."

"You shouldn't have to." The curtain was pulled aside as Nartan appeared. She drank in the sight of him, realizing she'd been tense since the police had taken him away.

She never wanted to feel that way again.

Marcus stood a pace behind Nartan, his eyes narrowing when he got a look at her face.

But nothing mattered as Nartan made it to her side. The tears she'd been fighting rolled down her cheeks, making her swollen eye smart even more. He slid his hand along her neck, cupping the back of her head and giving her the support she needed.

But the memory of him in the back of the police car remained. Caspian didn't know how to lose. Nausea filled her as she realized the only way to keep Nartan safe was to leave him.

~~~

Celeste woke up in Nartan's bed. She shouldn't have. But she'd been foggy from medication, her weakened senses unable to have the conversation she knew was coming. She rolled out of bed well into the morning and went into the bathroom.

Nartan was nowhere in sight, but a rumpled towel hanging on a hook proved he'd been there. She leaned on the vanity and studied her face. The entire left side was black and blue, but at least her eye was less swollen. Her lower lip was split but not badly enough to need stitching.

Of course not. Caspian wouldn't tolerate her being scarred.

She fought off a wave of nausea, refusing to let the thought of him make her sick. She leaned her head back, drawing in several long breaths before turning on the shower and letting the water run over her face.

It didn't wash away her dark mood, which only deepened when she stepped out and saw the backyard with the island.

She had to leave.

Nartan's paradise, his sanctuary, was being invaded and it was all her fault.

The hard truth dug its claws into her, flooding her eyes with tears. She wiped them away, struggling to find some way to console herself, but there was none. Leaving was going to rip her heart to sheds.

But she was absolutely determined to make sure Nartan never ended up so helpless again.

She dressed and pulled her bag out of the closet. After stuffing her clothing into it, she slung it over her shoulder and left the bedroom. She walked down the hallway toward the kitchen and the garage door.

"Celeste?"

Nartan looked up from the kitchen counter, where he'd been leaning over a large document of some sort.

She stiffened and turned to face him. "I need to go."

He came around the table and closed the distance between them, drawing closer when he noticed the bag.

"You need to go back to bed."

"You were arrested last night because of me," Celeste implored him. "You have to see reason."

Nartan pegged her with a furious look. "I have to?"

She nodded. Nartan's face hardened. She watched his eyes darken a moment before he moved toward her and scooped her off her feet. Her bag slid off her shoulder and hit the floor. He carried her through the house and back into the master bedroom before depositing her on the bed gently.

"Caspian doesn't know how to lose," she said.

He closed the bedroom door and leaned against it, a hint of satisfaction crossing his face as he surveyed her on his bed. His lips twitched as her words sank in. "And you think I do?"

There was a savage edge to his voice, one that made her hesitate and set her teeth into her lower lip.

"That isn't what I meant." Her resolve was crumbling. "I can't bear the idea of you getting caught in the middle…getting hurt because of me."

His expression softened for a moment. "I got caught with my pants down. I should never have brought you here before making sure it was safe."

"No…" She stood up. "It's me… I went to see him and set him off."

"You did *what*?"

She didn't care for the incredulous note in his voice. "You heard me. I wasn't going to take that wedding bouquet crap from him. So I went to his favorite spa and found him there." She nodded with satisfaction. "Caspian is such a slave to his vanity. Even years later, it was easy for me to track him down."

Nartan folded his arms over his chest. "What happened?"

She drew in a deep breath. "I told him I would never be back and to leave me alone."

"Celeste…"

"Don't lecture," she interrupted. "I know you want to protect me, but I need to be strong enough to face my past. I need to be worthy of you. I can't let him intimidate me into silence again."

He captured her, surrounding her with his heat and the scent of his skin that always overwhelmed her.

"Let me go… I can't think when you touch me."

"Good." He caught the back of her head, holding her in place. "I don't want you to think. I don't want you to do anything but let me deal with this."

She stiffened, pushing against his chest until he released her with a huff. She ended up crawling back onto the bed to put some distance between them.

"I can't just be your pet."

His eyebrows lowered. "That idea has merit all on its own."

"Don't use sex to end this conversation," she warned. "I can't handle knowing Caspian will come after you again. I love you too much…" The words were out before she could stop them from flowing straight from her breaking heart.

"I'm leaving you. At least if I'm not with anyone, Caspian won't have a target."

"The hell you are." He reached across the bed and lifted her up, cradling her gently but solidly and bringing her back to his side.

He buried his face against her neck, kissing the delicate, sensitive skin and setting off a soft tingling of need.

It was gentle but gained strength with every kiss and lick he trailed across her neck. He was too close to resist, impossible to keep her hands off. She moaned, the tension shattering as she arched toward him. He was everything she craved, the idea of leaving him too painful.

"You crave me as deeply as I do you…" His voice was a rich, deep tonic.

He rose up, grasped the waistband of her yoga pants, and pulled them off her.

"Wait…"

"So you can start thinking again?" He ripped his shirt up and over his head, betraying how on edge he was, but his touch remained gentle. "Not a chance, sweetheart. I'm going to remind you why you're going to stay right here…in my bed."

He pressed her thighs wide, settling over her mons. She gasped, her clit giving a crazy twist as she watched him in fascination. His breath touched her folds a second before he pulled them back and began to eat her out. She wanted to remember why she had to convince him of how right she was. Instead she was swept into the tide of need and desire that had always linked them. It was addiction, one so deeply rooted in her flesh that there was no way to resist it.

She arched and moaned, the pleasure building to a crescendo as he plied his tongue over her sex with a skill that left her moaning with rapture. She was helpless in its grip, withering and twisting as climax tore through her. He pumped her through the last few ripples, his fingers stroking her with a hard rhythm that made her hungry for something harder.

He didn't leave her wanting. He slid down the bed, standing up between her thighs, and freed his cock. It was hard and thick and everything she craved. He pulled her down to the edge of the bed and leaned over her, pressing her legs up to her shoulders as he plunged deep, shielding her from his weight.

"Tell me you want to leave now…"

She tried to think beyond the hard flesh inside her. "I can't see you…like that again…"

He worked his length in and out of her. "But that would mean you would never feel me like this again…" He thrust hard and deep, stilling for a moment as he whispered against her ear. "No one fits me like you, Celeste… I have to have you…"

She recognized the note of desperation in his voice, knew it because it mirrored the same feeling that was coursing through her.

"Then take me," she commanded. "Now. Hard."

He curled his lips back and fisted his hands in the comforter. Every thrust was hard, packed with all of the power in his body. She felt herself being driven up to another peak, the pleasure building every time he connected with her G-spot.

"Open your eyes," he rasped, his breath harsh and hard.

She struggled to look at him, her body starting its plunge into climax.

"Watch what you do to me…"

She heard how exposed he was in that moment and opened her eyes to witness him losing control.

"I want you to see what you do to me…"

She lifted her hips high to push him over the edge. His eyes narrowed, his neck cording as she felt his cock giving up the first spurt of his seed. It hit her G-spot, sending her over the edge as well. She locked her legs around him, binding him to her as he emptied himself.

But she kept her eyes open, locked with his as they twisted and strained toward one another. He collapsed, catching his weight just inches before his chest flattened her breasts. His eyes were glazed over with satisfaction. "Do you see? I can't live without you."

The confession was torn from him. She watched him bare his soul for her before rolling over and pulling her against his side. He locked her in place, his embrace as hard as his body.

"Trust me."

At that moment, she realized she didn't have a choice. She was responding to him just as instantly as she had always done. Nartan wasn't something she decided anything about. Control wasn't in her hands.

And she couldn't lie to herself any longer.

"I do."

He kissed the top of her head, smoothing his hand down her arm as his embrace shook. The tremor sent tears down her cheeks before she surrendered and closed her eyes.

———

"As your lawyer, I have to remind you that you could still end up in jail."

"Since I can afford to pay you, I hope you're going to keep that from happening," Nartan responded to Marcus. "That's not why you're here."

Marcus leaned over the map Nartan had laid out on the kitchen island. He peered at it with a critical eye.

"Why are you here?" Celeste appeared in the kitchen. She moved closer and looked at the map. "What is this?"

"A burlesque club your ex frequents," Nartan told her with a chill in his voice that sent a shiver down her spine. "I'm going hunting."

His tone was stone hard.

"Marcus…talk some sense into him." Celeste looked to her boss for a voice of reason.

Marcus pulled a pen from the countertop and tapped at a point on the map. "I'll take up position here."

She felt her temper shift into high gear, but the level of intensity coming from Nartan was too much to hit head-on. "Okay, fine. I'm going too."

She moved up and looked at the map.

"No, you aren't," Nartan informed her.

"Negative," Marcus added. "You're grounded on injury."

"Cut the Neanderthal bullshit," she said. "It's my butt on the line, so I'm part of this or out the door." She cut a look at Marcus. "Your door too."

"We settled this, Celeste—" Nartan started.

Her cheeks heated but she refused to shy away. "This is my fight, Nartan. It's my past coming back to haunt me."

"It's mine, and I'm taking it to him." His expression was like ice.

"How do you figure it's your fight?" she demanded.

Nartan faced off with her. "You're my responsibility and he poisoned my mare. I had to put her down."

Celeste gasped. "She died?" The magnificent creature that had carried her along the beach was gone. Her eyes filled with tears.

Nartan caught her in a gentle hug. "I'm going to track him down," he promised savagely. "For what he did to you."

He drew himself up and backed away. "Marcus brought over a couple of men to secure the house."

Marcus pulled his cell phone from his pocket and tapped in a text. A moment later, someone came through one of the patio French doors and another man through the garage.

"Paul and Kevin," Marcus introduced them. "Just got back from active duty. They're comfortable outside and competent."

Both were bulky and hard looking. They nodded toward her before slipping back out. She shook her head, rebelling against the idea.

Nartan let out a soft word in Apache. "Excuse me, Marcus."

For the second time, he scooped her off her feet and carried her back to his bedroom.

"I can't be your pet," she growled when he put her down and stood in front of the doorway again. "I…can't." Her voice broke.

Nartan softened, coming toward her and stroking her good cheek. For a moment, he was tender and everything that she needed.

"He breached the house I brought you to."

She looked up and drew in her breath when she witnessed the rage burning in his eyes. It was so deeply personal, she felt her belly knot. But she also felt something else. She felt protected.

"The place I want you to make into a home." He tapped her lips with his fingertip when she opened them to speak. "Do you remember what I told you about being rich?"

"Yes."

"Your love makes me rich." He stroked her cheek with the back of his hand. "And I will do anything necessary to defend it."

She shivered. The intensity glowing in his eyes shattered everything she thought she needed. It all fell aside, leaving her basking in the glow of his declaration.

"You shouldn't have to."

His lips curved. "Neither should you."

He rolled back until he was lying against the pillows. "Come here."

She crawled toward him, and he wrapped his arms around her. Everything churning inside her settled.

"Now look up."

Above the bed, the skylight allowed them a breathtaking view of the stars.

"I looked at the night sky when I was a boy, and every night through my youth and the days out on that claim with Tarak. I dreamed of the moment I'd find someone to share a home with."

He cupped her chin and angled his head so he could look into her eyes. "I'm going to go tell Caspian you belong to me." His eyes glittered with determination. "Deal with it. I intend to make sure he does."

"That won't go over well."

"Good." His expression turned savage. He stroked her jawline with a fingertip, letting her soak up the sight. "I understand why you went to see him and I respect it, even if I'm pissed about the chance you took."

Her lips twitched, rising into a smile. He tapped it with the tip of his finger. "Like I said, it was on my to-be-dealt-with list."

He returned her smile but it didn't stay on his lips long. His expression tightened within moments.

"So understand why I need to do the same thing."

"Ouch," she said. "Game point."

He nodded and kissed the top of her head before standing up.

"When I get back, you're going to tell me you love me again."

He sealed her lips with a soft kiss, one that didn't hurt her split lip. He tucked the bedding around her and then disappeared out of the door.

He was going out to fight for her. It should have disgusted her, but she discovered it sitting very comfortably on her shoulders.

Because that was who he was. She'd seen it the first day she'd met him. Instead of the thought chilling her, she found it far more comforting to know that he was honest.

⁓

Burlesque was more erotic than stripping. Caspian lifted his drink and inhaled its scent before taking a sip. He smiled, pleased with the quality of the spirits. Of course, he expected that level of comfort or he wouldn't frequent the establishment. A trio of dancers appeared, the overhead lighting perfectly timed with their entrance.

"I'm finished."

Caspian controlled the urge to jump as Gabon spoke from behind him. "You don't decide to be done."

"In this case, I am," Gabon answered softly. So softly that his words were almost too low to understand. The burlesque club was pulsing with music as three corseted women entertained on the main catwalk, their sultry movements causing the muted lights to catch the tiny sequins sewn to their costumes.

"Quitting on me will bring you more trouble than you can imagine," Caspian threatened.

"She's left you. Move on."

"Never," Caspian hissed. He turned in his chair to find the huge, hulking form in the shadows behind him. Gabon shifted back.

"She is mine."

"You're obsessed," Gabon decided. "I don't do obsessed."

"You do whatever I pay you to do."

Gabon shook his head. "You had her beat up. I don't play those games."

"What are you now? A thug with a conscience?" Caspian demanded.

"I'm a man who knows when the game is over." Gabon shook his head. "Wise up. You lost her, and Lupan isn't going to wait for you to come after him again." Gabon lifted one hand and pointed toward the door. "He's stalking you now."

Caspian stiffened, losing interest in Gabon as Nartan Lupan entered the club. He swept it, moving slowly along the outer edge until he came to the bartender. He reached out and shook the man's hand. The bartender's eyes narrowed as his hand disappeared beneath the bar for a moment to pocket the bribe Nartan had just given him. His lips moved and Nartan turned to look at the shadowed alcove Caspian sat in.

Rage filled him. Betrayal was something he refused to tolerate.

The bartender would suffer for his lapse in judgment.

Nartan was heading toward him.

He'd lost this battle but he would with the war. He always did. He quickly followed Gabon out the back and waited for his driver. But once inside his car, Caspian snarled, his poise deserting him as he watched the streets they drove past.

No one was going to tell him what to do again. He'd had enough of that in prison.

And yet there he was, being forced out by Nartan Lupan.

It was infuriating.

Enraging.

Celeste had turned slut.

Once he made it home, he tried to settle back in his office chair with a new drink. But Celeste's picture stared at him from the wall. So pristine. So perfect. Her wedding dress molded to her delightful figure and his ring shone on her finger.

"Got naked the moment they pulled into the garage."

The picture of Celeste in Nartan's embrace was on his desk.

Slut!

He hurled the heavy glass at the picture. Glass shattered, long shards falling out of the frame to the floor. His bodyguard entered the room, his gaze sweeping the scene silently.

"No one crosses me," Caspian declared ominously. "She and her lover need a lesson."

His bodyguard stiffened and shook his head. "I agree with Gabon. I'm just here until a replacement is sent over."

"You will help me teach them that lesson," Caspian snarled. "You will!"

His bodyguard didn't say a word and merely withdrew silently. But the man left behind doubt. Caspian found it eating away at him. Doubt wasn't something he allowed in his world.

It wouldn't be tolerated. He was the master.

So he'd take matters into his own hands.

That sent a jolt of satisfaction through him. It was thick and intoxicating. He turned and poured another drink, enjoying the burn of brandy mixed with determination.

Yes, he was the master.

Chapter 12

"I CAN'T KEEP DOING this."

Nartan looked up from his desk, his eyes narrowing. The look was familiar now. He leaned back in his desk chair and gave her his full attention.

"Caspian's succeeded in making you turn this place into the thing I hate." She pointed at the small, black security camera mounted to the ceiling in the corner of his office.

They were all over the house now. Two weeks later, her face had healed but her feelings hadn't.

"You had bars over the windows of your townhouse, Celeste." He stood up and came around his desk. "This is about the fact that I won't let you tag along."

She blew out a frustrated breath. "It is."

"It's nonnegotiable." He stood and went to the coatrack in the corner where his suit jacket was hanging. The office was neat and impressive, everything she expected of a man who owned such a premium stretch of the California coastline.

"Let's go over to Angelino's tonight," Nartan said.

He shrugged into his jacket, making it clear he was finished with the topic. Frustration chewed at her, but it was the same slow simmer that had been going for the last two weeks. She couldn't quite work it into a boil, but at the same time, she was failing miserably at letting it go.

He hadn't said he loved her.

That stuck in her throat. She was crazy to have said it herself, and the admission had left her feeling exposed.

"We've been spending too much time cooped up here." He moved closer, slipping his hands onto her hips with a familiarity that stole her breath. Repetition hadn't dulled the way his touch made her breath catch.

He pressed a light kiss against her lips before turning her around and giving her a soft swat on her backside.

"Put something ravishing on. So I can enjoy the idea of taking it off you."

His voice was rich with passion. She turned and eyed him over her shoulder. "Are you going to wait until we get home?"

His lips curved roguishly. "No promises."

"We might get kicked out. For indecent behavior."

"Sounds like fun."

She paused at the bedroom door. He smiled broadly and made a biting gesture. Heat was tingling along her body now, and she shook her head. The man was insatiable, and he made her feel the same way. Thank goodness she trained hard and was in great physical shape. She'd had more sex in the last month than in her entire life before, and she still felt anticipation building as she dressed.

A teasing of heat flickered through her passage as she put on a garter belt and snapped the stockings into place.

He loved garter belts.

She picked up a matching bra and reached around her back to hook it.

He liked her low-cut bras too.

This one barely covered her nipples but it supported her well, pushing her breasts up. Her nipples were pulling into tight little buttons as she pulled a dress out of the closet and slipped into it.

Nartan had pulled the Lamborghini out of the garage and flipped it around in the driveway. He was leaning against it when she came down the driveway. The stars were brilliant, the moon a silver sliver in the sky.

Her heels tapped on the concrete and he turned, holding out his hand. She watched the way he looked at her, his eyes filling with pleasure. He lifted her hand to his lips and pressed a kiss against the back before opening the door for her.

———

"They left the house."

Caspian smiled.

"They've gone up to Angelino's together and left the heat behind."

Caspian made a little sound of approval.

"What do you want us to do?"

"Wait. I am going to return the favor Mr. Lupan has been paying me by showing up where I like to relax."

He cut the line and stood up. Prison time was good for one thing, physical conditioning. His body was tight, the excess weight he'd had before his sentence worn away.

It was also good for something else.

Planning.

He had lots of plans. Meticulously thought-out ones that he was very ready to put into action. For just a moment, his attention settled on the new bodyguard in the corner of his office. He wasn't Gabon. But a disloyal man wasn't worth thinking about.

———

Angelino's was full. The moment they arrived, they were shown past the parties waiting in the lobby and bar toward the private section of the restaurant. Behind the sliding doors, there were mostly full tables. Nartan pulled out a chair in a corner alcove designed for privacy.

The meal service was perfect and the food divine. But all of it paled when compared to her dinner companion.

"You need to let me do this, Celeste."

She was on her second glass of wine when Nartan got to the topic she was stewing over.

"I could say the same to you," she countered. "It's my mess."

"No, it's ours, and I'm going to handle it."

There was determination in his voice that she hadn't heard before. She realized she was looking at the business side of his persona. The only other time she had seen it was the night in Alaska. It was a stark contrast to the man she'd been living with.

"What are you thinking?" he asked.

"That I've had the privilege of knowing your personal side, and I didn't realize it."

His lips rose just a fraction as his eyes filled with pleasure.

"In fact, the last time I saw you this focused was when you took that phone call." She didn't need to elaborate. His eyes flashed with instant recognition. "I think I'm ready to forgive you for that."

"Why?"

"You couldn't have built all of this without putting your personal life aside. I guess I'll have to give you some time to learn to change your priorities."

His lips rose higher. " I'm going to enjoy making you a priority…" He took a sip of wine. "As well as giving you my undivided attention."

Heat snaked through her belly, the pulse of anticipation increasing. "Excuse me. I think I'll freshen up before we leave for dessert."

He got up and pulled her chair out for her, then leaned down and growled next to her ear before she stepped away. She blushed as she walked to the restrooms.

Just like everything else in Angelino's, the restrooms were elegant.

Celeste leaned over to apply a fresh coat of lipstick with the use of one of the large, polished mirrors.

"Those bruises have healed rather fast." Laura came into view, studying Celeste's reflection.

"Excuse me?" Celeste popped the cap back on her lipstick and dropped it into her clutch.

Laura rolled her eyes. "I saw the police report."

Dread gripped Celeste's insides, but she kept her expression calm. "That was none of your business."

Laura fluttered her eyelashes, showing off a perfectly done makeup job. Her dark hair was piled on her head in a mass of curls that left her slender neck exposed. "Nartan Lupan is my business. Everything about him, even his screwups."

The frustration that had been stewing inside Celeste for the last few weeks suddenly found a target. "He's mine."

Satisfaction rolled through her as she delivered her words, but Laura only laughed softly.

"Who are you again?" she asked in a lyrical tone. "Oh yes, you're no one. Some stripper's cast-off who doesn't even know who her parents are. I understand your foster family wants nothing to do with you either. It must delight you to know the dog rated higher. Do yourself a favor— crawl back to your ex, because you will never keep a man like Nartan."

"Whatever," Celeste muttered, turning toward the door. But Laura slipped into her path. "As if I care what you think."

"You should," Laura informed her. "He might be enjoying you, but I'm the one he's going to keep for the long term."

"How do you have that figured?"

Laura shrugged a delicate shoulder. "I'm Apache. True blood. He's fucking you, but he'll come to me when he's ready to settle down. I have his grandparents' blessing."

She wanted to brush past Laura, but Celeste couldn't stop herself from looking the other woman over. Laura laughed again and slipped out of the ladies' room door, leaving Celeste with the sound echoing inside her skull.

She was shaking. She stumbled through the door, the need to escape driving her.

Nartan was leaning on the bar and Laura had slid up to his side. Her dress lay over her curves perfectly, and she was positioned so that he got a good view of her plunging neckline. She laid a hand on his chest and Celeste saw red.

I have his grandparents' blessing…

She turned and stumbled out into the entryway, pulling in a deep breath of cool night air. She suddenly didn't know enough about the man she'd fallen in love with. Her trust was so fragile that it was straining beneath the weight of Laura's words.

"What the hell are you doing, Celeste?"

Nartan hooked her bicep and whirled her around to face him. "You can't tell me you love me and then take off just because Laura showed up."

He was furious and pulled her off the main entryway into the foliage.

"It pisses me off that you don't have any more faith in me than that."

"Does it matter?"

Her question confused him. "Does what matter? You taking off? It sure as hell does."

"I told her you were mine."

His eyebrows shot up and a pleased look entered his eyes for a moment. "Then why the hell are you out here?"

She worried her lip. Nartan's gaze lowered to the telltale gesture and he grunted with frustration, crossing his arms over his chest. "I'll stand here all night, Celeste, so you might as well spit it out."

"She said she had your grandparents' blessing." Just saying it chilled her.

His eyes narrowed. "Not to my knowledge."

"Well, I'm telling you she claims to." Celeste stepped up to him. "What I want to know is, what does that mean to you?"

He cupped her elbows, bringing her close enough to feel his body heat. "Jack shit," he enunciated slowly and clearly. "If I wanted to be back with the tribe, I would be. I had that house built for me."

"But…your grandparents—"

"Have my respect. But I'm not letting them choose my wife." He squeezed his eyes shut and blew a hard breath out through his gritted teeth. When he opened his eyes, they glittered with determination. "You're the one I can't live without. The woman I brought into my house. I'd go back in there and set Laura straight, but I'm not giving you the chance to take off before I get it through your head that I want you."

"You didn't say you loved me."

His grip tightened on her elbows before he slid his hands around her back and crushed her against him.

"I told you…you make me rich." His breath was hard and his tone low next to her ear. He cupped her nape and raised her face so that their gazes met. "The single thing in this life that only my soul mate can do. It's more than love, Celeste. It's completion on every level."

She reached for him, wrapping her hands around his neck and pulling his head down so she could kiss him. He didn't disappoint her. He claimed her mouth, kissing her with a hunger that she matched. But they weren't close enough. There were too many layers of clothing between them for what she craved.

"Come on." His voice was rough. "Let's go home."

She was trembling with joy, the sheer volume of it astounding her. She'd never realized she could feel so happy, so content. So hopeful for the future.

Laura held back in the shadows.

A single tear escaped and made a solitary, wet trail down her cheek. She reached up and wiped it away. Bitterness welled up inside her as she watched the Lamborghini drive away.

The valet was looking at her, so she drew in a stiff breath and forced herself to walk to the curb. A sedan with tinted windows slid up before she had the chance to hand her ticket to the uniformed valet.

"Please join me."

She looked down and all she saw were the crossed legs of a man in a perfectly pressed pair of slacks.

"I don't think so." She opened her purse and pulled her valet ticket out.

"It will be worth your time."

She scowled at the man sitting back in the shadow of the car. "Shove off. I'm not an escort."

The valet holding the door open sent it closed. He looked away uncomfortably before one of his buddies brought her car up. She pushed a folded bill into his hand and slid behind the wheel.

Pulling into the driveway of the condo where she lived only renewed the sting of rejection. Alone, again.

She tossed her keys onto the desk in the hallway as her heels clicked on the tile.

"My offer is worth hearing."

She jumped, fumbling with her purse as she tried to find her pepper spray. Someone moved in the shadows, pulling her purse from her hands before she found it.

"Please sit."

She turned toward the garage, but there was a huge man between her and the door. He lifted one side of his suit jacket to show her a gun sitting in a chest harness.

Her mouth went dry.

"What do you want?"

The man merely gestured to the chair near him in her sitting room.

At least it was near the windows...

She stepped out of her heels and walked over to the chair, sitting as far away from him as possible.

"What do you want?"

"Not going to ask who I am?"

Laura scoffed at him. "Most people who break into houses don't introduce themselves."

"I am Caspian Devitt."

Laura forced the lump in her throat down. "What do you want?"

"What you want," he countered. "An end to the relationship between my wife and Nartan Lupan."

He'd stressed the word "wife," sending a chill down Laura's back. The guy was obsessed. Fear tightened in her belly as the sight of Celeste's half-healed bruises came to mind.

This guy was unstable.

And he was in her house.

She forced a half smile onto her lips. "I'm listening."

But she wasn't. Not really. She was trying to see if any of her neighbors were out on their porches. Looking for the blur of a jogger passing by. Anyone to run to for help.

"I will arrange for a man who looks very much like Nartan to arrive here. A few incriminating pictures should do what I want."

Laura fought the urge to throw up. She'd never met someone so evil before. She crossed her legs, hating how the slit in her dress exposed a large portion of her thigh.

The dress she'd been so happy to put on a few hours ago suddenly felt cheap and revealing.

"Let me think about it."

Caspian's eyes narrowed. "I require an answer now."

The huge guy lurking in her hallway shifted closer.

"I'm thinking about it."

She stood up and took a slow turn around the front room. The muscled guy tensed when she moved, but settled back when she came full circle.

"I plan to marry Nartan, so I can't have him slammed in the media…"

She slowly circled the chair she'd been sitting in.

"That is acceptable."

Laura slowed down as she passed the front door again. It was still unlocked. Her heart was racing but she resisted the urge to look toward the muscled guy.

"You will have to be nude."

Caspian's demand gave her a reason to stop and she stepped back toward the front door. He lifted an eyebrow at her outrage. The look sickened her but the doorknob was right beneath her fingertips. She closed her hands around it and turned. The hinges groaned just a bit as she pulled the door open and ran out.

"Stop her!"

She yanked her evening dress up as she ran. Her thin nylons didn't protect her from the rough asphalt. But she didn't stop running until she made it around the corner, her own breathing too harsh to allow her to hear any pursuit.

Panic was making her hear it anyway.

The warm Southern California weather came to her rescue in the form of a bunch of college students sitting outside their parents' condo. They looked up when she came barreling toward them.

~~~

Nartan groaned when his cell phone went off for the fifth time in a row. Celeste lifted her head from his chest and reached for it. She dropped it in his hand before she rolled out of bed and headed for a shower.

She hadn't even stepped into the water when Nartan came into the bathroom.

"Get dressed. There was a problem at Laura's."

Celeste snapped her mouth shut, holding back the argument that sprang to mind. Laura was still a relative.

They didn't have far to go. Nartan went past the construction for the new gate and turned toward the condos. Red and blue lights were still flickering from several police cars when they pulled up. Laura was leaning against one of the cars, two detectives in front of her.

It was still hard to see Laura next to Nartan. She folded into his embrace for a long moment before she pushed back and started talking.

A moment later, Celeste felt like absolute crap.

"It's over."

"I say when it's over!" Caspian hissed.

His new bodyguard shook his head. "She can ID you. Leave the country if you don't want to end up back in prison. You're still on parole. I'm heading out of state myself, just in case she got a good enough look at me."

Caspian bristled. Rage tightened every muscle of his body. His bodyguard never looked back, disappearing into the night.

He watched the lights from the police car for a few moments more. A blue Lamborghini pulled into the parking lot. Celeste got out, and a moment later, Nartan had his arm around her.

It was too much!

Caspian shook with the rage eating him. It burned away everything else, leaving only one thing. A word or idea. He wasn't sure which, only that he was consumed by it.

His!

Marcus jabbed a button on his cell phone and dropped it back into his jacket pocket. "The boys say the house is clear. Two more men have arrived. I'll take care of Laura."

Nartan reached out and shook Marcus's hand. Celeste looked across the parking lot to where Laura was looking lost. A bag was at her feet and she hadn't changed out of her evening dress. The street lamp made the sequins shimmer, but the dress seemed grossly out of place.

"Thanks, Marcus," Celeste muttered.

"Thank me by staying where my men can protect you," her boss ordered quietly. He exchanged a quick look with Nartan before he moved off to where Laura stood.

"Let's go home." Nartan reached out and cupped her elbow. "There's a manhunt on for Caspian. Something tells me he won't be able to go to ground and avoid getting caught."

"Caspian doesn't know how to do without his luxuries." At least she hoped that was true. She hesitated, looking back at Laura. "I owe her an apology…" The words were a little dry, but Celeste forced them past her lips. Knowing you had no place to call home was something she understood.

"Until Caspian is caught, you don't have time. Neither of you do."

Marcus was guiding Laura toward his car, while Nartan steered Celeste in the direction of the Lamborghini.

"I am sorry Caspian went after her," Marcus said.

"So am I," Nartan stated as he closed the door and sealed Celeste inside before moving around to the driver's seat. "Because now the police will get him before I can."

He peeled out of the parking lot as she gasped.

He reached over and clasped her thigh. "Don't argue with me, Celeste. Just let me be protective. It's the only thing keeping me sane."

Okay.

She didn't say it out loud, but he tightened his fingers on her knee as though he'd heard her.

He sped past the gate that had just been lifted into position that morning by a crane. Several large construction trucks were still sitting on the other side of the growing fence line with its sections of heavy iron panels.

The entire car suddenly slid sideways, the sound of crunching metal and glass filling Celeste's ears. Nartan cursed and grabbed the wheel, but they were spinning, raising a huge cloud of dust as the Lamborghini made donuts across the bluff toward the cliff.

Nartan was fighting for control, jamming his foot down on the brake. The car shuddered and stopped.

"What the fuck?" Nartan shouted as he looked through the windshield.

One of the gate trucks was facing them. It was only ten feet away. Whoever was behind the wheel turned off the headlights. Celeste blinked, still seeing spots from the bright lights. As her sight returned, she heard the driver shifting the truck into gear. The gears groaned, proving that the driver didn't know how to handle the manual transmission. He was struggling to get it in gear.

"Bail out!" Nartan shouted.

She fumbled with her seat belt and shoved at the door as the engine on the truck revved up. The door started rising, showing her a tantalizing glimpse of freedom as she heard the truck coming toward them. She dove through the door, rolling as the horrible sound of crunching metal came again.

Celeste rolled over and over to get away from the point of impact. She sat up just in time to see the Lamborghini slipping over the edge of the cliff. A huge dust cloud was choking her, burning her eyes, but she refused to close them. She strained to see if Nartan had made it. But all she could see was the truck.

There was a horrible crashing sound as the car hit the beach below.

A moment later, the gas in the tank exploded, illuminating the truck with a bright orange flare. The scent of burning gasoline filled the air. Superheated air hit her arms and face, raising her fine body hair.

It also showed her Caspian.

He stood in front of her, the dust cloud slowly moving with the wind. She struggled to her feet and kicked her heels off.

"You've been a very large disappointment to me."

"Too bad." She looked past him, but the truck was too massive to see around. "Nartan?"

"I think your lover is dead," he informed her gleefully. "I hope so."

"No." Her voice was a whisper and she felt like her heart had stopped beating.

"Don't worry, I plan to reunite you." Caspian lifted his hand, the moonlight illuminating the blade of a knife in his hand. "At the bottom of a cliff, they won't notice a few little holes in you. Especially when your body is burned to a crisp."

"Good to know!" Nartan surged out of the darkness behind Caspian. He grabbed the hand with the knife and brutally turned it around on Caspian. There was a harsh grunt as he drove it into Caspian once, twice, and a third time before flinging him away to lie in the dirt.

"She...belongs to me!" Caspian snarled as he tried to get up. His legs failed him, and all he managed to do was push himself closer to the edge of the cliff.

"No, she doesn't."

Nartan was moving closer to Caspian, rage in his voice.

"Nartan!" she shouted.

He fought to pull himself back, jerking with the effort before he turned to look at her.

She shook her head. "Let him be. He's not worth it."

In the distance a siren was heard. Caspian shuddered and went limp. Only then did Nartan move toward her. She reached for him, unsure if he was real. The steady chop of a helicopter blade joined the sirens coming their way. A searchlight hit the cliff, aimed at the burning wreck before moving along the bluff to them.

"This is the Los Angeles County Sheriff's Department. Stay where you are."

"Damn, you're lucky I'm a good lawyer," Marcus declared as he met them in the waiting room of the hospital. "I think you owe me one."

Nartan walked out of the lobby before ripping the sling off his right arm and dropping it in a trash can. He only shrugged when Celeste narrowed her eyes at him.

"It's not broken."

Paul and Kevin pulled up to the curb in a black SUV, and Marcus opened the door for Nartan and Celeste.

The moment it was closed, Nartan looked at Marcus.

"Dead on arrival," Marcus confirmed. "There will be an official investigation, but all evidence is pointing toward self-defense. Laura's testimony will close that deal."

"More like premeditated attempted murder on his part," Celeste said before her body decided to give out on her. The knowledge that Caspian was dead was the last straw. She collapsed against the seat, feeling every scrape and bruise she'd collected rolling across the bluff. Shock set in and her teeth started chattering. Nartan slid an arm behind her and pulled her close.

"It's over," he whispered against her head.

She settled her hand over his heart, absorbing the feeling of it beating. "Actually"—she smiled at him in the darkness—"it's just beginning."

Celeste awoke to another helicopter buzzing the house. She groaned as she turned over and rubbed her eyes.

"Damned press," she muttered as she stood up.

"I was about to agree, but on second thought…" Nartan replied from the rumpled bedding. He was enjoying the sight of her bare body.

"How can you be horny again?"

"Your fault," he said before someone rang the doorbell.

He rolled out of the bed, distracting her. He was just too gorgeous. He stepped into some jeans as the doorbell rang again. The helicopter hadn't left, so she hurried into some clothing, making a mental note to put in some shades before someone realized how much of a show they could get from the cliffside.

She wandered down the hallway, intent on coffee.

"Why didn't you call me?" Sabra was sitting in the kitchen, fixing her with a hard look. "My best friend nearly goes off a cliff and she doesn't call?"

Through the front windows, Celeste got a look at a helicopter with the Nektosha logo on its side.

"I didn't call because my phone is at the bottom of said cliff."

"I hear you two almost joined it." Tarak Nektosha was hard to read. He was contemplating her with eyes as hard as black diamonds.

"It's his fault." Celeste pointed at Nartan. "I warned him a relationship with me was going to be troublesome."

"She did." Sabra joined her friend in facing off against her husband.

"Nice to know Nartan hasn't lost any of his stubbornness," Tarak muttered as he accepted a cup of coffee from his wife. "Even if he did go and fall in love."

"Don't start," Nartan warned his buddy. The house intercom buzzed.

"You've got a truck and horse trailer coming up the drive." Paul's voice came through clearly.

Celeste felt a twist of pain go through her. The loss of the mare was still too fresh. Nartan caught her hand and pulled her toward the front door.

"Got something for you," he said.

"You didn't have to buy another horse for me."

He opened the front door and walked out. A full-size truck pulled up. It was beaten up and at least two decades old.

"He still won't let you buy him a new truck?" Tarak asked as the truck pulled up and stopped.

"I did and he gave it to my nephew," Nartan defended himself. "Feel free to show me how it's done."

A second truck was following the first—a brand-new model with a young man at the wheel. Nartan pointed at it and Tarak shrugged.

Nartan's grandfather climbed out of the cab of the first truck and lifted his hand in greeting. Nartan's grandmother was sitting on the passenger side of the cab. The younger man jumped out of his truck and ran over to open the door for her. He helped her around to where Tarak and Nartan were greeting their family in Apache. The older woman reached up and rubbed Nartan's cheek before she pointed at Celeste.

"Green eyes are good luck," Nartan's grandmother informed Celeste when she'd made her way over to her. "My grandson did not like hearing that when I met you. The young are stubborn when fate dictates."

The rest of the men had gone to the back of the trailer and swung the tailgate down. It raised a small cloud of dust before the younger man went inside and spoke softly. He appeared again, leading a horse that shook its white mane and sidestepped the moment it was free of the trailer. Nartan reached up and stroked her throat while talking to his grandfather.

He took the reins from the younger man and led the horse toward Celeste. The rest of the family seemed intent on them both as he got close to her.

"You make me rich, Celeste. This is a young, strong horse, the sort a bride would expect from a man hoping to marry her. You are worth a hundred more. I am the poorest man without you." He held the reins out to her.

Her mouth went dry and tears filled her eyes. She reached out and covered his hand with hers. "Together, we'll be filthy rich."

Tarak let out a yell that the other two men mimicked. Nartan caught her nape and kissed her. Deeply, to the delight of his family. She swatted him in reprimand before Sabra wrapped her in a hug.

———

The wood cracked in the fire pit, the logs shifting and sending a shower of crimson sparks into the air. Celeste snuggled closer, rubbing against Nartan as he held her on the lounge.

"This is being rich." Nartan stroked her hair as his words floated over her.

"This is being loved." She kissed his shoulder. "But I should warn you…"

He lifted her chin so that they were looking at each other.

"My birth control pills were in my purse. I sort of forgot about them, with your family being here. Now—"

"It's too late," Nartan finished for her.

She waited to see what he'd make of it, rolling her lip in to worry. He tugged her chin down to free her lip and stroked across it with his thumb.

"I told you, nature finds a way."

He leaned down and kissed her, filling her with every bit of happiness that she'd never expected to find. And she kissed him back, seeking to return it to him.

———

"Sure you want to sit in the back of a truck all the way home?" Marcus asked.

Laura nodded and closed the gate of the trailer. Everything she wanted from her Malibu condo was packed and in the back of the horse trailer. The sleek, two-seat sports car she'd been driving was being left behind to be sold. Sports cars and the reservation didn't mix.

"Best way to get all of this home anyway," she said. "Thank you. It was nice to meet you."

Marcus watched her for a long moment, but Laura had come to realize that was just his way. She tucked a strand of hair that had escaped her ponytail behind her ear and nodded.

"Guess it's time to go."

"Not just yet."

Nartan appeared from behind the trailer. Celeste was hanging back.

"I want to say…we want to say we're sorry."

"Don't be." Laura raised her voice enough that Celeste could hear her. "I'll be just fine."

Nartan extended an envelope. "This will cover your investment in the condo."

Laura felt her insides twist. But she accepted the feeling because she deserved it.

"You still don't get it, Nartan. I came here for you. Send me the money when the property sells."

His face tightened and Laura shook her head. "Don't worry about it. It wasn't meant to be." She looked past him to Celeste and closed the distance between them. "I'm sorry I was a bitch to you."

Celeste opened her mouth, but Laura turned and walked back to the truck where Nartan's cousin was waiting. She climbed up into the cab without another look back.

Yeah, she'd been stuck in her girlhood fantasies too long.

It was time to find her future.

It looked like a perfect day to do it too.

⁓

"She loves you."

Nartan nodded. "But like a girl. I think I may just have gotten a glimpse of the woman Laura is going to be."

Celeste linked her fingers with his and walked back to the Jeep with him.

"I think you're right," she offered softly. "And I wish her well." She cut him a sidelong look. "Just so long as she's no longer casting her sights on you."

Nartan pulled her close and kissed her hard.

"Wouldn't be able to see her anyway. I'm far too preoccupied with you."

Read on for a preview of the first book in the highly charged erotic romance series, Redemption, from *New York Times* and *USA Today* bestselling author Sarah Castille.

AGAINST
THE ROPES

Chapter 1

Oh, betraying lips

"You come in. You fight. It's simple."

Me fight? He can't be serious. Do I look like I pound on people for fun?

"Sorry. I think there's been a misunderstanding." Forcing a tight laugh, I shuffle back to the red line marking the fighters' entrance to Redemption, a full-service gym and training center that is home to one of Oakland's few remaining unsanctioned, underground fight clubs. Maybe I should have read the rules posted at the door.

"No, you don't." The hefty blond grabs my shoulders and pulls me toward him. My nose sinks into the yellow happy face tank top stretched tight over his keg-size belly. The pungent odor of unwashed gorilla invades my nostrils, bringing back memories of school trips to the San Diego Zoo. Lovely.

Gasping for air, I glance up and flash my best fake smile. "I'm just here to sell tickets. One of your fighters, Jake, asked my friend Amanda to work the door and she asked me to help her. Why don't we just pretend you didn't see me cross the red line and I'll get back to work?"

If I were a different type of girl, wearing a different—and lower cut—shirt, I might try another kind of technique to get out of this predicament, but right now, a smile is all I've got.

It backfires.

"Mmm. Pretty." He releases my shoulders and paws at my hair, mussing it from my crown to the middle of my back. What a waste of two hours with the flat iron.

"I'm not too sure about pretty." My voice goes from a low quiver to a thin whine as he strokes my jaw with a thick finger. "But I am small, fragile, delicate, easily frightened, and given to high-pitched screams in situations involving violence." In an attempt to make my lies a reality, I suck in my stomach and tuck in my tush.

He frowns, and for the first time I notice the missing teeth, jagged scar across his throat, and the skull and crossbones tattoos covering his arms like sleeves. Not quite the cuddly teddy bear I had thought he was. More like a Viking berserker.

My heart kicks up a notch, and I hold up my hands in a defensive gesture. "Listen. I was chasing after some deadbeat who didn't buy a ticket. He came in just before me. Tall, broad shoulders, black leather jacket, bandana—I only saw him from the back. He was in line talking to people, and then suddenly he breezed past the ticket counter and went through this entrance. Did you see him?"

A smile ghosts his lips. "You'll have to talk to Torment. He deals with all line crossers and ticket dodgers. Usually takes them into the ring for a lesson in following the rules. He likes to hear people scream." His chuckle is as menacing as his breath. Maybe he ate a small child for lunch.

"Let's go. I'll introduce you." His hand clamps around my arm and he tugs me forward.

A shiver of fear races down my spine. "You're kidding, right? I mean, look at me. Do I look like I could take on someone named Torment?" My smile wavers, so I add a few eyelash flutters and a desperate breast jiggle to the mix. Unfortunately, my ass decides to join the party, and my thighs aren't far behind.

Wrong message. His heated gaze rakes over my body, and a lascivious grin splits his wide face from ear to ear. "Torment likes the curvy ones."

Now there's a slap in the face. But maybe I can use the curves to my advantage. If I can't talk my way out of this mess, I'll just wiggle.

"Come on. He'll decide what to do with you."

Heart pounding, I scramble behind the self-styled Cerberus deep into the belly of Hell. I wish I had written a will.

Upon first glance, Hell disappoints.

The giant sheet-metal warehouse, probably around 20,000 square feet, boasts corrugated metal walls, concrete floors, and the stale sweat stench of one hundred high-school gym lockers. The ceiling is easily twenty-five feet above me. At the far end, a few freight containers are stacked in the corner, and a circular, metal staircase leads up to a second level.

Our end of the warehouse has a dedicated training area and a fully equipped gym. Half-naked, sweaty, pumped up alpha-males grapple on scarred red mats and spar in the two practice rings. Fight posters and pennants are plastered on the walls. In one corner a man dressed as a drill sergeant is barking orders at a motley group of huffing, puffing fighter wannabes.

My stomach clenches as the drumroll of speed bags, the slap of jump ropes, the whir of the treadmill, and the thud of gloves on flesh create a gut-churning symphony of violent sound.

"Hey, Rampage, you get us a new ring girl?" A small, wiry, bald fighter with red-rimmed pupil-less psycho eyes points to the "FCUK Me" lettering on my T-shirt and makes an obscene gesture with his hips. "Answer is yes, honey. Find me after the show."

I berate myself for my poor choice of attire. But really, it is my sister Susie's fault. She sends me the strangest gifts from London.

Rampage leads me toward an enormous raised boxing ring in the center of the warehouse. Spiky-haired punkers, clean-cut jocks, hip-hop headers, businessmen in suits, and leather-vested bikers fill the metal bleachers and folding chairs surrounding the main attraction.

I've never seen a more eclectic group. There must be at least two hundred people here with seating for probably two hundred more. But there's no sign of Amanda. Some best friend.

We stop in front of a small, roped-off area about ten feet square. Rampage opens a steel-framed gate and shoves me inside. "You can wait in the pen. It's for your own safety. We can't have people wandering too close to the ring."

"I am not an animal," I mumble as the gate slams shut. He doesn't even crack a smile. Maybe he doesn't go to the movies.

I walk to the back of the pen for a good view of the ring and instantly recognize the man with the black bandana, despite the fact he has changed into a pleasantly tight pair of white board shorts with black winged skulls emblazoned on the sides. "That's him," I shriek. "That's the guy who didn't buy a ticket."

Amusement flashes in Rampage's beady black eyes. He stalks over to the pen and throws open the gate. "You get that guy to buy a ticket, and we'll call everything off. I won't make you face the ring."

My brow crinkles. "Isn't he a fighter? Does he even need a ticket?"

"I made you an offer. You gonna stand around talking or are you gonna take it?"

I lean up against the gate. "This has got to be a joke. And guess what? I'm not playing anymore. Just let me find Amanda and I'll get out of here."

Rampage glowers at me and his voice drops to a menacing growl. "You get up those stairs or I'll take you up myself and I can guarantee it ain't gonna be pretty."

I sigh an exasperated sigh.

"I'm going. I'm going." What the hell. Even if this is some kind of joke, the guy in the ring has mouth-watering shoulders and a great ass. I can also make out some tattoos on his back. It can't hurt to get a closer look. Maybe make a new friend.

Stiffening my spine, I climb the stairs and slide between the ropes and onto the spongy canvas mat. Hesitating, I take one last look over my shoulder. Rampage smirks and waves me forward.

My target is leaning over the ropes on the other side of the ring talking to an excessively curvy blonde wearing a one-piece, pink Lycra bodysuit. Her mountain of platinum hair is cinched on top of her head in a tight ponytail. Her huge, brown doe eyes are enhanced by her orange, spray-on tan and a slash of hot pink lipstick. She is pink and she is luscious. She is Pinkaluscious.

She rests a dainty, pink-tipped hand on Torment's foot and gazes up at him until he slides his foot back and away. Ah. Unrequited love. My heart goes out to Pinkaluscious, but really, she could do better than some two-bit, cheapskate fighter.

"Hey, Torment. I brought you a treat." Rampage's voice booms over the excited murmur of the crowd.

In one smooth, quick movement, Torment spins around to face me. My eyes are slow to react. No doubt he caught me staring at his ass, and now I am staring at something even more enticing. Something big. My cheeks burn, and I study the worn vinyl under my feet. Someone needs to make a few repairs.

Footsteps thud across the mat. The platform vibrates under my bare feet sending tremors through my body.

Swallowing hard, I look up. My eyes widen as well over six feet of lean, hard muscle stalks toward me.

Run. I should run. But all I can do is stare.

His fight shorts are slung deliciously low on his narrow hips, hugging his powerful thighs. Hard, thick muscles ripple across the broad expanse of his chest, tapering down to a taut, corrugated abdomen. But most striking are the tattoos covering over half of his upper body—a hypnotizing cocktail of curving, flowing, tribal designs that just beg to be touched.

He stops only a foot away and I crane my neck up to look at his face.

God is he gorgeous.

His high cheekbones are sharply cut, his jaw square, and his eyes dark brown and flecked with gold. His aquiline nose is slightly off-center, as if it had been broken and not properly reset, but instead of detracting from his breathtaking good looks, it gives him a dangerous appeal. His hair is hidden beneath a black bandana, but a few tawny, brown tufts have escaped from the edges and curl down past the base of his neck.

His full lips quirk into a faint smile as he studies me. A lithe and powerful animal assessing its prey.

My finely tuned instinct of self-preservation forces me back against the ropes and away from his intoxicating scent of soap and leather and the faintest kiss of the ocean.

"Excuse me…Torment. I…thought you forgot to buy a ticket, but…um…I don't think you really need one. Do you?"

"A ticket?" His low-pitched, husky, sensual voice could seduce a saint. Or a young college grad trying to supplement her meager salary by selling tickets at a fight club.

My heart thunders in my chest and I lick my lips. His eyes lock on my mouth, and my tongue freezes mid-stroke before beating a hasty retreat behind my Pink Innocence glossed lips.

He steps forward and I press myself harder against the springy ropes, wincing as they bite into my skin through my thin T-shirt.

"Are you Amanda?"

With herculean effort, I manage to pry my tongue off the roof of my mouth. "I'm the best friend."

He lifts an eyebrow. "Does the best friend have a name?"

"Mac."

"Doesn't suit you. Do you have a different name?"

"What do you mean a different name? That's my name. Well, it's my nickname. But that's what people call me. I'm not going to choose another name just because *you* don't like it." My hands find my hips, and I give him my second-best scowl—my best scowl being reserved for less handsome irritating men.

His gaze drifts down to the bright white "FCUK Me" lettering now stretched tight across my overly generous breasts. With my every breath, the letters expand and retract like a flashing neon sign. I hate my sister.

He leans so close I can see every contour of bone and sinew in his chest and the more intricate patterns in his tribal tattoos. The flexible ropes accommodate my last retreat, and I brace myself, trembling, against them.

"What's your real name?" he rumbles.

"Makayla." *Oh, betraying lips.*

He smiles and his eyes crinkle at the corners. "Makayla is a beautiful name. I'll call you Makayla."

Heat roars through me like a tidal wave. He likes my name. "So…about that ticket—"

He snorts a laugh. "I don't need to buy a ticket."

Why is he standing so close? Has he not heard of personal space? My body trembles from the exertion of pressing back against the ropes, and my brain clicks into babble mode. "I guess the joke's on me. Rampage said I would have to fight you if I didn't get you to buy a ticket. Not that I believed for a second I would have to fight. Well, maybe I did until we got here and I saw the ring and the blood spots on the concrete and I remembered my stepdad is a policeman. I mean I'm a girl and you're a guy—"

He looks at me aghast and cuts me off. "Shhh. It's okay, Makayla. I'm not—" He takes a step toward me. In my effort to dodge away, I lose my footing and the ropes propel me right into Torment's chest. He steps backward and falls to the floor pulling me on top of him.

No way. I am not that heavy. Sure, I enjoy my desserts, but not enough to send a two-hundred-pound man tumbling to the ground.

For a long moment, neither of us moves. One of my legs is tucked between his muscular thighs. My breasts are pressed against the warm, bare skin of his hard chest. My head is nestled on his shoulder and my hands rest lightly on his thick biceps. We breathe together. Our hearts pound together. I melt into him, not wanting what should be a humiliating moment to end.

Torment snakes an arm around my waist and I hold my breath, daring to hope he will pull me closer, but instead he rolls us so we are each on our side and rests one hand in the curve of my waist, propping his head up with the other.

"Are you hurt?"

I shake my head, not trusting myself to speak.

"Is this what you plan to do to every person who doesn't buy a ticket?" he murmurs. "If so, I might have to offer you a permanent position."

"You…own the club?" My eyes find yet another tiny tear in the mat. Really, he should keep his equipment in better repair.

"Yes, I do."

"But Rampage—"

"Set you up." He finishes my sentence for me. "I'll deal with him when we're done here. I don't allow mixed fighting at the club, and I don't force people to fight who have not already agreed to do so. I also have a zero-tolerance policy for hazing beautiful new staff members."

He thinks I'm beautiful. Or maybe it's just a figure of speech.

His warm hand strokes the dip of my waist and the curve of my hip, back and forth, up and down—a seemingly absent and casual caress. And yet, he appears to be a man very much in control of his body. A solid, heavy, muscular body.

"I didn't really knock you down, did I?" My mouth blurts out my thoughts before they make it through the filtering process. As usual.

He gives me a slow, sexy, devilish smile but his sensual lips remain firmly closed.

Well, I'm not going to complain. He can pull me on top of him any day.

"Hey, Torment. Thirty minutes. Time to wrap." Rampage's voice cuts through my perfect moment like scissors.

In one swift, easy movement, Torment rolls to his front and pushes himself to standing. He easily pulls me to my feet. "I've got to go and get ready for my fight."

A sliver of disappointment slices through me. "Sure. I've got to get back to the door, anyway. My boss might be upset if he knew I was rolling around on the mats with one of his fighters."

Torment chuckles. "Your boss wants you to stay and watch the fight."

"No can do, Boss." I can't help wrinkling my nose even though it isn't my best look. "I've got a serious aversion to violence. Unless you've got a mop and a bucket handy, you do not want me anywhere near that ring."

"If you don't like violence, why are you working here?"

I shrug and my cheeks heat. "I needed the money. Amanda promised I wouldn't have to go inside. I was planning to go home when you guys locked down for the big event."

He studies me intently for a moment and then lowers his head until his lips are so close I can feel the heat of his breath on my cheek. "Stay."

Yes! God, I want to stay. So hot. So sexy. I could watch him all night. But no. I can't. One punch. One drop of blood. One vomit bag, please.

"No. I can't. Really can't. Not a made-up can't. It's a physical thing. Basically, I can only stomach violence if I know no one is actually getting hurt. Boxing, wrestling, even karate or judo, all fall into my no-watch zone. Just not me."

He stokes a finger along my jaw. Blazing heat shoots straight to my core, and my breath catches in my throat.

"Have you ever seen an entire fight?" He tucks a wayward strand of hair behind my ear and strokes his hand over my head.

Oh, lovely hand petting me. So gentle. If I had a tail, I would thump it.

"No. Not even on TV."

"All the more reason for you to stay. You can't sell tickets to an event you know nothing about. I would be remiss in my duty as your employer if I didn't ensure you were familiar with the services we are offering, especially if I needed you to come back and help out again."

Again? I thought this was a one-shot deal to cover for the regular ticket girls who couldn't make it tonight. "I was doing okay."

His hand drops to my shoulder and tightens. "Dressed like that, I can imagine you were."

Jeez. Again with the shirt. Doesn't anyone understand it's a joke and not an invitation? "Amanda will be waiting for me. She's taking me home."

"She and Jake went into my office as soon as ticket sales ended. I don't think you'll be seeing her anytime soon."

I knew it. She couldn't keep her hands off him. No wonder she needed a wingman tonight. She didn't want help on the door. She wanted full coverage.

He tucks a warm finger under my chin, tilting my head back so he can mesmerize me with the chestnut depths of his beautiful eyes.

"One fight. My fight. I promise it won't last long."

Mesmerized, I say, "How long is not long?"

Triumph flares in his eyes, but in an instant it is gone, replaced by concern. "How long can you last?"

"I don't know. A couple of minutes, maybe, if no one gets hurt."

A rough sound erupts from his throat. "You don't want me to hurt my opponent?"

"And I don't want him to hurt you," I say softly.

Burn cheeks burn.

His eyes widen and the look he gives me is speculative,

thoughtful, considered. "One minute and I'll win by submission. No one gets hurt."

"Cocky."

His smile sears me to the core. "You have no idea."

Chapter 2

My heart isn't so easy to please

Twenty minutes later, I am seated in the front row between a thoroughly chastised Rampage and a "submission artist" named Homicide Hank. Wiry thin and lanky, with overly long arms and a shock of wildly unkempt red hair, Homicide claims to have been sent by Torment to translate the fight into Makayla-understandable terms. More likely, Torment needed someone to keep me from screaming and running away as I am now *persona non grata* in Rampage's books for getting him in trouble.

Courtesy of Torment, I have a protein shake, a protein bar, an energy drink, a bucket, and a wet cloth. He sure knows how to treat a girl.

While we wait for the fight to start, five ring girls warm up the crowd cheerleader style. Rampage puts his fingers in his mouth and whistles, "Go, Sandy," at Pinkaluscious.

Homicide shakes his head. "Torment doesn't like all the pre-show hype, but it distracts people from the lockdown. We secure the doors in case of a raid by the California State Athletic Commission."

"Why doesn't Torment just get a license and have his events sanctioned?" I ask.

"He won't do it," Rampage says. "He wants to be able to fight when and how and who he wants to fight. He wants to be able to take on a two-hundred-sixty-pound judoka or a Five Animal kung fu master without some big ass government official telling him he's in the wrong weight class, or he doesn't have enough fights under his belt. He wants to keep it real. He's not in it for the money or the glory. And he doesn't want to follow a whole lot of rules. Most of us think the same. That's how we all found our way here."

"No rules?" What would stop someone from bringing in a weapon or causing a fatal injury?

"Four rules," Rampage says. "No eye gouging, no groin shots, no biting, and no fish hooking—that's when a guy sticks his fingers in his opponent's mouth or nose and tries to tear the tissue."

My stomach clenches and I reach for the bucket. "Please don't tell me any more."

Rampage frowns. "If you can't even hear about it, how are you going to watch the fight?"

Bucket on head. Face cloth over eyes. Torment has given me lots of options.

"Torment said it would only last a minute, and he would win by submission. I'm not sure what that means but it didn't sound so bad."

Homicide chuckles. "It means he's gonna put Flash in a bone-breaking arm lock or leg lock or a choke that can put him out cold. If Flash doesn't submit—" He makes a disgusting cracking sound with his throat.

I dry heave into the bucket.

"I'm not sitting next to her." Rampage gets to his feet. "She's gonna spew all over me."

But it's too late for him to leave. The crowd suddenly comes to life, cheering and clapping as Torment and his opponent, Flash, climb into the ring.

My breath catches in my throat. Flash is none other than Mr. Psycho Eyes and supposedly my post-fight date for a little FCUK.

Jake joins Torment in his corner. Jake's blond hair is mussed and his T-shirt is inside out. Nice. Amanda must have pulled out all the stops in Torment's office. At least his fly is closed.

"Jake is Torment's cornerman," Homicide explains. "He'll coach him and tend to his cuts."

"Why does Flash have three guys in his corner?"

"He's a show-off. Likes to pretend he's a sanctioned amateur."

Jake checks Torment's gloves and helps him with his mouthpiece. Beside each other, they are a tableau of masculine perfection, all broad shoulders, tight muscles, tattoos, and slim hips. They are almost the same height, but Jake is slightly leaner and his muscles less defined. Still, with that chiseled jaw, deep voice, and those dazzling baby blues, I can totally understand how Amanda fell under his spell.

And where is Amanda?

"Thanks for covering for me." A poke in my back and a clipped, sarcastic tone reveal the location of my missing friend.

I look over my shoulder and glare as she settles herself on the chair behind me.

"You left me and now look what's happened," I say. "I'm sitting in a fight club about to throw up into a bucket of protein bars."

"You left *me* to chase after a guy." Amanda crosses her arms under her ample and perfectly-formed breasts, drawing the attention of every male in the vicinity.

"I thought he was a ticket dodger. You know I would never just run off."

Rampage and Homicide insist on introductions. Of course they would. Amanda in a burlap sack could make any man drool. Amanda in a simple, fitted, green sheath dress and gold kitten-heel pumps, her soft golden curls cascading down her back, her perfect features glowing from an hour of doing the nasty with Jake, will bring them to their knees. If I am a desert on the dating front, Amanda is a monsoon.

The bell rings. The cornermen step out of the ring. My pulse races. How is Torment going to win a fight without anyone getting hurt?

Torment wastes no time. He throws a right hook and catches Flash a glancing blow to the jaw. He follows it with a one-two punch and then a kick. Flash backs away and dances around.

"He's just playing with Flash," Homicide says. "Torment is one of the top underground fighters on the circuit. He is only a few fights away from the underground championship belt. Flash only has about ten fights on his card."

"Why would he challenge Torment?"

Homicide shrugs. "He thinks he's something special because he was an enforcer in a street gang in San Diego. In this club you can challenge whoever you want, regardless of weight or experience. We never turn down a challenge. But in the ring, skill usually wins out over strength, speed, and aggression. Flash doesn't have a chance."

Even I can tell Torment is highly skilled. There is stark beauty in the precision with which his body moves. He keeps to a tight circle near the center of the ring, moving back and forth only to strike or defend. If he wasn't wearing gloves, I might think he was dancing.

Suddenly Torment lunges forward and grabs Flash's left leg. Flash keeps his balance. Torment grabs the other leg and slams Flash to the floor, falling on top of him.

"Nice double leg takedown," Homicide calls.

But Flash is quick. He rolls to his side and gets up on one knee. Torment tries to push him back. He flattens Flash but just for a moment. Like a jack-in-the-box, Flash pops back up. Torment grabs him around the waist and falls back and to the side, pulling Flash on top of him.

"Oh no." My hand flies to my mouth.

"Don't worry. He's nasty off his back." Rampage says, as if that means something to me.

A few seconds later it does. Flash lifts his right arm to throw a punch. Still on his back, Torment grabs Flash's right wrist and pulls Flash toward him. Then he wraps his right leg over Flash's neck, hooking his foot into his left leg, which he has just wrapped around Flash's midsection. He pulls Flash's head down against his chest with two hands. Flash flails, trying desperately to escape, but he's obviously in pain.

"He's locked him in a quick triangle." Homicide says. "Match over."

My heart thuds in my chest. "He's putting pressure on the carotid artery. Flash will lose consciousness. Stop him."

Homicide gives me a sideways glance. "That's the point. It's a submission hold. Flash knows what will happen if he doesn't tap out or break the hold."

"How did you know about the artery?" Rampage asks. "I thought you weren't into fighting."

"She's an intermediate-level EMT and a pre-med grad." Amanda ruffles my hair. "And she's damn good. She's just figuring out what to do with her life, but I already know she's meant to be healing people. She's got a gift."

"Stop it." Tears well up in my eyes, and I bat Amanda's hand away. She's the big sister Susie never was and the mother I always wanted all wrapped up in one golden, best friend package.

I turn my attention back to the ring. Flash's legs are no longer flailing.

"If he loses consciousness, I will consider it as 'someone getting hurt.'" I grumble quietly but Homicide hears me.

"He'll tap out," Homicide says. "If he doesn't, the referee will stop the match."

As if on cue, Flash taps the mat twice. Torment releases his grip and Flash rolls off him and lies spread eagle on the mat. The crowd is a frenzy of cheers and clapping. The retro bass of "Eye of the Tiger" pounds through the warehouse. The ring girls run a circle outside the ring, bosoms bouncing, miniskirts flapping, high heels clacking as they cheer, "Torment. Torment. Torment."

My God. If this is what happens after every fight, his ego must be blimp size.

The referee holds up Torment's hand and announces a win by submission in forty-six seconds. Flash staggers to his feet and wavers. He takes a step forward, then back, then sideways. He blinks several times and reaches for the ropes.

"Something's wrong with him." I tug on Homicide's sleeve. "Where's the doctor?"

"We don't have a ring doctor." His face tightens. "After the CSAC decided to sanction amateur MMA events, the ring doctors became afraid to work the underground circuit. The penalty for working an unsanctioned event is a license suspension. No doctor wants to take that risk."

"You must have someone here to look after injuries."

"It's every man for himself," Rampage answers. "Torment always takes the seriously injured guys to the hospital, but other than that, it's the luck of the draw if we've got a medical professional at a match."

I glance over at the ring. Torment is watching Flash and frowning. He calls out and Flash spins around then crumples and falls limp through the ropes. He lands on the concrete floor with a thud.

I jump up, knocking over my barf bucket. Protein bars spill across the floor. "Do you have a first aid kit?"

"Down by the ring. I'll get it for you." Rampage bulldozes a path through the crowd, and I race over to Flash.

Torment and the referee are already with him. His cornermen hover uselessly in the background.

"Makayla, you shouldn't be here," Torment snaps when I kneel beside Flash. I ignore him. He broke his promise. Someone got hurt after all.

Flash is conscious but moaning. He rubs his head and lets loose a string of swear words that would put a fifth grader to shame.

"Flash, I'm an EMT. Can I examine you?"

Flash's eyes focus on me and his lascivious smile makes my skin crawl. "Yeah, FCUK. I knew you'd come lookin' for Daddy Flash. You're wanting what I promised you. Don't worry, baby. A little injury isn't gonna stop me from putting my—"

A low growl startles us both. I look up. Torment's jaw is clenched and his eyes have narrowed to slits.

"Calm." I place my hand over his. "Although rude and obnoxious, he is my patient. I won't be very happy if you hurt him…yet."

Other than a bump on the head and the telltale signs of drug abuse around his nostrils, Flash seems fine. His cut man—the cornerman responsible for tending injuries—helps him to a folding chair near the training area. While the next fight gets underway, I check his vitals and ice his head. Torment hovers beside me. Although I don't look at him, I feel his presence like a protective cloak over my body.

I warn Flash about the possibility of a concussion. I tell him I think he blacked out because of the combination of restricted blood flow to his brain and drug abuse. His lips tighten and I know I've hit the mark.

After ten minutes, Flash starts to come down from his high. He apologizes for his behavior. He moans about his defeat and his humiliating fall from the ring. A tear trickles down his cheek. I try to console him as best I can. I pat his back and tell him he was brave to challenge one of the best fighters in the league and he isn't the first person to fall through the ropes.

I glance up at Torment. He is watching me, his brown eyes darkened by intense emotion. For the briefest second, he lets me in, and the need and longing I see behind his mask take my breath away. Suddenly his eyes shutter and the moment is gone. Maybe I imagined it.

Still can't get enough? Keep reading for an excerpt from a fresh, hot, contemporary erotic romance from Terri L. Austin.

HIS
EVERY
NEED

Chapter 1

ALLIE CAMPBELL FROWNED AT the black SUV parked in her drive-way. One of Monica's friends? Damn it, if her sister ditched school again, Allie was going to handcuff herself to that kid and haul her delinquent butt into class. And even though Monica was an adult—*technically*—and could make her own decisions—*really stupid ones*—she was going to graduate high school this year if it killed them both.

Allie parked on the curb and shoved open the driver-side door. It groaned, sounding as tired as it looked. And for a Ford Festiva that had seen seventy-five thousand miles too many, it looked exhausted.

Before she could grab groceries from the backseat, a man strolled around the side of the house, clipboard in hand. Middle-aged and slightly paunchy, he waved at her with a tape measure.

"Great, you're home. Would you mind letting me in so I can get some measurements, ma'am?"

Allie shut the car door with a bump of her hip and adjusted her purse strap. *Ma'am*? Twenty-five wasn't ma'am territory. She walked across the narrow strip of yard, stopping directly in front of the stranger who wore a polo shirt with the name *Dave* embroidered on his chest.

She had been on her feet for the past nine hours soothing unhappy hotel guests. The Festiva's air conditioner was on the fritz. Again. And her polyester uniform—hot and itchy on a good day—stuck to her in all the wrong places. Add the *ma'am* comment, and she didn't have any niceties to spare. "Who are you and what are you doing in my yard?"

He pointed at the truck. "Dave Buchanan, home appraiser. I'm taking measurements for the owner."

Allie glanced at the white magnetic sign affixed to the truck's door. Sure enough—Dave Buchanan, Home Appraiser. "My dad is the owner, and he didn't mention this to me."

Dave examined the clipboard. "Says here Trevor Blake ordered an inspection." He shrugged. "Maybe he forgot to tell you?"

Who the hell was Trevor Blake? "No, you've got the wrong house. Would you mind moving, so I can pull into my driveway?" She turned and walked toward her car. Crisis averted. No need to have another pointless argument with Monica. At least not about this.

"Nope," Dave called after her. "This is the place. I need to get inside. I have a couple more houses to see this afternoon."

A small tingle shot up Allie's spine. She spun around to face Dave, if that was even his real name. Was this some kind of scam to get into her house? If so, he'd picked the wrong place. They didn't have anything worth stealing.

Pulling her phone from her pocket, she glared at the man. "If you don't leave immediately, I'm calling the police."

He shrugged. "Whatever, lady. It might speed things up."

Well, that wasn't the response she was expecting.

He squinted down at the form. "The signature says Trevor Blake. There's a second one here too—a Brian Campbell?"

Alarm bells started clanging in her ears. This had to be a mistake. She speed-dialed her dad's cell number, her eyes tracking the stranger as he pointedly looked at his watch.

"Yeah, Al," he answered, "I already know. School called this morning. Monica never showed up. I don't know what to do with her. I'm out of ideas." He sounded weary.

Allie pinched the bridge of her nose. "It's okay. I'll deal with it. Listen, a guy's here at the house, says he's an appraiser?"

There was long pause on the other end. "Damn, he's there already?"

She blinked. Something was wrong. Seriously wrong. Her dad didn't make a sandwich without asking her opinion. "You're not thinking about refinancing, are you? You never even mentioned it."

"I, uh." He cleared his throat. "I don't know how to tell you this, honey."

His answer scared her. The afternoon sun seemed brighter, hotter, making her skin feel prickly. A bead of sweat slid down her back. "Just say it." For some reason, her voice didn't sound like her own.

"We…" He trailed off. "No, not we. Me." He stopped. "This is my fault. I did this. I lost the house, Al."

Despite the dry Vegas heat, Allie went cold all over. "What are you talking about?"

Dave tugged on his earlobe and wouldn't make eye contact.

"I'll explain it all tonight." Another drawn-out pause. "I didn't know how to tell you."

She shook her head, gripping the phone like it was a lifeline. "Tell me now. And who is Trevor Blake?"

"He's an investor. English guy." His breath sounded ragged, his voice shaky. "I borrowed money for the business. But when your mom…" He didn't finish. He didn't need to.

Allie staggered backward a few feet until her ass hit the Festiva's taillight, her stomach in free fall. She felt a little woozy. "No," she whispered. "It's all we have left." *Lose the house?* They'd already lost so much. "The business will pick up. We just need more time to pay off this loan. I could get a second jo—"

"No. The business is busted. It's over. You don't know how sorry I am." She heard his pain, as clear and sharp as her own. "Trevor Blake's the new owner."

A thousand thoughts flooded Allie's brain. How were they going to survive? Where would they live? How much time did they have before the new owner kicked them out?

No, she couldn't think about any of that. She needed to fix this. Now.

She gathered herself together and pushed off the car. "Dad, I've got to go. We'll talk about this tonight." Without waiting for his reply, she hit the end button and tossed her hair over her shoulder as she strode back to Dave, shoving her phone into the pocket of her slacks.

Another day, another freaking crisis. She needed to get rid of this guy before her youngest sister got home. If Brynn thought they were losing the house—well, Allie had to make sure that didn't happen.

"Mr. Buchanan?"

A red-faced Dave looked at her with pity. "Sorry. These things are tough," he said. "The economy's bad for everyone right now."

God, Allie was so tired of pity. So tired of empty platitudes. She squared her shoulders and clung to her purse strap with both hands. "This isn't a bank thing. We're not in foreclosure." Realizing how defensive she sounded, she swallowed and tried for a softer tone. "Can I see that?" Allie nodded at the clipboard.

"Sure, of course." Dave handed it over and stared at the Garcia's house next door. With its freshly painted exterior and decorative yucca plants, it was the complete opposite of Allie's raggedy place with peeling brown paint and a crumbling driveway.

She read through the form, making a few mental notes. "Mr. Buchanan? I need you to put off this appraisal until tomorrow." She held out the clipboard.

"Not possible. Look, I'm sorry for your troubles, but I've got a job to do."

All right, Dave, time to pull out the big guns. Allie widened her eyes, glanced up at him through her lashes, and took a deep breath. "Please? Just twenty-four hours, that's all I'm asking." She placed a hand on his forearm and squeezed. "Please, Dave?" she whispered.

He gulped and licked his lips, his eyes darting back and forth. Finally, he let out a gusty breath. "Okay, what the hell? But I'm coming back tomorrow. And I'm getting in the house, one way or another."

Allie smiled. "Thank you." *Ma'am my ass.*

He sniffed and hitched up his jeans before climbing into his truck.

She had bought herself some time, but how was she supposed to get their house back in twenty-four hours? And what if she couldn't?

She closed her eyes for a second. Focus. One thing at a time. Groceries first.

Allie made three trips, hauling bags into the house. As she shoved a box of cereal in the cupboard, she heard the front door slam. "Brynn, is that you?"

She stuck the milk in the fridge and glanced at the kitchen doorway to find her fifteen-year-old sister propped against the jamb. With a bulging backpack, she looked like a turtle ready to topple over. Brynnie was pale. And too thin.

"How was your day?" Allie asked.

Brynn studied her thumbnail and shrugged.

"You hungry? I could make you—"

"No, thanks."

Allie grabbed four potatoes out of the bag and dropped them in the sink. "What about your geometry test? Did you kick ass and take names?"

Brynn scuffed her toe over the worn, beige linoleum, causing a high-pitched squeak. "It was easy. Boring."

"Your art teacher emailed me this morning." Allie glanced over her shoulder. "She said you didn't want to enter your drawing in the art show this year."

"So?"

"That's the drawing of Mom, right? The one of her in the hospital." Their mother had been beautiful, even if she had lost all her hair and forty pounds. Her frame was thin, her face gaunt, but her smile was radiant. Brynn had captured that. "Mom was proud of that picture, Brynn. And your teacher said you could win an award." Allie scrubbed at the potatoes and blotted them with a paper towel.

Brynn rolled her eyes. "Who cares about awards? I'm not showing it. Ever. And why're you making so many potatoes? Dad will be late and Monica won't be home." Digging a hand in her pocket, she whipped out her phone, her thumbs flying over the keyboard.

"Have you heard from her?" Allie asked.

"Right. Like she talks to me."

"She skipped school again today."

Brynn ignored her.

"Did Monica even get on the bus?"

"No." Brynn paused and glanced up. "One of her stupid friends picked her up at the bus stop. As usual."

Fantastic. Banking her anger and frustration, Allie dried her hands on a dish towel. "We're having pork chops for dinner tonight." Pork chops were Brynn's favorite. That's why Allie'd bought them, even though they weren't on sale. She knew the chances of Brynn coming out of her room for dinner were almost nonexistent, but she kept trying.

"I'm not hungry. Sometimes...I just wish we could all be together again." She said it so quietly, Allie barely caught the words.

"We can be. I'll text Monica and tempt her with chocolate cake. A family dinner would be nice." The cheerful note Allie forced into the words grated on her nerves. She knew what Brynn meant. But if she thought about it right now, she'd completely fall apart. And she couldn't do that in front of her little sister.

"Monica would never pull this crap if Mom were here. I miss her so much." Brynn pressed a hand to her abdomen. "I remember how it was before she got sick."

Allie remembered too. The house had been filled with chatter and laughter and the smell of her mother's sweet perfume. But the chatter had been replaced by Monica's bitching and Allie's nagging. Deep lines of stress and worry etched their way across her dad's face, and he seemed older than his fifty years. Losing Mom changed everything. For all of them. And Brynn was right. Monica wouldn't dare act like this if Mom were alive. Allie was doing her best, but she made a poor substitute parent. And Monica resented the hell out of her for it.

Allie glanced away from the pain in her sister's eyes. "Dinner will be ready soon. Do you have homework? When is that English essay due?"

"I know what I need to do," Brynn said. "You don't have to keep reminding me. I'm not a six-year-old."

Allie stepped forward, her hand outstretched to pat Brynn's shoulder, but her sister turned and walked out of the kitchen. As Allie's arm fell, so did the fake smile that left her cheeks sore.

She wanted to follow Brynn, hold her close, tell her everything would be all right—even though it was a lie. *Everything will be fine. It gets better. We'll be okay.* Lies. She said them over and over and felt like a fraud every time.

A hug wouldn't make Brynn feel better. Wouldn't bring her mom back. Wouldn't heal her family.

Allie glanced at the wooden doorjamb Brynn had been leaning against and the growth marks her mother had charted. Each sister had a different color. She traced a finger over her own red marks. This was her family's history.

Crossing her arms, Allie cast her eyes over the dated kitchen, took in the red-and-white-checkered curtains and the rooster wall clock. Her mom loved that stupid rooster.

Allie made a promise. *Take care of the family.* She was supposed to hold everything together, but she was failing. Big time.

Losing the house would be like losing her mom all over again.

She had to talk to this Trevor Blake, make him understand, beg if she had to. Allie was prepared to do anything to keep the promise she made. She would take care of everyone—starting with the house. She was going to get it back.

And she wouldn't take no for an answer.

—⁓—

Trevor Blake sat behind his polished desk and stared at the girl—woman, really—who'd come to plead her father's case. Her lips were full and pink. Her cheeks were bright with color. She was flustered, nervous, hand trembling as she repeatedly tucked her pale hair behind one ear.

Lovely. Although that uniform should be burned. The bright green waistcoat hid a spectacular pair of breasts.

"So, that's why we have to keep the house." She looked at him and waited.

Chin propped on his palm, he stared at her. Truly lovely. He roused himself and straightened in his seat. "I don't care, Miss Campbell."

With wide blue eyes, she stared back. "Excuse me? I don't understand."

Trevor placed his elbows on the desk and steepled his fingers. "I said I don't care. Not about your problems, not about your house. I don't care about any of it."

She blinked a few times. "But my mother died six months ago. We're still trying to recover."

"I'm terribly sorry for your loss. Now, if you'll excuse me, I have work to do." He gestured toward the door.

She shook her head and a few blond strands slid over those amazing tits. "No, I won't excuse you. Didn't you hear what I said? I don't know what my father owes, but we can pay you back. We just need time."

"I was only half listening, really." He leaned forward, his gaze resting on her face. "You're rather beautiful. I find it distracting."

With a clenched jaw, she clutched the armrests of her chair until her knuckles were white. As she took a deep breath, the green buttons on the waistcoat strained and looked ready to pop right off the bloody thing. Very distracting indeed.

"Please, I'm trying to keep my family together, Mr. Blake. Since my mom died, that house is all we have left. Surely you understand that?"

"I don't have family, Miss Campbell. Relatives are considerably more trouble than they're worth." A pain in the bloody ass was more like it. He flatly refused to acknowledge his own.

"Please?" Her voice was a breathy whisper and she tugged on that full bottom lip with her teeth. "Can you give us an extension? Just a month or two. I promise we'll pay every cent."

He bit back a smile. Oh, she was good at this. Very practiced. Most men probably tripped over their own cocks to give her what she wanted. But he wasn't most men. And her sad eyes left him as unmoved as her tragic little family drama. "Do you know what I do, Miss Campbell? Who I am?"

She met his gaze. "Who are you, Mr. Blake?"

"I am, for lack of a better phrase, an investment angel. When I loaned your father money to expand his business, he put your house up as collateral." He lifted his shoulder. "But he's hemorrhaging money, an astounding feat given that he has a commercial refrigeration repair business and we're in the middle of a desert. He even sold off the tools and equipment, which were also mine." He raised a brow in annoyance. Brian Campbell had gone behind his back. Did he think Trevor wouldn't find out? And even though the loss was trivial, Trevor hated losing money, no matter how small the amount. "How your father's managed to keep his head above water this long is something of a mystery."

"What? No, you're wrong. He wouldn't do that without telling me." She scooted to the edge of her seat and placed her hands on top of his desk. Her nails were ruthlessly short, the skin around them red and rough. "You can't do this. My sisters will be out of a home. I'm begging you."

"I am sorry for your plight, but it changes nothing. Now, I trust you can find your way out." Dismissing her, he turned his attention to one of the computer screens and checked the commodities prices. Wheat held steady, oil down, gold up.

Hmm, he'd made a nice little sum today. Not a fortune, but tidy.

When he glanced back, she still hadn't moved. The heat drained from her cheeks, leaving her pale. That lush bottom lip trembled.

Trevor sighed. *Oh God, not tears.* He narrowed his eyes and gave her a nasty, calculated smile. "You know, Miss Campbell, with assets like yours, you could make money in this town. I'm sure you could work a pole as well as the next girl. Or there are the brothels. Prostitution is legal in parts of Nevada, after all." Just as he'd planned, the tears that clung to her lashes didn't fall. Color flushed her cheeks. He'd lit the fuse, and now he waited for the explosion. *Anger—so much better than tears.*

She leaped to her feet and slammed her palm on his desk. "Fuck you. Take your loan and your investment angel bull crap. Just…" Her gaze darted from his face to the multiple computer screens and her mouth flattened into a straight line. Angry eyes met his. "Fuck. You."

He took in her pink cheeks, the determined tilt of her chin, then his gaze slid downward, landing on her breasts, which were rapidly rising in agitation. "If you'd like, I'll be happy to oblige."

"My God, do you think this is funny? My mother is dead, my father is now unemployed, my sisters are about to get kicked out of their home, thanks to you, and you're joking about sex?"

He splayed his hand over his chest. "I never joke about sex, Miss Campbell. I take my fucking very seriously."

She froze for a moment, her lips forming a perfect O before she turned and stalked across the room to the fireplace. Clasping the edge of the marble mantel, she remained silent.

Even in those hideous black trousers, her ass looked nice and firm. She was rather magnificent.

He was a bastard for saying those things to her, for taking her family home. But it was business. It wasn't personal. Why didn't people understand that?

She swung toward him. "All right. If that's the only way, then I'll do it."

"What?" Her ass had him in a bit of a daze. What had they been talking about?

"I accept."

He replayed the last couple of minutes over in his mind. Then it finally hit him, like a cricket bat to the head. She was offering to fuck him in exchange for her house. Dear God.

She licked her lips and glanced at the door.

Already regretting her hasty offer? Good, she should be. And of course, the idea was ridiculous. She was hardly the type to offer up her body in exchange for anything as mundane as a small house in a rather shabby part of the city.

He stood and stepped from the behind the desk, strolling toward her slowly, purposefully. His gaze lowered to her mouth. She audibly swallowed but stood her ground. He liked her spirit. She was tall, but he towered over her, forcing her to crane her neck to glare up at him.

He placed his hands on the mantel and caged her between his arms. With his head angled, he leaned forward. Their lips were only inches apart. Her pupils dilated, her breathing became shallow. If he leaned just a little closer, those breasts would graze his chest. *So tempting.*

She smelled good enough to eat—a light, fresh fragrance that wasn't too delicate, wasn't overpowering. It made his cock stand up and pay attention. "All right then, I'll forgive the debt if you agree to cater to my needs. At my beck and call, fulfilling my every whim, for as long as I want you. How does that sound?" Dropping his hands, he pulled back and smiled. Positive she would throw his offer and probably her fist in his face, he waited. Baiting her was rather delicious. But he needed to get back to work. He couldn't spend the rest of the afternoon taunting Allie Campbell, as delightful as that sounded.

She stared at him with those impossibly blue eyes. "All right," she said after several seconds, "for one month, but I want it in writing."

His jaw dropped for an instant, gobsmacked. "Sorry?" He'd just been teasing her. He couldn't have a mistress. Didn't want one. Especially one that came with so much baggage. A party girl who knew her way around? Possibly. A woman who had sisters to take care of, a widowed father? He resisted the urge to shudder.

"I said yes." She tilted her chin and studied him. "You expected me to say no, didn't you? Are you trying to welsh out of it?"

Was she challenging him? Questioning his word? He crossed his arms over his chest and regarded her coolly. "I've never *welshed* on anything in my life."

She mimicked him, also crossing her arms, and nodded. "Good."

"Three months, not one, and there's a catch, Miss Campbell." He smiled at the panicked look in her eyes.

"What's that?"

Ah, now he had her. "You have to comply with whatever I tell you to do, when I tell you to do it, no matter how...depraved"—his voice deepened on the word, drew it out—"or the deal is off."

Her arms fell and she shook her head. "No. Forget it."

Excellent. "Well then, good day." Turning, he walked back to his desk.

"Wait," she said, a thread of desperation in her voice. "Two months. And I won't do anything that could hurt me."

He wasn't sure what possessed him to turn around, but when

he did, he saw a flicker of fear in her eyes. And it made him feel…
He rubbed his chest. He didn't know what the feeling was, but he
didn't like it. He quickly dropped his hand. "But a little pain can
be very pleasurable."

Instead of running for cover, like a sensible girl, she met his cool
gaze with her own.

"Then we'd need a safe word or something. And no other partners."

Truly, he'd never been into pain, either delivering it or receiving it. Doling out the occasional light spanking—well, quite. But
that wasn't painful. That was foreplay. As for other partners, he
didn't like to share. Not that he was planning on actually having
Allie Campbell.

So. Tempting.

He told his cock to shut up. He'd never let it do the thinking
before and he wasn't about to start now.

But what was he to do? Knowing there was no way out of his
offer, not without *welshing*, he stalked toward her and held out his
hand. "You're mine for two months. Deal."

She hesitated for the briefest moment. "Deal."

When she placed her hand in his, he felt a rush of anticipation.

"And you'll forgive my father's debt, let us keep the house, and
pay off the existing mortgage," she said in a rush.

He sighed. "Fine."

Her face relaxed a bit. "Fine."

Bloody hell. He wasn't sure when things had gotten so out of
hand, but somehow Trevor had acquired himself a mistress.

About the Author

Dawn Ryder is the erotic romance pen nan[...]
of historical romances. She has been publis[...]
than eight years for a growing and appre[...]
hugely committed to her career as an au[...]
authors and to her readership. She resides i[...]